DEATH RITES

ALSO BY

ALICIA GIMÉNEZ-BARTLETT

Dog Day
Prime Time Suspect

Alicia Giménez-Bartlett

DEATH RITES

*Translated from the Spanish
by Jonathan Dunne*

Europa
editions

Europa Editions
116 East 16th Street
New York, N.Y. 10003
www.europaeditions.com
info@europaeditions.com

Translation by Jonathan Dunne
Original Title: *Ritos de muerte*
Translation copyright © 2008 by Europa Editions

Library of Congress Cataloging in Publication Data is available
ISBN 978-1-933372-54-9

Giménez-Bartlett, Alicia
Death Rites

Book design by Emanuele Ragnisco
www.mekkanografici.com

Cover photo © Leslie Richard Jacobs/Corbis

Prepress by Plan.ed – Rome

Printed in the United States of America

DEATH RITES

1.

Shortly after my second separation, I resolved to locate a small house with a garden in the city. A difficult objective, but I managed it. It was something more than a whim, I liked to think. Too many years of apartments with functional furniture and a deep-freeze. I was now being offered the chance to live alone in a peaceful place, and I fancied it was an opportunity for change. The house was in a district, Poble Nou, not far from the city center. Nearby there were other houses as old and decrepit as the one I'd bought, flanked by a swath of industrial warehouses, transport companies and bus depots. A somewhat desolate landscape, notwithstanding valiant efforts to freshen up the neighborhood. On Sundays, however, the companies closed their doors, the trucks disappeared and were replaced by an unusual calm.

I suppose at the heart of the matter was an attempt to be better organized, to tend plants in the back garden and to eat a good, hot meal from time to time. Though deeper impulses beat under the surface of that decision. Having my own house was like tying a rope to a post, setting foot on the ground, putting down roots. A premise which conditioned everything else, as did being blond, ugly or born in Japan. For any serious project you only have first to decide on the stage set; the rest is normally a smooth series of consequences till the happy ending.

The builders spent six months renovating the interior and, by the time they finished, my scant savings were being squandered on such apparently absurd things as gas pipes and win-

dow frames. The police don't earn much money, so accumu-
lating such a sum again was a remote impossibility, a mere illusion. I was satisfied, all the same, because everything had
worked out more or less well. The day before moving, I examined the result, which had the appearance of being solid and
ordinary: happy doors painted white, good light . . . In the
kitchen, the made-to-measure cupboards stood out alongside a
fine, old oven that had escaped refurbishment. Next to it, I
had a glass-ceramic hob installed, the latest technological
craze. Here I would cook complicated dishes, stews that would
make even grandmas edgy, broths that needed a whole day
simmering. As far as possible, I would bid farewell to pre-
cooked food, takeaway pizzas, hot dogs, Mexican tacos, chop
suey packed in individual plastic containers. I would stop eating out at the slightest excuse. A change is a change and, contrary to belief, has to start with the details, the breeding
ground of any truly existential experience.

Pepe helped me with the move; it was inevitable that he
help me. I knew I shouldn't have let him come near my new
home, but I thought that fearing his presence at this stage was
childish, so he helped me. Besides we had separated on such
friendly terms that rejecting his offer would have been
improper, almost rude. He turned up dressed as always in a jersey and frayed jeans, his glasses slipping down the bridge of his
nose. His uncomplicated air of extreme youth made me shudder. How could I have married such a young, helpless boy?
Above all, how could I have done so when it was my second
marriage following on the heels of a first marriage that had
been turbulent, difficult, and had ended in a bloody and
painful divorce? The police specialists in the Department of
Psychology would have had a lot to say. Except that they were
too busy solving cases to have an opinion about private affairs.
Nor would it have occurred to me to ask them. I had ended up
joining the police to fight against the broodiness that used to

overwhelm me in every situation. Action. Only practical thoughts in working hours, induction, deduction, but always at the service of criminal matters, no more intimate, inward absorption at the counter of a bar.

Pepe placed the boxes of books in the lounge. He stood staring out of the window, in a daze, covered in sweat and dust. He had probably forgotten to eat.

"Have you eaten?" I asked.

He shrugged his shoulders melancholically and smiled, as if eating were a luxury reserved for another class of human being. I cut short the urge to make him a sandwich. I had played mother for too long and it was no longer expedient.

"Who's looking after the bar?"

"Hamed," he answered.

"Is it still going well?"

"Yep."

He retained the air of a stray dog, but I had ceased to be a paid-up member of the Society of Protective Ladies.

I stood the volumes of *Law and Criminology* next to the window and went to the kitchen to serve some drinks, stout for Pepe and a sweet anisette for me. No more acts of charity on my part, no more volunteering or passion: work, food, evenings of music and reading, a return to basics, plain life at its most elementary level.

Pepe took a sip from his glass and got foam on his nose. He wandered around the room full of jumbled boxes, yawned:

"Is there anything else?"

"The plant pots, Pepe, are in the hallway if you don't mind fetching them."

It snowed that winter, a reason to remember it, in Barcelona snow is not very common. However, the flurry of events that winter was such that I would have remembered it anyway, without having to see my newly planted garden covered in white. A year chock-full of events. I moved to a new house, an independent life, and circumstances, rather than fate, got me my first case and led between boxes and snowflakes to my meeting Sergeant Garzón. Of course the initial, idyllic impression I was under at home soon vanished. The pipes froze and I learned that living in a neighborhood tucked away from the rest of the city isn't always the height of pleasure. The small patio I had managed to refloat finally foundered. The geraniums dried up and the earth turned rock hard beneath a layer of frost. Sad images. I sat shivering in front of the failing fireplace and tried to concentrate on a book about New Police Technology, recently translated into Spanish from a distant Chicago English. Most of the examples in the text had no equivalent in our long-suffering police force, so different from the FBI. I knew from memory that such complex technological devices would take years, if not centuries, to reach Spain. Knowledge, however, doesn't take up any room, even if it doesn't enable others to make room for themselves. In fact, despite my brilliant training as a lawyer and my police studies at the Academy, I had never been assigned a significant case. I was labeled "an intellectual." I was also a woman. All I needed was black or Gypsy blood in my veins to complete the picture of exclusion. From the beginning I was posted to the Department of Documentation, where I looked after general affairs: archives, publications and the library, which ended up according me a purely theoretical status in the eyes of my colleagues. I demanded to take part in active service from time to time, a request that was granted. I was involved in isolated cases of robbery which didn't even need investigating. I hadn't been inspired to join the police by action movies or crime novels: chases, fights, lots of whisky and bad manners . . . However, being kept in a permanently speculative, bookish state inevitably produced a feeling of frustration. I was like an entomologist confined to a laboratory without a field book, condemned always to observe insects eternally dead under the microscope. This disenchantment hadn't left me on my trips outdoors: violated ATMs, filing reports on bag snatching. I once had to question a group of young pickpockets, who made fun of me, calling me "doll," when the most basic understanding of the genre indicates it should have been the other way round. Despite all this, I didn't lose hope, nor did I go crying to my bosses. I thought that, whatever happened, my entry into active service and my prestige would coincide, marked by some inscrutable destiny. I also believed that a woman cannot go about her workplace whimpering without provoking a fatal response. I bided my time in silence and, when another inspector walked past me in the corridor and asked, "How's our little intellectual?" on the inside I always thought, "One day you'll see," while on the outside I greeted him with a couple of ironic chews on my gum and simply smiled.

The only solution for a frozen pipe is to cross your fingers and pray for the worst not to happen. The worst is for it to crack and have to be changed. I had just come home after a hard day's work and was planning to take a shower when I noticed it. The noise when I turned on the taps was like a warning call from the Other Side. I sensed that there was no immediate cure and sat down wrapped in a bathrobe. It had been a chaotic day. When it snows in Barcelona, people emerge: they are less tense, in less of a hurry, but in their cars. Driving becomes impossible and you have to wait with civic patience for the traffic jams everywhere to clear. It's all smiles to begin with, the salesgirls come running out of the shops holding up their hands to the snowflakes. Then, if the snow lasts, a generic bad mood sets in, horns blare, meetings run late and pedestrians discover that their footwear fails to keep out the wet. There was nothing for it. I served myself an anisette and put on a CD of classical music. It had belonged to Hugo, but I took the CD collection with me. I left Pepe's behind, heavy metal and traditional African songs, too much for my deformed taste, Irish folk was about as ethnic as I could get. Having struggled for a while to light the fire, I sat down to read. The room was full of smoke, the geraniums were dead and the pipes about to burst, but then hadn't I chosen this house for the enjoyment of moments like this? A good book of police science, piano music by Chopin, solitude, the silence of night . . . Suddenly the phone rang, as always happens when you encounter a certain peace. It was the chief inspector. His voice surprised me, he never rang me at home. But I was even more surprised by the official tone with which he addressed me.

"I am waiting for you at the station, inspector. Your presence is required, a matter concerning field operations."

To ask "Is something up?" struck me as ridiculous, but I wasn't used to being summoned unexpectedly and had no idea what to say. The chief inspector sensed my consternation down the line and exclaimed:

"I know it's after ten o'clock!"

"That's not a problem, I'm on my way."

The poor man probably thought he was disturbing some family scene: me seated next to my husband, watching television or helping my youngest son with his math, or ensconced in the final preparations of a soufflé . . . No one at work knew anything about my private life. It seemed to me an essential condition not to lose people's respect. I had witnessed female colleagues giving their nannies advice over the phone in front of everyone. "Throw a handful of rice in his food, his stomach's a little upset." Though they may well have been able to solve the mystery of the ten little Indians, they were forgetting that certain rules, certain forms, had to be respected. I'd never caught a male inspector phoning home out of concern for his children's gastronomy. And things hadn't reached the neutral point where it's possible to show a certain weakness without paying the consequences.

"Don't worry, I'll be as quick as the traffic permits."

Maybe all those years my superiors had believed they were doing me a favor. Posted to a service that didn't require "walking the streets," working set hours at a safe distance from crimes and their ugliness. A good position for a woman. But I had no domestic affairs to attend to or babies to feed, with neither of my husbands had I spent evenings watching TV and, while I hadn't entirely given up soufflés, this was a practice that could be combined with a moderate dose of action.

I got dressed again and slipped into a fur-lined raincoat. The sidewalk was covered in filthy slush, with ugly tire-tracks running alongside the curb. There was now more water than snow, which had settled only in the two or three trees in the street, white and shiny, magical, as if the night were taking place in a Norwegian forest, far from the depots of Poble Nou. A night for listening to Chopin.

When I arrived, the station was quiet, with no signs of aggression or butchery. I wondered again why they had called me.

"Inspector González has had a skiing accident. I want you to replace him while he's off work."

That explained the call but not why it had come at such a late hour. It didn't even occur to me to inquire.

"Very good," I replied.

"If you'll wait here for a moment, I'll introduce you to Sergeant Garzón, who will be your partner. I mean he'll be under your command."

This is what the chief inspector meant and he did well to clarify it because, if I was an inspector, it was due to the merits of my graduation, I had never had anyone under my orders since starting.

"Sergeant Garzón has recently been transferred from Salamanca. A very pleasant fellow."

I nodded. I decided that logically this Garzón must be a novice they wished to break in. I harbored no illusions about "the troops" that might be placed at my disposal. And besides it was still unclear why they had called me in. Was it to make an urgent delivery of credentials in the imperial style? Possibly, the chief inspector had a reputation for being majestic and rhetorical.

"He's a tough guy who will serve you well. He has a lot of field experience."

My theory about the raw recruit crumbled away. The chief inspector stood up and opened the door of his office. Changing tone completely, he roared out:

"López, tell Garzón to get in here!"

There was no answer from the corridor, the chief inspector grew impatient:

"Where the hell . . . ? López!!"

While I was thinking how quickly a reputation for diplomacy can be ruined, a frightened-looking policeman appeared, saluting in military fashion. The chief inspector didn't bother with an explanation and bad-temperedly repeated his order. He then smiled again and turned to me:

"It's been a difficult evening, though you may not believe it."

Garzón finally entered. My immediate reaction was that this guy was not tough but in need of a truss or some other orthopedic accessory owing to his age. Almost sixty, fifty-seven at least. I was wrong about the years but still right not to get excited. He was on the verge of retirement, grayish, somewhat unsophisticated, with a belly. He reluctantly shook my hand as if we'd had a children's spat and been obliged to make it up.

"Let me introduce you to Petra Delicado, our intellectual gem. Since she joined Documentation, everything's been perfectly dated and arranged. She's taken the necessary steps and now we receive foreign magazines and books published by the UN, UNESCO, Interpol and the FBI."

"Hmmm . . ." muttered Garzón.

"And this is Fermín Garzón, a man with experience and a hard worker. You'll get on."

"Hmmm . . ." I repeated. Contrary to appearances, his hand was not damp and limp like a provincial cop's, but warm, dry and strong. We both remained silent.

"You'll have guessed I didn't bring you here at such a late hour just for this," the chief inspector laid his cards on the table. "The truth is I want you to take charge of a case of rape. The victim's already made the relevant statement and will have to be questioned again before she leaves."

Like two synchronized automatons, Garzón and I both nodded.

"Sergeant Garzón's already had the chance to examine the file and will fill you in on the facts. Then I suggest you have a beer together to get to know one another."

This much was new. Chief Inspector Coronas had allowed himself to go beyond the strictly professional and take an interest in the beers of our free time. I didn't like it and I'd swear Garzón didn't either. He threw me a sideways glance and pulled a smiling grimace, which was like an old cork in a bottle: difficult to extract.

I didn't have a lot to say to my new colleague when we entered the corridor. Fortunately he was the one who started talking first.

"Well, the case doesn't need much explaining. A seventeen-year-old girl has been raped. She was going to meet her mother, who's a cook in an old people's home. While she was waiting in the street, a young man accosted her. He put a knife to her throat and forced her into a doorway."

"Was she mistreated?"

"In part, though the only wound is on her arm as you'll see."

"Was it a normal rape?"

"Just penetration."

"Would the girl recognize the young man?"

"Why don't we go in and question her?"

He wasn't very communicative or felt uncomfortable giving details when there was no pressing need. This, in principle, was an encouraging sign. I detest the tendency at work to talk insubstantially, the habit of repeating the same ideas a hundred times disguised by a variety of synonyms. It wasn't a bad start.

In a cold office we were met by the victim and her mother, a fairly miserable woman, her clothes reeking of oil, who kept dabbing her eyes. The girl was white and helpless like a laboratory mouse. She sat with drooping shoulders and stared at the ground. They made a strange pair, as if they bore not the slightest relation. Coronas, a middle-aged man who fancied himself as an innovator, had obtained a grant to change the station's decor. A few months earlier, a removal van had appeared before our astonished eyes. They took away the old, somber office furniture, all except the archives, which, since there wasn't enough money, stayed put. They brought instead geometric chairs and cheaply designed tables with metal legs and lots of colored plastic. The result was ambiguous and failed to erase a certain sordidness, although the old funereal atmosphere of a police station had now been twinned with the air of a Social Security office. The bulging wooden cabinets with their ancestral cigarette burns and holes bored by generations of woodworm had been consigned to history.

"My daughter hasn't done anything," was the first thing that woman said when she saw me come in. "She didn't provoke him."

"Please sit down."

I again flicked through the police file in front of them, looked at the girl and asked:

"Did you see his face?"

"No."

"Was it covered?"

"With a ski mask, only his eyes were showing."

"And what were they like?"

"I don't know. He was tall and thin, that's all I know."

"Did he speak to you?"

"He said if I didn't keep quiet he'd kill me."

"Did he have an accent, anything special?"

"I don't know, the mask covered his mouth and he spoke softly."

"Do you always wait for your mother in the same place?"

The mother intervened:

"She doesn't come every day. I don't want her out on her own at that hour, but she insists."

I didn't even acknowledge her. I carried on addressing the victim.

"Had you told someone you were going out that night?"

The mother again butted in.

"Why would she tell anyone anything? She's a polite girl, what happens is I have to work because my husband's dead, you see, but she didn't provoke that pig nor is she out and about at that hour in the street."

I stood up and slightly raised my voice.

"If you don't stop interrupting, madam, I'll have to ask you to leave."

She clenched her jaws and said something I couldn't understand. I then heard myself saying:

"Go and wait outside!"

Even I was surprised by my outburst, but I couldn't have carried on putting up with that Gorgon who insisted on exculpating herself. I saw how my new colleague remained static and open-mouthed, standing next to me. The mother had a proud expression on her face and, on leaving, imperceptibly touched her daughter on the arm. I then noticed it was bandaged just above the wrist.

"Is that what the rapist did to you?"

"Yes," she replied.

"A stab wound?"

"No. When he left and I thought he wasn't going to harm me, he brought his arm close to mine, pressed hard and I felt a very sharp pain."

"Could we see the wound?"

There was a moment of stupefaction. The doctor had just attended her and the cure was finished. Sergeant Garzón spoke for the first time.

"There's a forensic report and photographs. To see it now, we'd have to remove the bandage."

"So? I'd rather see it with my own eyes, she can then go back to the clinic."

I didn't wait for anyone to give me their consent, I was the one who was supposed to be in charge. I slowly unwrapped the bandage in the middle of a complete silence.

"Interesting!" I exclaimed.

The wound was very strange, superficial and an unusual shape, nothing like a scratch or a stab wound. It was in fact a perfect circle drawn by a succession of tiny pinpricks.

"Have you seen this, Garzón?"

He approached and looked over my shoulder. I sensed the touch and warmth of his potent belly.

"I've never come across anything like it," he said.

"Did you notice how he did it or if he was carrying something?"

"I only know he accosted me, but I didn't see anything."

"What movements did he make?"

"He just applied pressure."

"Did he talk to you, say something?"

"Almost nothing."

"Did he talk softly?"

"Like he was shouting, but in a whisper."

"Would you say he was trying to distort his voice so you wouldn't recognize it?"

"I don't know."

I paused. The girl's impassive face did not encourage me to pursue any particular line.

"Did you think at any point you might recognize him?"

"I already told you I didn't see him."

"I know, but there may have been a gesture, his way of walking . . . "

"No."

"No detail that might have been familiar, not even a hint of one?"

"No."

I sighed.

"Do you always wait for your mother in the same place?"

"Yes."

"At the same time?"

"Yes."

"Are there lots of people at that hour?"

"Not many."

"Days before that, had you seen anyone suspicious, someone looking at you or passing you repeatedly?"

"No."

"Are you absent-minded? I mean, could a guy have gone by every day without you realizing?"

"Perhaps."

"Was the man nervous when he attacked you?"

"He didn't seem so."

"Were you afraid, did you think he might kill you?"

"Yes. He seemed very sure, like he wasn't joking."

I looked her in the eye.

"Did he enjoy himself when he raped you? You know what I mean. Was he excited, panting, or was it merely an obligation?"

She looked at me with disgust. She may have been thinking all this amused me, that I felt a kind of morbid curiosity.

"I already told you he was cold and calm."

She was cold as well. She answered without getting emotional or upset. Her thoughts were obvious: my questions were going nowhere, the interview was a waste of time. All she really wanted was to leave.

"All right then. Go back to the doctor and he'll replace the bandage."

She slowly stood up, holding one arm with the other, trailing a piece of gauze along the ground. She was hunched over and pale. As she passed by, Garzón gave her an awkward smile and said:

"Don't you worry, we'll catch that bastard!"

"What do I care?" replied the girl, and her expressionless, languid eyes settled on the empty ashtray, which would always be empty because it was forbidden to smoke in that office.

We entered the corridor. The victim's mother stood up when she saw us and ostentatiously asked Garzón:

"Can we go now?"

"Yes, madam, a patrol car will accompany you."

She passed in front of me, inches from my face, and gave me a furious look full of scorn and hate. I had the impression she'd spit at me any moment, but she controlled herself.

"Hell, I get the impression she doesn't like me!" I commented to my companion.

"Well, rape's pretty serious and it is her daughter, you understand."

"Do you think my approach was too harsh?"

It was as if a wasps' nest had landed on him, inciting him to give an obvious answer:

"Do I think . . . ? God forbid I should have an opinion! Who's in charge is in charge, and that's it."

That was all I needed. No doubt Sergeant Garzón felt

offended at being under feminine orders. Hugo, my first husband, a man of cynical intelligence, always used to say, "Expect
the expected, the biggest cliché, the most commonplace, that's
what will happen, whatever's customary, whatever's ordinary: a
stiff Englishman and a Frenchman with a baguette under his
arm, that's the script of reality." He appeared to be right.

"Shall we have that beer?" asked Garzón.

It was clear that, though he didn't want to, he planned to
follow the chief inspector's instructions to the letter. We
crossed the street and went into the bar the Jarra de Oro, a
bona fide branch of the station which never closed before
three.

"Will you have beer as well?"

"Yes," I murmured. "Where are we going to start?"

"Tomorrow I'll comb the neighborhood. I'll go and see the
most notorious thugs, those on probation, any with a sexual
past. We'll meet in the evening and I'll tell you if there are any
suspects."

"Over in Trinitat is the local detention center."

"I'll have to go there as well."

The landlady was humming while washing glasses. A few
strands of hair had escaped from her disheveled bun. She had
bags under her eyes and looked tired. I thought the following
morning she'd wake up early to start again and wondered
where she got the heroic energy from. I couldn't think of anything to say, but we were there to share some impressions. In
the end, I came out with a really dumb question:

"How do you like Barcelona?"

"It's O.K.," he replied. It seemed that the incursion into
friendly territory would end there, but after a pause he added:

"Shame so many people speak Catalan."

"Don't you understand anything?"

"No."

"Perhaps you should do a course."

"At my age I can't do a course. The age is a good and a bad one, at which you realize just how few things you know and how little you feel like learning new ones."

Maybe my new colleague was not so conventional after all. Maybe he had a weakness for philosophy.

"No age is good," I ventured, touching upon the existential.

"Who was that Italian businessman who manufactured cars?" he asked abruptly.

"Agnelli?"

"Yeah. Well, he didn't mind if he was old or young, he wore silk shirts, he was tanned and healthy, I don't imagine he cared if he learned or not."

"But he'll have had his problems."

He looked at me, astonished by the length of my stupidity, the breadth of my ignorance.

"Right. Excuse me, but I have to go. I'll see you tomorrow. I doubt very much I'll have the information I told you about before seven o'clock. I'm also helping the Civil Guard out in a case of smuggling."

"Drugs?"

"Tobacco. These things are on the rise again."

He left the bar with his jacket slung over his shoulder. He hadn't let me pay for the beer. Agnelli's shirts. He was a little disconcerting, I'd need more time to form a rough idea about that man. I couldn't start the car. I grew angry. The following day I'd have to get up early, leave everything arranged for there to be some continuity during my absence from the Department of Documentation. It was cold and late. Such was a real cop's wretched life, long nights in shady bars, extremes of temperature, violence, unpleasantness and the untimely early rise, the mouth bitter from cigarettes and coffee; a whole mythology.

The water and snow had stopped. The air was still, as if the cold had frozen all of life. I went out into the back garden of

my house, iced like a cake. A hot shower, or listening to
Chopin, would have been ideal. But I decided to go straight to
bed. I could hardly have enjoyed such refined music after seeing the rape victim's empty eyes when she said, "What do I
care?" and the terrible imprint on her arm.

2.

I was surprised that Hugo rang and, after the initial distrust,
pleased even. Since our separation, we had stopped phoning each other so often. There were moments of greater
interchange, but always for practical reasons or legal matters: the
divorce proceedings, the gradual liquidation of our common
assets. All these communications were awkward, ironic or cold.
Hugo always considered himself an abandoned husband and me
a crazed and thoughtless woman who had recklessly altered the
prosperous conditions of my private and professional life. This
time I was also surprised by his polite, even friendly tone. He
wanted to sell the last piece of property we shared, a parking
space in Ganduxer, and for this he needed my signature and
agreement. I felt that an unforeseen payment of money would be
fantastic and told him he could act as he chose. Then, quite
unexpectedly, he proposed having a cup of tea to discuss the
matter. Unbelievable, he had never agreed to something like this
though I had tried on numerous occasions. I envied those civilized couples who were able to visit each other after their
breakup and chat without problems. But, for him, meeting over
a cup of something smacked of reconciliation—hot drinks were
symbolic. As a result, we had always met up in lawyers' offices,
judicial lobbies and other similar venues that discouraged conversation. This time would be different and I wondered why.

"I could do with the money," I told him.

"I suppose a policeman earns just enough."

"I get by."

"You'll have gotten by better before as a lawyer."

"I recently bought a house and that's why I could do with the money."

"I guessed as much."

With this string of monosyllables, he presupposed my investment had been a clumsy one. If our appointment was going to be laced with similar injections of wit, it would have been better to meet up in a notary's office and, having completed the transaction, to take off. But something always stopped me standing up to him, maybe guilt, maybe the conviction that, deep down, he was right in his opinion about my recurrent recklessness. During our relationship we'd had terrible rows and shouting matches. After the separation, my anger disappeared and his abated till it was replaced by an irony too weighed down with hate to be effective. Taking the decision to abandon the ruinous building of our marriage had forever deprived me of reason. You must never be the first, it's better not to move, all you have to do is rebuild with willpower what is then destroyed in moments of sincerity.

Hugo looked distinguished and tired, as if he'd recently recovered from an illness by taking the waters in a spa. The passage of time favored him, his gray temples and careful appearance. As Mother Nature's springtime waned, money and experience had come to the fore. Agnelli's shirts, as Garzón would say. We had arranged to meet in the Jarra de Oro, where his prosperous look contrasted with the simplicity of the drinking proletariat. He raised his eyes heavenward as he always did prior to a speech. His characteristic histrionics wouldn't have changed so late in life. Well, I'd listen to everything he had to say, as always with humility, with restraint, without revealing the good things my current life had in store. There was no way I could share with him my new plans for a homely existence and geraniums in the garden. In his eyes, I was a wretch and I would behave accordingly.

As soon as we sat down, he gazed at the corners of the ceiling as if all the moral misery of the Jarra de Oro had gathered there. He also viewed with disdain the waiter, who carried his daily map of stains on his apron.

"Bring us two teas."

He had chosen for me, no doubt without realizing.

"I only drink tea now," he confessed. "Coffee does me in. You know that after your departure I had a very serious ulcer which took a long time to heal. Although I'm better now, I still prefer to be careful."

The ulcer always put in an appearance, even on the phone. The moment of our separation, which he invariably termed "your departure," was already seven years old, but his ulcer behaved like the nails of the Cross and left an indelible mark which became worthy of adoration over time. And I was the Roman soldier with my hammer at the ready, I and only I was the one who had caused his suffering. Armed with a pointed spear, I had riffled through his intestines until I made them bleed. He produced a sheaf of papers and didn't dare leave them on the stained table, but passed them to me:

"That green document you're holding has the conditions of sale, I hope you find them interesting. Only the green one, the others contain financial details that I'll take care of."

His complacency regarding the obviousness of the green document was meant to highlight my inability to manage practical, administrative tasks. His conversation was as perilous as a minefield, but for some time now I had been equipped with a detector.

"I've no problem with that. The price seems right, everything's O.K."

"You have to sign your authorization. Then, when the sale goes through, you'll have to appear before the notary."

The waiter arrived with the teas. Hugo checked the brand written on the label hanging from the bag.

"Is this where you have breakfast every day?"

There was censure and scruple in his voice.

"Not just breakfast . . . this is where I meet up with colleagues, we drink beer and coffee. It's like an annex to the station."

He looked around.

"We must be surrounded on every side by cops."

I shrank a little under my skin.

"I don't know, maybe."

If he launched into an attack on the degradation brought about by moving in police circles, then it could be said that the scheme of our infrequent meetings was identical: the ulcer, money and the degeneracy of having become a cop. I endeavored to shore myself up against the idea that Hugo was always right. I attempted to take a shortcut and gain time till we finished our drinks.

"Have you heard from the Gálvezes?" I improvised.

He looked at me as if I was mad.

"The Gálvezes? No, I haven't. Things are not the same as when we were together, Petra, I thought you'd have realized. My friends are different, my life is different . . . I'm sure it doesn't matter to you, but the fact is next month I'm getting remarried."

Here he had caught me by surprise. I threw up both hands in an awkward gesture.

"Wow! I'm very happy for you, Hugo, believe me."

"It's seven years since we broke up, I don't think this news can make you sad or happy."

The smile I wore on my face stretched. I drank my tea and burned my tongue.

"All the same, I wish you every happiness."

"She's a lawyer."

"I thought this time you'd have switched profession."

"She won't become a cop, I assure you."

I smiled. Hugo blamed me not only for having abandoned

him but also for deserting my position in our solid lawyers' office. An act of madness. According to him, this had razed my already weakened ability to lead a balanced life. Change, burn . . . "Some people have the gift of destroying everything they own of real worth." His sayings remained inside me for a long time, torturing me. I longed to disappear immediately.

"I think I must be going."

"It's a bit late for you to be worried about my well-being."

I smiled again like an idiot. He could now go on to review my life, one wrong decision after another on the road to chaos: a respectable job vaporized, a convenient relationship broken off, an absurd second marriage with a much younger man, which also ended in separation . . . By his mere presence, Hugo placed before my eyes the pernicious consequences of my recklessness, making them look like a misshapen comedy of errors. They probably were.

"I really have to go."

He hurried his tea. As we approached the bar, I spotted Sergeant Garzón. I wondered how long he had been there. I had no choice but to introduce them.

"Sergeant Garzón works with me."

"On a case," he specified.

Hugo stretched out his hand unenthusiastically. He looked at me with sympathy. This was my own doing. I had swapped the security of a real home for the company of shady cops with boldly striped shirts and a prominent bellies. I'd had the courage to break up a pair of brilliant, enviable lawyers to come and root about in a dive like the Jarra de Oro. This was something I would have to grow to accept. He left with his head held high in a supine gesture of contempt and I remained, shrunken and minimized, next to Garzón. He suggested having another tea. I tried to step back into my professional role.

"Have you unearthed something?"

"Nothing special. I checked out the neighborhood, asked a few questions . . . No one saw anything, not a scrap of evidence."

"Did you talk to the local lowlifes?"

"To little effect. At least I don't think it's one of the regulars."

"Then we'll have to pay a visit to the reformatory to see if it's one of theirs."

"Well, it's up to you . . . "

"What, isn't this a lead you would follow?"

"As I say, it's up to you . . . "

If the sergeant carried on offering passive resistance to all my proposals, I'd have no option but to draw his attention to it. Of course there was the possibility of winning him over by fair means. I tried it by breaking one of my golden rules on work and private life:

"Do you know who that gentleman I just introduced you to is?"

I noticed in his eyes a fleeting look of surprise, which he instantly repressed. He recovered his elegant skepticism.

"Not if you don't tell me . . . "

"My first ex-husband. And don't think I'm making a mistake. I've two ex-husbands and he's the first!"

I let out a supposedly mischievous and amusing laugh. I'd managed to hit him on the waterline. His jaw dropped a little and a spark of curiosity glimmered in his pupils.

"Right," he commented without flinching. "Well, I've been widowed, thank heaven."

"Thank heaven?"

He gave a childish start.

"I mean that fortunately I never had to divorce my wife, we stayed together till the day she died."

There appeared to be strict censure in his way of talking. I got annoyed. I abandoned my policy of appeasement. Must I put up with all those who reproached me? Was I perhaps

Sigismunda, condemned even before birth? I drank down my tea and eyed him perversely.

"Changing subject, Garzón, do you have any idea why this case was given specifically to you and me?"

He was completely defenseless. I moved in mercilessly for the final kill.

"Well, since you don't know, I'll tell you. We were given this case because there was no one else, it's that simple. I found out this morning. The rest of our colleagues are involved in a highly complex operation, something to do with drugs. One of those stories that end with photos in the paper and lots of confiscated material." He seemed to have received the blow but he resisted. "As usual they don't want people brought in from outside and, had it not been for the lack of staff, they'd have left us where we were full-time, me with my archive and you with your smuggling. I don't think they trusted us with a job of such responsibility. After all, you're almost retired and I'm only a woman."

My wickedness made his face resemble a dead man's.

"I've still some time before I retire but, all the same, I've always obeyed orders, no questions asked."

"Well, that's fine by me since I'm your new boss. So let's start right away by doing something useful. Go and fetch the car to take us to the reformatory, I suppose the director will agree to see us."

I was chuffed by my own military style. The truce was over. If Garzón was a penguin who did not allow the ice to be broken around him, I'd lavish all the severity a woman can muster. I wasn't being paid to wear kid gloves. No doubt I had been kept very safe from prejudice in the Department of Documentation, where the secretaries always smiled on passing you a book. But this was not some quiet backwater, we had ventured outdoors, this was the Wild West, cops' cops, criminals, rapists . . . You had to whirl the whip overhead when someone thought to come and wish you good day.

The traffic was slow and thick as usual. We waited at the traffic lights, endured waves of horn blasts, but Garzón remained unperturbed at the wheel like the driver of a hearse. The director of the reformatory was a woman in her fifties, elegantly poured into a cheviot suit with discreet jewels. When I explained the reason for our visit, she smiled sarcastically:

"Needless to say, I've kids in here who've been charged with sexual offenses, it seems obvious. You won't want to interview them all . . . "

"We thought it'd be sufficient to select those who were allowed out on probation . . . "

"Listen, inspector, to be honest I'm a little tired of the dynamics employed by the police. As soon as a girl turns up raped in this city, the first place you come looking is here."

"Don't you think that's normal?"

"This is a center for reform, we're supposed to reintegrate these youngsters into society, but if you don't stop pestering them . . . "

I wasn't prepared for her aggressive tone. This was definitely not the Department of Documentation. I'd have to sport armor and offensive weapons if I did not wish to lose the respect of my subordinate.

"I understand but this is hardly a summer camp, you have criminals here and may I remind you that this time the rape occurred in this very neighborhood?"

Garzón silently watched the unexpected and heated exchange. The director looked at me with deep hatred in her eyes, threw up her hands and feigning patience said:

"O.K., don't get all official on me. I'll go and see what I can find out. What did you say the date was?"

As she left, tense and with a little color in her cheeks, I murmured under my breath:

"Her boys must be real saints."

My colleague continued unperturbed, rapt as he was in

monastic recollection. Inside he'd be thinking we women had an innate tendency towards hysteria and fratricidal confrontation. What I had to do was get used to being fierce. Garzón defended his turf, however limited it was; in the same fashion, the director defended those entrusted to her care with genuine team spirit. In this world, which was new to me, I had to find some turf to defend and starting with my authority wasn't a bad idea.

"They must all be darling angels," I whispered again, pretending to be in a bad mood.

Suddenly Garzón responded:

"They may not all be devils. One or two will have been reformed."

"You know you can't make a silk purse out of a sow's ear."

What till that moment had been mere indifference was turning into a deep-seated aversion towards me. Garzón despised me. The director sighed as she came back in.

"Let's see . . . " She rummaged through sheets of paper.

"The only one with a sexual history to go out that day was Jorge Valls. But I doubt he had anything to do with it. His manners are exemplary. He's been with us for a year and has always behaved well. He's been studying computers during his time here and every day helps to clean the kitchen. He never steps out of line, never kicks up a fuss. For the last three months, we've been letting him out the odd weekend. I really can't believe . . . "

"Why was he sent here?"

"A strange case, according to the psychologists, unusual for his age. He would wait for girls at the school gate and show them pornographic material, groups in the middle of an orgy, nudes . . . "

"Is that unusual for his age?" asked Garzón.

The director gave him a pleasant look:

"This perversion is considered more common among old

people. They make up for their physical inabilities by indirect experience. Youngsters tend to act directly, some masturbate or expose themselves, but he . . . " She looked through her papers again. "No, Jorge didn't expose himself either."

"Strange, why do you think that is?"

The director appeared content to have found in Garzón a civilized and sensitive interlocutor. He obviously wanted to show me how it's possible to deal with people without assaulting them.

"Actually we don't know what exactly to attribute it to, the psychologists are very careful with their questions, things sometimes take years to come out. But his is a disastrous family background. The father's an unemployed alcoholic, the mother takes off for months without so much as an explanation. A horror, in short. This boy has lived in an atmosphere of moral deterioration."

"You mean society's been to blame," pronounced Garzón like a sad lefty.

The director replied at once:

"It always is." And the two of them looked at each other with smug understanding and then turned their gaze on me as if I were some poor misfit.

I gritted my teeth and asked:

"What time did he go out that day?"

"From five to eleven."

"I need to speak to him."

"I'm afraid dinner's about to be served."

"It won't take more than a moment."

She accepted my request, which further deepened her animosity towards me.

The visiting room was as gloomy as the rest of the place. Pictures and photographs hung from the wall and had evidently been carried out by inmates as manual work: bucolic scenes, birds. A dried pine tree stood in one corner with a small imitation pearl stuck to each branch. A pointless effort without a trace of beauty. The dusty emptiness was palpable. Jorge Valls arrived almost immediately, a boy with small, penetrating eyes, dressed vulgarly. I introduced myself. He appeared to be intimidated and crossed his legs, keeping one hand in his pocket.

"You've been told why we're here, I imagine."

He nodded.

"Then perhaps you could tell us where you were at the time and on the day in question."

"Yes, I was at home, with my mother."

"It's obvious you're on your best behavior. You've learned how to use computers and don't get into fights. You do what you have to. At least in here."

"Outside as well."

"But it must sometimes get boring always being a saint."

He blushed, strained his neck uncomfortably.

"I was with my mother, watching TV."

"A mother's a mother, she might not find it difficult to lie."

"There were also neighbors. They saw me."

"My, my, you do have a good memory!"

"The neighbors drop by every afternoon to see if my mother needs anything."

"Good folk."

"That's right." He grew bolder in the face of my continued irony. "Besides, anyone can tell I don't go about raping girls, I never would."

"I'm quite sure of it."

He looked at me with a puzzled expression, Garzón as well.

"You don't go about raping girls because you can't."

"What do you mean?"

"You can't get it up or it's tiny, something like that."

The boy turned imploringly to Garzón as if he'd suddenly set him up as judge.

"Hey, tell her to stop being rude, I never insulted her."

Garzón stuttered without knowing what to do. In the end, he said:

"Well, we can check what you say about your mother and the neighbors."

I pretended not to have heard either of them.

"You've spent the last year boring the psychologists silly when the only problem is you can't get it up."

He got to his feet and started shouting.

"I want to go, I don't have to be here and answer your questions, I know that!"

He made as if to leave but I intercepted him.

"We'll check it out and I swear if what you've said about the neighbors isn't true, I'll come for you and personally investigate whether or not you can rape."

He left the room a wreck. Garzón's eyes were on stalks as if he'd witnessed a pileup on the freeway. A distant silence took hold of us. The typical smell of boiled vegetables, rotten and familiar, floated in the air.

"Shall we go, sergeant?"

He walked next to me, slightly dazed. I tried to provoke him, maybe now he'd react.

"Do you think I went too far?"

He emitted an indecipherable gurgle.

"Would you say the intensity of treatment was adequate?"

He snorted:

"What did you say those things for?"

"To make him nervous."

"Why?"

"It's always better if they're nervous. Anyway, this guy's in here for attempting to pervert schoolgirls, I wouldn't say he deserves special treatment. Or don't you agree?"

"I don't know, inspector. If you don't mind, I'd prefer not to give an opinion."

He retreated back into his attitude that "orders are orders." We made for the exit, strolling down the gray building's dismal corridors. Bunches of synthetic flowers, ashtrays on the ground, a depersonalized, hollow limbo people passed through with only the hope of getting out at some point. This blasted sergeant was not to be fooled, he kept up his respect-ful disdain. More bloody acts would be necessary to show him what I was capable of.

Back home I served myself a glass of anisette. Lying on the sofa, I fell to wondering who my new partner really was. A run-of-the-mill cop, one of those fifty-somethings who has spent their life drinking milky coffees on the corner, waiting for orders from a superior. Needless to say, brutal with detainees and suspects, I was sure of that. Only he couldn't accept my using the same methods. A woman should be dif-ferent, show understanding towards the weak, solidarity with her sex, restraint in her expression, and regret for the presence of so much evil in the world. Poor Garzón, he was going to find himself with a difficult pill to swallow, and he didn't even know Shakespeare or Don Juan Manuel, so the "Taming of the Shrew" wouldn't serve as a spiritual example. Limited hori-zons, linear life, far from the deep chasms and sudden lifts of my own. Well, now I had a case, something I'd always wanted, it was absolutely essential I believed in my role and returned to a time when I thought that being in the police would make my days interesting, close to the heart of things. But maybe the case had arrived too late, like all wishes that come true. It had caught me off balance, in the process of putting down roots, a house with a backyard, the firm intention of resisting the onslaught of love's passion, something like turning up at the banquet of life convinced that eating's not good for you. But it's difficult to retreat in the heat of the action; a stone always splashes on the surface of a calm lake. Whatever, there was no use thinking, sooner or later this case would be taken off our hands, I was expecting it and, when the moment arrived, was sure it wouldn't matter. It would be different for Garzón. However much he said he'd seen it all before, having just been transferred, he'd be keen to cap his impeccable, gray career. Though maybe he simply wanted to be discharged, to be able to go back home, where a bowl of hot soup would be waiting, and to enjoy the pensioners' meetings and a game of billiards. A reasonable plan, quiet for both of us. But I couldn't say to him, "Come on, sergeant, that's enough fooling around, let's get the job done and move on to something new." No, I had to stay where I was, defend my duty, demonstrate that I had it in me to take the reins of an investigation: a woman cannot afford the luxury of backing down, especially if she's a para-trooper, a policewoman or a bus driver. And as for Garzón, he'd have to put up with the orders of a greenhorn like me, having crawled down all the alleyways of the country, arresting drunks and jailing prostitutes. Too much for us, hopefully they'd soon take us off the case.

I was in a foul mood. According to my life's new regula-tions, now was not the time to order a takeaway pizza but to set about cooking. Some frozen peas would suffice. I left the door open to listen to the music from the lounge. A perfect sys-tem which would end up working well. No neighbors above or below, no gossiping witnesses of mediocrity. At nine, however, the doorbell rang. It was Pepe.

"My cat's died," he exclaimed as soon as I answered.

I let him in with an almost violent gesture. I was about to offer him a drink, the correct thing to do, but I realized this couldn't go on.

"Pepe, you can't come here every time your cat dies."

"But I only had the one left."

"You know perfectly well what I mean. Before it was almost normal, I still lived in our old apartment, but now I've a house and I want to enjoy it. We're separated, remember?"

"It wasn't my intention to bother you. We're friends and I like to pay my friends visits."

"What if I wasn't on my own?"

"I'd have left straight away."

It was important he didn't stay for dinner, that would have upset my first day of normality, much more than I could permit. We were good friends, he was right, and I'd always have the impression that I'd used him according to the swell of my personal criterion and then spewed him on to the beach, wet and alone. Though it wasn't true. How could a man be left wet and alone who was only twenty-eight and had his whole life in front of him? He said he'd drop by from time to time, repair the sockets, drink a beer, and that was all right. But he'd turned up on two successive days. Too risky, too absurd as well.

"I think she was run over. She was in the back of the bar, she came and went as she pleased, as you know, she was pretty independent. I found her lying with trickles of blood in her mouth, she couldn't breathe. I took her to the vet, but there was nothing doing."

I had never shared his mysticism about cats. When we were married, it annoyed me to see his purring animal about the place, on the bed or curled up between my high heels.

"I'm truly sorry. Have a beer and then go, tomorrow I have to get up far too early."

He sat down, observing the small lounge. The boxes were next to the wall, waiting to be unpacked.

"If you like, I'll help you with that tomorrow."

"No, thank you, not tomorrow. I've been assigned a case and have a very busy day."

"That's what you wanted."

"It's only temporary, there was no one else to take it on. I'm sure they'll relieve me as soon as another inspector becomes available."

"Is it a murder that is beyond your experience?"

"It's not a murder, it's a rape."

Neither of my husbands had ever fathomed the ins and outs of police work. For Hugo, what I did amounted to a kind of monotonous librarianship, but in a sordid environment that didn't suit me. Pepe, on the other hand, seemed convinced that a policeman's sole aim was to tackle elusive killers. In both cases: too much television.

"A ritual rape?"

"Forget about it, Pepe, it's a bit late to be discussing it."

When I first met him, I was greatly amused by his ability to turn things on their head. He struck me as a sweet, attractive boy, a break from all the obstacles of reality. He lived in the world on a different level. I could climb or descend his stairs as I liked.

"I don't think I'll get another cat."

"Good idea."

"I'm fed up of losing the things I love. The fewer the ties of affection, the better."

"You know that's always been my philosophy."

"Yep, I know."

At the time, I had not wanted us to get married, it was enough to live together. But he insisted. His mother, a very traditional woman, had been widowed, refusing to go down to the registry office would have involved a terrible fuss. And what did it really matter? Then, after a few months, his traditional mother hooked up with a taxi driver and took off to Madrid. Didn't even say goodbye to her son. She relied on me to assume her maternal responsibilities and abandoned him. Later I abandoned him, and now his blasted cat had died. But he still wasn't going to stay for dinner.

"I found out a way to regenerate frozen plants. It might work with your geraniums."

This interested me and I listened attentively.

"But it's not something that can be explained in five minutes. If you like, I'll come and try it out one of these days."

Another proffered hand. I'd never be rid of him.

"You can come and teach me, I prefer to learn."

"Are you also going to learn how to fix sockets?"

"I might do so. At the station they're organizing some DIY courses for detectives, I think I'll sign up."

It was such a ridiculous lie he should have gotten offended, but he probably believed me, he probably entertained such a possibility in his pretty archangel's head, overworked cops taking a rest from bloody murders and ritual rapes to unblock drainpipes. He was left with no beer and no fire-lighters for kindling conversation, so he stood up and walked straight towards a cupboard.

"The exit's that way," I pointed.

He unhurriedly changed direction, put on his anorak and made to leave.

"I'm sorry about your cat."

"Me too, she was a very understanding cat and kept me company."

Even Mother Teresa of Calcutta, exposed and inured to the most atrocious human miseries, would have taken pity on him, would have sat him down at her table and served him up a plate of rice. But not me, I even cursed him because the peas were overcooked. But there was no point in losing hope, tomorrow was another day; all the tomorrows, with a bit of luck, they'd turn out better.

I was in the Department of Documentation, rearranging some papers, when Garzón himself got in touch with me. I rarely received calls there, so I was a little surprised. I immediately recognized his cracked smoker's voice.

"Petra? I'm sorry to bother you but I absolutely had to call. I'm afraid to say another girl's been raped. The case is ours because she also was marked with the flower."

"The flower?"

"You know, that strange circle on the arm."

The flower. So it turned out the sergeant wasn't only merciful, he also had a poetic vein. It would be interesting to know what other spiritual qualities were hiding behind his belly. I made a beeline for Homicide.

We had a rapist on our hands, and things were going to get ugly, as they say in bad movies. A rapist in the true tradition, including sacrificial rites and all the rest. Pepe may not have been so wide of the mark. This time the attack had taken place in the neighborhood not of Trinitat but of Verneda, so we'd avoid having to pay another visit to the hateful director of the reformatory. Also on this occasion there were no obvious signs of violence, except for the flower. The aggressor, a tall and apparently young man, wearing a mask, had accosted the victim as she was returning home from work. He had threatened her with a knife and taken her to a nearby, poorly fenced lot. He made her climb up on to a beer crate he had no doubt prepared and jump inside. Once inside the lot, he raped her.

"The girl has declared there was prior upper molestation," said Garzón.

"And what's that?"

"Mammary suctions and the like."

"Do you mean he fondled her tits? Is that what you're trying to tell me?"

He eyed me with aversion.

"Yes, that's right."

Where had this policeman come from, my God, from a seminary? And why had he fallen to me exactly? There were already lots of women working for the police and more than once he must have bumped into one, spoken to her. Why the hell did he say "mammary suctions"? Did he never swear in front of a woman? Did he shout out "testicles!" instead of "balls!" in moments of tension?

"Did the rapist come? I mean, did he excrete his semen into the woman's body?" I inquired bad-temperedly.

"It seems not. The girl has just come out of the clinic, she's with a social worker. In an hour we can question her again."

"Again? Has someone already done so?"

"The chief inspector."

"First warning, we'll be back to our normal routine before you know it."

He didn't reply. We had to pace up and down for an hour, I was about to clear off and leave him there. However, I tried to regain my composure. We went to the coffee machine.

"Do you take milk?"

"Yes."

We sat down on a bench in the corridor like a couple of pupils who've been thrown out of class.

"Listen, Garzón, let's be honest, you don't like women very much, do you?"

He looked at me with a flush of panic. I found it necessary to clarify what I'd said:

"I mean you'd rather have a male colleague, a male boss."

It seemed I had given him the opportunity to get something off his chest. He turned towards me with coffee-stained lips:

"Well, inspector, since you ask, I'll tell you what I really think. To start with, I'm not a male chauvinist. I think it's fair for women to work, it's normal, I accept it, there's no problem. But then, when push comes to shove, having female colleagues in certain jobs makes things very difficult."

"But why?"

"Look what happened at National Rail. According to the new guidelines, a woman can be a porter, an engineer, a mechanic . . . but then what happened in practice? Women didn't have enough physical strength for certain jobs and had to be helped, they needed separate cabins to get changed in . . . in short, a real mess."

"I don't understand you. What does this have to do with our case? For this job, we don't need physical strength, we don't need to get changed . . . "

"It was just an example. We have other problems."

"What, having to say 'suction' instead of 'fondle'? Is that what bothers you?"

"I feel a little embarrassed, yes."

"Well, don't hold back for my sake, sergeant. I also say 'cunt,' 'balls' and 'fuck.'"

He swallowed.

"Hearing you say it is also embarrassing, excuse me, it must be a question of manners."

"What the hell do you want me to do, use sign language? The result could be even more shocking."

He gestured impatiently.

"Don't make it difficult for me, it's just that we're dealing with a case of rape and the allusions are constant. It's not only that. With a man there's something to talk about, even if it's soccer, but with you . . . I suppose there weren't many women at the station in Salamanca, just the ID girls."

I suddenly took pity on him, his attempts to turn prejudices into rational arguments, his defensive hostility towards me. I understood him. But it's very dangerous first to understand, then to take pity. And I'd decided not to do it anymore.

"You can go home, sergeant. I think I can manage to question the girl on my own."

He didn't understand a word. He was open-mouthed as if he'd been told to throw himself off a cliff. I didn't fully understand my reaction either, but knew I absolutely had to be on my guard at the first symptoms of pity. Dostoevsky called it humankind's only salvation, but he obviously wasn't talking specifically about women.

"As you wish," said the sergeant.

He was offended, he stood up and walked down the corridor surrounded by a halo of injustice that could be seen at a hundred yards. I also felt pretty bad. I hadn't done the correct thing, the correct thing would have been to shout at him, "Listen, Garzón, don't give me that about National Rail. I'm your boss. So stop messing around and act normal!"

People are much better at being told off than at handling civilized coldness. But I had banned repentance as well as pity, so I interrupted my thoughts and went to get another coffee. I watched the small wonders of technology working in the machine, fairly useless advances, since the entire workforce preferred to carry on crossing the street to the bar, where, aside from the stimulus of caffeine, they enjoyed other incentives such as conversation and tumultuous noise.

The biting wind produced by Garzón's silent wrath did not settle. An official called me over, the victim was ready to make a statement. I threw the plastic cup in the wastebasket and got to my feet. All this irritating feminist business with the sergeant was preventing me from concentrating on the case. Or maybe it was the certainty I had that they'd soon relieve me. If this case turned into that of a large-scale serial rapist, it would quickly gain notoriety and be taken off our hands, mine and, of course, my belligerent colleague's. What should I do then? Protest? Things weren't so bad in Documentation, I'd go back there.

Before the second victim, I had the same impression as before the first: a small, frightened, defenseless mouse ready to flee. She wasn't accompanied, her parents had already left. I was told one of her brothers would pick her up as soon as we let her go. Her hair was curly and dyed blond, spoiled by the mistreatment of hair sprays and perms. Barely seventeen. Like the first, she didn't seem very keen to talk. She worked in a local hairdresser's.

"I wash hair and help to clean the salon. I lock up at nights."

After this final duty, she was surprised by the rapist. According to previous cases I had consulted, a large number of rapes occurred at the weekend, at the exit of bars and discos. This helped to direct the investigations more easily. You could check those who attended local places of entertainment, the circle of friends, the odd guy whose behavior had been strange all through the evening, the odd thug. Such a path was blocked on this occasion. That said, the subject of the girl's friends and relations could not be left out, especially now there were two victims presumably of the same rapist. The mark was a clear link between both girls, though they'd never even met.

She corroborated that she hadn't seen his face, but his complexion and stature coincided with those described by the first victim, as well as the mysterious manner of marking her arm.

"He brought something close to me, applied pressure and I felt a strong pain."

"Was he carrying the object he marked you with, holding it or something?"

"I couldn't say."

"Was he wearing it on his wrist, a bracelet maybe?"

"I don't know. I suddenly felt this pain, a sharp jab, and started to faint."

Her small, unattractive face was blurred, as though it was being erased. She was so fragile I was afraid she'd fold back on herself any moment like a simple umbrella or a spring box.

"You'll have to give me a list of all your friends' names. You've probably lots of friends, and the odd boyfriend too."

"It wasn't my boyfriend. Or one of my friends."

"We just want to ask them a few questions." She burst into tears. "I'm not accusing them."

I suddenly understood what it was.

"You don't want them to find out, is that it?"

She carried on crying without answer. Of course it was. She was subject to passive dishonor, sully, shame. Standing before her lover would never be the same.

"Listen here, you're not to blame for what's happened, you mustn't feel ashamed."

She nodded impatiently:

"I know, I know, they already told me."

The social worker had done her job. I felt fairly stupid trying to teach that girl a woman's basic rights. I watched her mouse-like face; she was like one of those mice we've caught in the trap and can observe at leisure, the soft fur, the eyes like two minute buttons. Hour after hour of washing hair, talking about the events of last Saturday, the horoscope, the hairdo, the fashion, the illustrated magazines. It probably hadn't been her boyfriend or any of her friends, trapped mice like her, their long, unpleasant tails following them wherever they go. Well, what had we done the first time? Follow a circumstantial, insignificant clue. The boy at the reformatory wasn't lying, we checked out his alibi and it was correct. This time we had to dig deeper, take better aim.

I brought Garzón up to date over the phone. He answered with monosyllables. "Right. Right." He'd undertake to find out the friends' addresses, to locate and question them.

"We need to do the same with the friends of the cook's daughter. Did you get that?"

"Will do."

Bare and efficient like the mechanism of a watch. Perhaps like this, within the parameters of simple authority and the strict dictates of duty, our relationship would improve. Clearly we had to lighten the emotional load. Because of the blasted emotional load, athletes lose decisive competitions, business-men make false steps and the police can botch an investigation. Coldness.

On leaving the station, I headed for my gym. I always did this. A cop needs to stay in good shape, this is what I'd been taught at the Academy, though for sitting in the Department of Documentation it was never necessary. I attended a packed class of rhythm and muscle-building. I was the oldest student but, dressed in leotards and sweating, the age barriers soon faded. In the changing room, all these young girls made the same stupid remarks they'd have made had I not been there. They asked my opinion about lightweight problems, tried on new swimsuits and laughed. It was a pleasant experience, I managed to forget about everything in that frivolous environment. But that day, with a two-kilo dumb-bell in each hand, things were not the same. It was difficult for me to separate my classmates from a brutal and tragic context. Any one of them could be raped as she left class, marked with a flower. They all seemed to me in danger of being pushed towards a nightmare that would destroy their minds, if not their lives. At any moment, for no good reason. I glanced at them all, their legs drawing circles in the air, their necks out-stretched. I understood that enjoying life was not now going to be easy. The most fragile girls appeared to be that son of a bitch's ideal victims. So far this was their only point in common.

"And their social class," said Garzón a few days later. "The two of them were low-income workers with no professional qualifications."

"True. You don't think we're getting ahead of ourselves by linking the two cases?"

"I'm sure the two rapes were committed by the same guy. No one else goes about marking girls like that."

Suddenly he realized he'd been too informal and spontaneous, he remembered he was angry.

"Well, it's just my humble opinion."

Investigations among the victims' friends had not shed a glimmer of light. But they were personally revealing to me. It had never occurred to me to consider the great mass of dispossessed youth wandering the city streets. They were not outcasts or criminals. In fact they were all more or less integrated into the social wheel. The wheel, however, as I found out, seemed to pass over them and crush them without thinking. If they weren't unemployed, they filled jobs that had come out of the labor subsoil. Couriers who delivered small packages for hours, riding fragile motorbikes, breathing the city's polluted air. Checkout girls, eternally on their feet, fixed to their cash registers like another mechanical part. They caught buses from outlying suburbs to the center, returned home at night with just enough time for dinner. The few I questioned had tired, discolored eyes, barely managed to assert their youth by dressing carelessly or cutting their hair according to the latest vulgar fashion. Trainee mechanics, salesgirls, waiters, a whole lumpen in bloom. They knew nothing about the rapes, they had no intuitions or suspicions. Nor were they indignant at what had happened, they simply answered. Someone had raped their friends, sure, it was out of order. But heaps of pointless things could be loaded on their plebeian backs. They were used to bearing the weight, watching these things fall on top of them with no great surprise.

"What do you do on Sundays?"

"This and that."

"This and that?"

"Play games, go to the disco."

"What about Salomé?"

"Salomé? The same. I'd see her some Sundays, others not."

The families' situation was not much better. The fathers were workers, or unemployed. Almost all the mothers had a second subsistence job: washing stairs, cleaning windows in a bank, sewing hems for a dressmaking factory.

"Some panorama! These kids don't have it easy, don't you think?"

Sergeant Garzón didn't have a clue what I was talking about.

"Who does?"

Now he would tell me he'd had to pull a cart full of sacks when he was young, or some other atrocity. But no, he stayed quiet. Was I the one who had it easy, a spoiled brat who'd ended up joining the police, an "intellectual gem" as the chief inspector described me? I was forced to keep up my surly attitude because, as soon as I lowered it, there were Garzón's dog eyes observing me.

"It seems obvious the conversations with all these boys have led us nowhere. Do you suggest another path of investigation?"

He raised his rural doctor's eyebrows in my direction.

"And don't say you'll do as you're told, I know that already."

He blushed slightly and nodded:

"I'd check out the bars in Verneda. The guy could be a regular. He may have been drinking a lot that night to egg himself on."

"Good. O.K. then. Well, don't just stand there! We can go right now."

He adopted an expression of suppressed irony, as if he were making fun.

"Inspector, the kind of bar I'm talking about opens only at night, as you should know."

I pretended not to notice the impertinence.

"Fine, I'll see you tonight. Tell me where and what time."

The idea of a nocturnal outing finished me off. I had planned to spend a quiet evening in my new home. I couldn't find the right moment to enjoy it, to integrate into it, to stamp it with my own style. Had it been an illusion to suggest such a life? I refused to accept such a big cliché. The rape case was a passing situation, soon everything would return to its usual course. And I proposed to control this course myself, as well as the current. No unexpected floods, thaws or droughts, a regular, moderate flow of water.

I returned home intending to rest a little, take a shower, eat. I needed to gird up my patience at the maddening prospect of going out at night with the seductive Garzón. I just hoped I didn't bump into Hugo in the street, it would have been unbearable to have him witness that graceless professional activity. I turned on the heating and checked the frozen geraniums. Maybe Pepe had come to revive them with his new invention and not found me at home. I went to the kitchen and selected a sachet of readymade soup. "Soups for Your Home," declared a colorful announcement with a photograph underneath of an attractive woman holding a steaming tureen in both hands. She and the tureen created a home together, that was it, I didn't even need the geraniums.

Having eaten, I sank into a bath in which I had dissolved some strawberry-flavored bath salts. It felt good, like forming part of a sensual fruit salad. I closed my eyes. How long would it be before they took us off the case? Would they give us the remotest chance of solving it? Affairs at the station must be extremely complicated for us still to be on it. The truth is at this stage in my career I was resigned to not taking part in active service. But the thought of losing the case now triggered in me a small internal rebellion. What was going on? Was I acquiring a taste for Homicide? It didn't seem to offer many advantages: irregular hours, depressing environments, greater responsibility. And all far from the brilliant Theory of Evil that could be constructed with books and archives in the Department of Documentation.

The phone rang. I immediately thought it was the sergeant, but it was Hugo. He needed further details of mine to draw up the contracts of sale. Did he really not remember my ID number? It must surely appear in one of our divorce papers, so either he hadn't bothered to look for it or he wanted to talk to me for some reason. He was friendly and even relaxed, the topic of his forthcoming marriage came up. He was very busy with the preparations. They would honeymoon in Paris and the office had to carry on running in his absence.

"Elvira's very classical, she won't travel to an exotic country, she considers it vulgar. She'd rather go for walks by the Seine, dine in restaurants in the Latin Quarter."

It was the first time he'd said her name, it sounded good. When we were married, he tried several times to persuade me to change my name legally. He found Petra undistinguished. The fact that this was my grandmother's name was an accident that shouldn't determine the rest of my life. He preferred Celia. I almost did what he wanted, but fortunately refused. Since then, however, I'd been unable to tell anyone my name for the first time without feeling a pang of guilt. Petra really was horrible, it might not have been a bad idea to replace it.

"I don't care where we go. We've our life in front of us and will have many opportunities to travel the world, don't you think?"

"Of course you will."

A mysterious situation. Why was he telling me all this? The

tragedy of the modern American man resides in phone calls with his ex-wife, a battering that's difficult to take: demands for an increase in maintenance, unexpected reproaches dating back a thousand years, unsettling moments of tenderness that resurface. Maybe the Hispanic case was the reverse and it was the turn of us ex-wives to endure past visits. The thought of Hugo phoning for a chat each time he fought with Elvira made my flesh crawl. Something unimaginable during all those years when his wounded honor was the sole support of our silent relationship. Though perhaps it was just that Hugo, before getting married, wanted to make sure that his new circumstance would not allow me to stop feeling guilty. I had left and, in the annals of the civilized world, the woman never leaves.

"Sure, Hugo, you've plenty of time to go visiting places."

What else could I say? And, having said it, I again felt guilty, like always.

Garzón was waiting for me in a pub, a dive that resembled a warehouse. He'd already started questioning the owner, a kind of giant with a brass earring in his right ear. The owner was so annoyed you could see it, the cops sniffing around in his bar was not good for business, the sooner we cleared off the better. His customers, however, did not seem too bothered by our presence. There were lots of skinheads and girls in black tights and plastic jackets. The music bounced off the bare walls and returned to the center of the room with a growling echo somewhere between the eye of a storm and the sound of a liner out at sea. I wanted to make a beeline for the exit and, for the first time, admired Garzón's professionalism. He was undaunted, immune to the din and hostility, asking the owner questions in his ear, showing him photos of the rape victims, checking times without flinching, as if his whole life had been spent in joints like this one. After a while, he signaled to me and we left. I hadn't opened my mouth or followed the conversation.

"He doesn't know anything but, even if he had, I doubt he'd have told us something. He struck me as a complete . . . bad sort."

I realized that this pause should have given way to the word "bastard," but the sergeant was still making concessions to my femininity. We went to the second bar on his list, which wasn't exactly a tearoom either. Till then I had failed to appreciate my colleague's command of what in police circles is termed "street culture." The tone he adopted for questioning was neutral but firm, and he showed a leathery politeness that turned into a veiled threat if his interlocutor lapsed for a moment. He was neither shameless, nor cynical, nor fawning. He had visited many bars in his life, I was sure of that. This owner was a fairly harmless type who insisted on inviting us to a beer, but he didn't talk. He knew nothing and nobody that might help us.

By the fifth drinking-den, I thought I was going to plunge into despair. Theoretically a search of bars should have been something attractive, a compendium of sociology and neocultural immersion. But theories hang on quality and completely ignore repetition. I was fed up with seeing stripped walls, icy counters, fed up with the sergeant's identical questions. I was sick to death of strident music and beer. It was almost one in the morning and I'd begun to wonder if all this time would count as overtime or be paid at the normal rate, though most likely it wouldn't be paid at all, being considered an occupational hazard. I couldn't bring myself to ask my colleague, such buns would not fit in our interpersonal oven. So we carried on knocking back beers among youths from various urban gangs who'd completely lost their memories in the face of our questions.

"Are we getting anywhere like this, Garzón?" I asked finally.

He looked at me as if this were a question that didn't need answering. He armed himself with patience and sighed.

"You see, in cases of rape, you don't tend to get very far

when dealing with people. Nobody knows anything. Everybody thinks it's serious and is paralyzed by fear, they don't digress, don't give clues they're not sure of. It's normal for them not to know much, these things happen very privately. In cases of smuggling or robbery it's another story, then it can work well with informers. Still, this is something we're obliged to do, we have to rule out possibilities."

I observed him with curiosity, impressed by his knowledge.

"Have you ever had contact with informers?" I asked.

"It's my specialty, I give them confidence. I'm using them at the moment to investigate the smuggling of tobacco."

"Oh, yeah! How's it going?"

"Not bad."

My feet hurt. Three hours wasted on the obligatory ruling out of possibilities. Three hours scouring joints that, to a certain extent, were not a novelty for me. I knew something about them, not in vain was my dashing second ex-husband: owner of an environmentalist, pacifist, anarchoid bar in which, alongside traditional alcoholic drinks, they served gluten balls as snacks. I bought the bar for him, it was the solution to his problems. Pepe had graduated in sociology but, needless to say, he never even thought of trying to find a job in that field. I met him in the crowded bar of the court-house, where he worked as a waiter. We got on well, I thought he'd make the ideal antidote to the seriousness of my former life. Some time later, when we decided to get married, I suggested using part of the money raised by the sale of my and Hugo's apartment to set up the bar he so wanted. He joined forces with a Maghribi friend of his called Hamed and they set up the Ephemerides, a place where their philosophy and way of doing things prevailed. He felt happy, he could coexist there with people of his own age and orientation: neonatural-ist enemies of science, conscientious objectors, Green Party supporters, modernized Stoics, antinuclear protesters and practitioners of the most unbelievable arts. A somewhat shabby guild, but a loyal brotherhood. We hadn't checked out their kind of gang tonight, though it was fairly unthinkable for a friend of the rape victims to have emerged from the Ephemerides. From the Ephemerides or any other place we'd visited, because basically these girls didn't look as if they'd ever come close to any urban tendency, they were too anodyne, gray, seemingly swept along by the torrent of the city, with no platform to grab hold of.

We'd finished. There were no more names on Garzón's list. I felt so depressed, frozen and exhausted that I asked the sergeant if we could go into a final bar, this time not for investigative reasons, just to have a short, sharp drink to overcome the effervescent effect of so much beer.

"Tomorrow we have to get up early," he argued.

"O.K., if you don't want to come, I'll go on my own."

I entered a crestfallen musical establishment, one of those sad places designed for mature and lonely people to form a relationship with no strings attached. There were eye-catching, gaudy women, advanced in years and flesh, and semi-bald men in their fifties, wearing alpaca suits and fat imitation Rolexes.

I ordered a brandy. Out of the corner of my eye, I saw that Garzón had followed me. He leaned on the bar and ordered the same as me. We didn't talk to each other. There wasn't much to say. In the background, they were playing one of those overcooked, doughy boleros.

Tell me why we separated.
Tell me why time interfered with our love.

A smartly repugnant man toyed with the cameo hanging from a woman's fleshy neck. He lifted it in the air, then let it fall on her ostentatious breasts veiled only by a thin blouse of artificial silk. I looked at Garzón, who had shrunk inside himself and was drinking in short sips the unhappiness oozing from his glassy, unlit eyes. I deduced that the bolero was stirring his inner soul.

"Good music, right?" he said to hide his sudden surprise at being observed.

I cracked a joke. He turned to face me, once again amazed by my stupidity.

"Boleros tell the true story of love. If you pay attention to the lyrics, you'll see it's all there."

Now I was the one to be amazed. I judged it inappropriate to admit I found the music grotesque and coarse.

"I hadn't thought about it."

"Well, think about it."

No one will ever know how much I've loved you, no one will ever know how far my passion's gone.

"I used to dance to them with my wife. You know, at family parties and celebrations."

His eyes grew even more opaque.

"Did you love your wife a lot?"

He took a long swig and abruptly livened up:

"You've formed a wrong idea about me, inspector."

Things had taken an unexpected turn. I protested just to give him a suitable colloquial entry.

"No, what I . . . "

"You have, I know what I'm saying, a false image, that's what you have of me. You've taken me for an unfeeling male chauvinist, for a man of little sensitivity, and I assure you that's not true. I have a very high opinion of women, I literally put them on a pedestal. I believe they're wonderful beings, full of spirituality, perfect and beautiful like a flower."

The sergeant's capacity for comparison was clearly limited, the rapist's mark was like a flower, women were like a flower . . .

He smiled at me, I think for the first time. Who then would have dared explain to him that flowers are just perishable matter, it's easy to fall off pedestals, and spirits are characterized by being ethereal and so neither count nor take up any room?

"I understand you, Garzón, but what you have to realize is that all these feminine virtues in the workplace get in the way more than anything, they hamper our relationship. I'd like you to think of me as a colleague."

Garzón downed his drink, sniffed the air in distemper and concluded:

"For me a woman's always a woman. Is that all?"

"You can take me home, please."

As we crossed the bar towards the exit, one of those crumpled flowers—tattered spirit on tottering pedestal—let out a coquettish, hysteriform laugh aimed at her dressy gallant. I shuddered. We drove home in silence. It had been a failed attempt at a rapprochement, sealed by his "Is that all?" which put paid to the possibility of a peaceful agreement. No doubt the sergeant, moored at the hard bank of the wheel, was cursing himself by now for having allowed that stupid bolero to spark off his emotions unnecessarily.

"I want you to start investigating the girls' families tomorrow."

"Their families?" he asked in surprise.

"Remember there may be cousins, uncles, men nearby, who've become obsessed with them."

"Then how do you explain the mark? Those girls had nothing to do with each other, no family in common."

"It doesn't matter, one thing could lead to another along paths we don't know. In any case, we're so lacking in clues we need some thread to pull on."

"As you wish, inspector, will do."

I heard the car behind me pulling away in the cold of night. Someone had slipped an envelope under my door. Intrigued, I opened it, it may have something to do with the case, the confession of a witness who preferred to remain anonymous. But my intrigue disappeared when I saw a photograph of Milena sprawled on the sofa. There was a note from Pepe: "I thought you'd like to keep a memento of the poor cat. I'll pop by in case you need more copies. See you soon."

This was the limit, Pepe knew I'd never been able to stand that lazy, wheedling animal. It was such a poor excuse to turn up at my house it should have made me smile. Contact with ex-husbands, a strange business. Marriage was a fatty substance which always left stains on the skin, however much you scrubbed it with soap. I'd already conjectured about Hugo's motives for reappearing, Pepe's were much more direct, in fact since our divorce he hadn't stopped returning. I tore up the blasted dead cat's photograph and immediately regretted the gratuitous, ill-humored gesture. I was already annoyed at having had to put up with my work colleague's feeble clichés, at the cold I'd suffered, at the horrible bars, pedestals, pure spirits and the flower, most of all the flower. It's easy to be level-headed and balanced when surrounded by intelligence and comfort, such are the honeyed fruits of civility.

4

A few days later, there was a third rape with the same mark on the arm and the case became fodder for the national press. The downpour began. The journalists wanted to know details, and they got them: the victim was eighteen years old, attended an evening class in design and dressmaking, lived in the neighborhood of Gracia and also hadn't seen the rapist's face. However, the stature, complexion, method and, above all, the hateful mark on the arm seemed to indicate it was the same young man, equipped with a strange weapon that left a circle of precise pinpricks on the skin. These details, published in all the accident and crime reports, made up the official version. But, as always in such cases and without anyone knowing the system, leaks soon appeared. One headline almost hit the mark: "The Investigation of These Mass Rapes Is in the Hands of Two Inspectors Who Curiously Belong Not to Homicide But to Documentation." In a scarcely concealed tone of reproach, another said: "The Inquiry Seems to Be Making No Progress. Utter Confusion Reigns in Police Circles." Hunting season was open.

This time it had been difficult to get anything out of the girl: she was in a state of shock, in the care of psychologists who had knocked her out with sedatives. Furthermore, we were dealing with a high-strung family. The father, a metalworker, kept flying off the handle, swearing to wreak revenge, denouncing justice, the police, any institution with the slightest responsibility. The mother cried all the time and was also administered sedatives. It seemed the girl had put up resistance, for which she not only got the mark on the arm but received a punch on the nose. As usual the rapist had barely said a word and had acted very cautiously, sheltered by the darkness and loneliness of the street.

When the chief inspector summoned me, I had no qualms in embellishing the situation.

"We've already lots to go on," I began. "He's obviously someone with a personality disorder, you know, resentful of women and so on. He opts for girls who are clearly helpless, thin, short and fragile. He isn't motivated by fits of passion. He's cold and calculated. He chooses the girls, follows them for a few days till he's worked out their movements and carefully picks his moment. He's astute, doesn't speak, always covers his face, switches neighborhood. He's proud of his misdeeds, otherwise he wouldn't perform the macabre rite of marking each girl with the flower. Something must have provoked his crime-fest or else a gradual charge over time has led to an explosion, which is why the rapes have occurred in such quick succession. He is not, however, a particularly cruel or morbid individual. There are no other signs of abuse or violence, nor does he appear overly to enjoy the rape itself, he doesn't come, he marks the girls and leaves."

The chief inspector eyed me with a certain amount of surprise at the end of my exposition. The truth is I also felt surprised by the whole series of deductions I had managed to thread together. It gave the impression we'd made progress in the investigation, which in fact we hadn't. We were still at the start, clueless, irresolute, not knowing which way to turn. Every step we had taken ended in a path of frustration and we were out of new ideas. Garzón carried on combing bars like an experienced hairstylist and, now that the case had become a serial crime, I had meetings with the police psychologists in an attempt to draw up a profile. But the fact is psychology as a science resembles a mix of intuition and fantasy, nothing like a science. Every time I spoke to the young team I had explained the case to, every time they started a sentence with that perpetual "It would seem that . . . " I felt a wave of despair. What followed was so obvious it could have come out of a manual: "childhood problems, dominant mothers, unresolved Oedipus complexes, probable intermittent impotence, the inability to build ordinary emotional relationships . . . "

One day I squared up to the chief psychologist:

"Listen, don't you think this is all a bit simplistic?"

He was barely more than twenty-five and at the station was considered a brilliant prodigy. He had finished complicated masters and theses and his judgments were met with blind faith. He looked at me with eyes used to incredulity.

"What did you expect, inspector? Human behavior is extremely varied, unpredictable, full of twists and turns, but it always revolves around the same identical points, the most everyday things: love, jealousy, envy, resentment, control. That's what makes Shakespeare's work still relevant."

"Please don't talk to me about literature; that's even worse."

He burst out laughing.

"Anyway, we'll do what's always done in such cases. I'll give you the medical histories of individuals who psychologically match your rapist and who are out in the street having served a sentence or who are in open prison or on probation. It's all I can do to help you."

He had pretty hazel-colored eyelashes and long hair tied back in a ponytail. I guessed what he might think of me: another sullen cop, incapable of theorizing or dealing with abstractions. He may have been right, it's just that I was, as never before, in pressing need of a concrete detail, a clue, of some solid ground to push off from. How could theories be put into practice, in what way should speculation take form?

It was fine to articulate hypotheses, but then, a few steps later, you came across misshapen reality. What places needed scouring, who needed questioning? This was something I had not had to face in my world of text printed on paper. I took the files the psychologist handed me and went over them at home. Most of them were vulgar stories, the brilliant youth was right about that. Guys who appeared in the photograph on the front page looking disgusted or afraid, making slight grimaces that gave nothing away. Family backgrounds that were sometimes normal, others on the brink of marginalization. Youngsters who had it in for women, the children of mothers who had abandoned them or been too possessive or overly protective. A miscellany of assorted women who all, however, nursed crime. I had fortunately avoided creating one of those monsters, having consciously deprived myself of the pleasures of motherhood. A couple of them owed their unbalance to unhappy love affairs or adult sexual disturbances, but generally the mothers took the lion's share. I had to tell the sergeant all this, study the new material with him. We'd been working apart for the last two days, which he must have found a relief. But now we absolutely had to sit down together. I called the station. He wasn't there but, having identified me, they gave me his home number. A woman answered, which surprised me, and, when I said his name, she remarked rudely, "Ah, the cop!" She then went to inform him and over the phone I heard the background noise: the clatter of plates, a radio turned up loud, knocks at a door . . . I deduced he lived in a boarding house. He picked up the phone with suppressed alarm and didn't seem very happy to recognize me.

"Do you want me at the station?"

"Listen, sergeant, I hate to abuse your kindness, but it's so cold and late . . . What do you say we meet informally in my house? We might even work better. If it's O.K. with you, I'll give you my address."

"Go ahead. I'll be there right away."

If my request was inconvenient for him, he'd decided to make concessions, but, when he arrived, he rang the doorbell with all the indications of being on an official mission. He was visibly embarrassed when he came in, but calmed down after a while. He looked at the parcels of books next to the door to the garden.

"The thing is I moved fairly recently. Do you like my house?"

"It's very nice."

I hadn't often seen him smile. His Mexican mustache, which was streaked with white, had only moved to drink or talk. He had carefully combed his hair and smelled of cologne water as when we saw each other in the office in the morning.

"Can I offer you a drink?"

He hesitated. According to his antiquated protocol, the correct thing would have been to refuse.

"I also have coffee."

He still couldn't make up his mind.

"I'll bring them both, I guess that'll help to keep us awake."

I left him on his own, sitting bolt upright in an armchair, more uncomfortable than if he'd been tied to the electric chair. I realized he must be feeling unwell, I'd dragged him out of his room and forced him to come to my house, where there was a greater sense of intimacy. I had to remember that till now our relationship hadn't been at all friendly. He was in my territory and finding it difficult to behave naturally. I thought the best thing would be to get straight down to work.

"Come close. This is what I wanted to show you."

He drew up to the table and the files occupied all our attention. We read them one by one. He took notes separately, studied each report, went back, compared.

"We need to reject all those whose weight and stature don't match the description of the rapist," he said.

"And then how would you proceed?"

"First see what neighborhoods they live in, where they go, question them and immediately check out their alibis."

I saw a mammoth, repetitive task before me, like starting all over again a hundred times. I was invaded by a stream of laziness, a gust that gripped my brain. How many more routine acts would we have to carry out from a position of ignorance? I realized I wasn't completely absorbed in this case and would be willing to drop it as soon as they asked me, which wouldn't be long. That was why I felt lazy; it was like leveling mountains so that others could walk on flat ground. Especially now that the case had acquired importance thanks to the press. Our days were numbered, perhaps this was what I wanted, I'd had enough of playing cops and robbers. I once thought that withstanding the sordid environment of a police investigation would be extremely hard, but began to realize that the greatest hardship lay in the terrible monotony, boredom, the constant feeling of going backwards. Garzón carried on happily before me, doing what he'd done all his life without a hint that it bothered him. A female bookworm and a newly arrived retiree from Salamanca. The strange thing was that we were both still on the case. Probably the chief inspector hadn't dropped us to avoid feeding scraps of meat to the journalists, who'd have crucified him, nailing speculation followed by speculation.

"What do you make of all these files, sergeant?"

He shook his head, shuffling them on the table.

"The truth is it's a complicated case."

"I agree with you. A psychopathic serial rapist is much more than I was expecting to start off with. I thought these things only happened in the movies."

"Well, I hadn't exactly come across many psychopaths in Salamanca. Though, to be honest, I don't believe our man is crazy. I have the impression he's a rich kid fed up with what he has, unable to find satisfaction. So he visits working-class neighborhoods, picks a socially inferior girl, has a change and enjoys himself."

"Garzón, I didn't know you were a Marxist!"

He turned his bland eyes on me, eyes of a fried fish. This was the last thing he needed to hear.

"Never, in all my life, never have I gotten involved with politics of any kind. I've always strictly followed the orders of my superiors and done my duty."

He was really annoyed. By this stage he was openly wondering why, among all the members of the force, he had ended up with me.

"Don't get me wrong, I just meant that, for you, the social explanation of facts is definitive."

"I prefer not to delude myself. While it's true there are lots of crazy guys out there who are off their rocker, the poor are not in the habit of prissily tattooing flowers on girls' bodies. They tend to be more direct."

"Don't be so sure, everyone does what they can with their imagination, in this there are no classes. The girls have a point in common which makes me think it's someone unbalanced. The three of them are fragile like porcelain figures. This guy, Garzón, doesn't dare face up to a corpulent woman."

"Maybe."

I saw his brandy glass was empty. I poured him a little more without asking. He pretended not to notice. He piled the files up on the table.

"Well, this is all sorted, we can start tomorrow. If we find one that fits, it would be good to arrange an ID parade."

"But his face was covered . . ."

"We'll cover them all up, maybe the complexion . . . By the way, inspector, there's a TV journalist who's been following me, the director of one of those crime shows."

"Did you tell her anything?"

"Yeah, that this is not the United States, the police here simply investigate."

"Well done."

"But she'll be back."

"We might have been taken off the case by then."

"Are you still on about that? Frankly I don't care what they do to us, I'm on this case now because it's my duty, but if they send me elsewhere, I'll go without a word of complaint."

"The boss is always right?"

He was about to tell me where I could get off when the doorbell rang. Garzón started, but I immediately imagined who it could be at a time like this. I showed Pepe in, who seemed to get bogged down in his own footsteps. I introduced them by name without any further explanation.

"I've come to rescue the geraniums," he said.

"Did it have to be a night rescue?" I asked him.

"No, but since you're never at home during the day . . . "

Garzón showed no signs of making a move. I was trapped and felt obliged to offer Pepe some coffee. He accepted with pleasure. As I entered the kitchen to prepare it, leaving them on their own, I thought to myself anything could happen. To my surprise, when I returned, an icy air had taken possession of the deserted room through the door to the garden, which stood wide open. I found them outside, leaning over the alleged corpses of the geraniums, happily sharing impressions as if this were a *déjeuner sur l'herbe*. Garzón was saying something I couldn't make out and rubbing moist earth on the stalks, giving them a kind of massage. I didn't have a clue what was going on, but realized this was one of the most absurd situations I had ever experienced and I wasn't prepared to put up with it. Pepe had to go, unaccompanied; I didn't trust what he could tell Garzón if they left together. I served more coffee, turned up the heating. They were still outside, exchanging agricultural tips and fingering the plants that were the emblem of my new home. I waited with Franciscan patience and only after twenty minutes did they decide to come back in. They entered, merrily wiping their hands. Garzón made straight for his coffee.

"Your colleague says it's not necessary to pour hot water on them, as I was going to advise you, if you just rub earth on their stalks, they tend to react." He turned to Garzón. "Where did you learn so much gardening?"

"My parents were farmers, in a village near Salamanca."

"For me it's just a hobby. I was told how to revive geraniums by a guy who comes to my bar, someone who grows crops without artificial fertilizers."

"You have a bar?"

"That's how I earn a living. Do you have any idea how to prune a *Ficus Benjamina*?"

"I think so."

"I've been given one and don't know where to put the scissors."

"Not the scissors! *Ficus Benjamina* has very liquid sap and the clean cut of the metal could make it suffer a hemorrhage. You should prune by hand, using your fingers, and stanch the wound using some cotton."

"Wow, I can't believe it!"

I didn't even dare interrupt them. Clearly an irrepressible common understanding had arisen between them. I sat watching the performance, which included the rare sight of Garzón smiling, contented even. In this new light, his face was not disagreeable. His eyes assumed a lively expression and his mustache puckered, losing part of its walrus-like ferocity. It was obvious he was a pleasant chap and the only problem he had was with me. I brought out the worst humors his bulky body could secrete, I filled him with black omens till he literally couldn't take any more. I did not remember making a worse impression on anyone in my entire life. But I had tried to be friendly, neutral, polite. In vain. From now on, I would renounce any further stratagem, I understood our failure to get on was inevitable and didn't plan to receive an intensive course of gardening just to please him. Whatever happened, whether they took us off the case or we managed to solve it, when it was all over, I would never see Fermín Garzón again, or only in passing.

"And a rhododendron cutting, how would you acclimate it?"

I was obliged to forestall the botanical disquisition that was coming.

"Gentlemen, I'm very sorry to bother you, but it's really quite late . . ."

Pepe stood up.

"I'll be off, I also have an early morning."

We gave each other a peck on the cheek. He took his leave of the sergeant with furor. I went with him to the door and, on my return, found that the sergeant was also preparing to make a move.

"I've selected a few guys on the list who look interesting. If you don't mind, I can have everything organized to start questioning them at nine."

"That'll mean getting up very early."

"I'm used to sleeping little. Your brother's nice," he threw in maliciously.

"He's only my second ex-husband, hardly a brother."

He smiled ironically. I was indignant inside. It was one thing for him to want to keep our professional relationship on a frozen footing, quite another to go on the offensive. I watched through the curtains how his little car refused to start. I decided to turn a deaf ear if he came looking for help. But in the end it started and disappeared down the street, letting out small clouds of smoke from the broken exhaust. I sighed, the photos of those strangers lay on the table. The whiffs of Garzón's cheap aftershave still hung in the air together with the smell of incense that Pepe's jerseys always gave off. I felt nervous, a number of foreign presences, too many for the *sancta sanctorum* of Poble Nou. I cleared away the cigarette butts and coffee-set in a foul mood. I was going to put on a little music before sleeping but decided it would sound banal and tainted after that prosaic work meeting, something like celebrating a wedding in a brothel. The garden through the glass resembled a gaping hole. There were the geraniums, like Lazarus, waiting for that pair of losers to resurrect them.

To save time, we divided the work. Garzón would question some of the chosen men in the boardroom, I would question the others in the office. When someone is on probation and is summoned as a possible suspect to make a statement, they tend to take it rather personally. I learned this easy lesson on that morning in January, having received more looks of hatred in a short while than ever before. I noticed the extreme tiredness these men felt, how they were aware nobody expected them to be reformed. They were branded for life, had been turned into cannon-fodder and found it extraordinarily arduous to express their innocence naturally. They faltered, turned away and hid their eyes like some honorable citizens who cannot confront a customs officer without feeling guilty. I realized that what I had to do was remain patient, talk slowly, insist: "What time did you arrive? What time did you leave? What were you doing there?" Everything they said was recorded. Hour after hour of twanging accents, cocky voices, verbal diarrhea brought on by nervousness, hesitations and stammers. Together with my own voice, which I listened to in a kind of stupor, the inquisitive tone of a school-mistress rather than a cop, immutability, pauses that I considered significant, a somewhat pathetic comedy.

In the middle of one of these exhausting tugs-of-war, Garzón popped his head around the door.

"May I?" he sang out, and this turn of phrase appeared so dated to me I didn't know what to say.

"May I?"

"Come in, Garzón, for Christ's sake!"

He chewed the words under his mustache, a millimeter from my ear and in a very low voice:

"A guy's just confessed."

I looked at him in surprise, his face was expressionless. I ordered a guard to take the man who was with me and we went out into the corridor.

"Has he really confessed?"

"He's a maniac with a chip on his shoulder, aggressive too. I suppose he's fed up of being called in for questioning and has decided to toy with us for a while."

"Then why did you call me?"

"He's confessed and you're the boss, you'll decide what we have to do."

Good old Garzón, he was throwing me in all conscience to the lions.

"O.K., let's go then."

My legs were trembling, a violent sex offender deliriously acting out was perhaps too much for me. When we came in, a couple of guards made him stand up. I ordered them to leave. Garzón introduced me:

"Inspector Delgado, who's going to do the questioning."

He looked me straight in the eye and I could see him clearly. He was tall and handsome, defiant.

"Sit down."

He sat down and placed his hands on his knees. He was grinning idiotically.

"So it was you."

"That's right, I already told this pig."

"Well, now you can tell it to me."

"Not again!"

Contempt in his mouth was like saliva, a natural secretion.

"You can start by telling us what you were doing on the dates in question."

He rolled his eyes.

"Come off it, that's enough! I've given you all that, it's all recorded, why don't you have a listen and get off my back!"

"You'll address the inspector with respect!"

"Leave it, Garzón, leave it."

I sat down and unbuttoned my jacket.

"What did you mark them with?"

He silently tore a piece of skin off his finger with total concentration.

"Answer, please."

He gave me a mocking look.

"I don't remember."

Garzón was unable to control himself and started towards him.

"Listen you . . ."

I gently stopped him.

"Please, sergeant, come and sit down next to me."

Turning to the suspect, I asked:

"Try and remember."

He focused his steely eyes and said:

"With a watch."

My mind went into overdrive, I reflected.

"Explain yourself better."

"It was with a watch. Or don't you know what a watch is?"

"You marked them with a specially prepared watch, is that what you mean?"

"Well, it obviously wasn't a normal watch!"

"Can you describe it for us?"

"Yeah, it had two hands, a face and a nodule to wind it up with."

"I see."

From where I was, I could hear Garzón's jaws crunching.

"And where did they make it for you?"

He stopped grinning. He took the back of his chair in both hands and twisted around. He raised his voice.

"Listen, I've had about enough of this. I'll tell you what I did. What I did was stick my cock in first and then the watch. Those girls kept on asking for more, so I opened wide their filthy cunts and stuck it in them, that's what I did. And they all creamed their pants, don't think they were crying."

Garzón stood up, went over and began to shake him. I took him by the arm, made him come and sit back down.

"No violence, please."

I cleared my throat, asked in a gentle tone:

"What's your name?"

"Tomás," he answered.

I lit a cigarette, trying not to let my hand tremble.

"Fine, Tomás, I won't ask any more questions. What you're going to do now is get undressed."

He smiled in astonishment.

"You're joking!"

"No, I'm not. There are things we have to check. Get undressed."

"No way, you've no right . . . "

"Get undressed."

Garzón took a cigarette from my pack and, without lighting it, twiddled it around his fingers.

"Please get undressed."

"No fucking way, I'm not doing it, there's a law, you know . . . "

I stood up, went to the door, slid the bolt across. The boy watched me nervously. I went up to him and, with a slow fury that gave me lots of strength, took him by the lapel and pulled towards me.

"If you don't get undressed right now, I swear to God we'll beat you to a pulp. That's the law."

He consented and began silently removing his clothes. Garzón gave off the same static, burning heat that comes off a bar grill. He was down to his underpants.

"Take those off as well. And stand up."

He was stark naked. His young, dark flesh contrasted with the cabinets and the walls, the photo of the King. He had a beautiful penis, a scrotal sack that was full and fertile as the vine. He didn't know what posture to adopt, which way to look.

"Right, let's start over. You say you marked them with a watch."

"Can I sit down?"

"No. You raped them and marked them with a watch."

He covered his genitals with his hands.

"Hands off! Keep talking, we're listening."

All we had to do now was wait. The clock ticked on the wall. He moved the weight of his body from one leg to the other.

"Listen, how long are you going to be?"

"Shut up."

The sergeant finally lit his cigarette, sent out smoke signals of agitation, coughed. I didn't take my eyes off the man, I stared unashamedly at his genitals. He shrugged his shoulders. Every minute that passed, he withdrew his body a little more.

"This is illegal," he said.

"It's also illegal to rape girls and mark them with a watch."

He stuttered.

"I didn't do it," he said in the end.

"That's not what you said a moment ago."

He took hold of his trousers.

"I just read it in the papers, then you called and I thought . . ."

I interrupted him:

"Leave those trousers alone, whatever you have to say, say it as you are."

He stirred, his voice adopted an anxious, imploring tone.

"Can't you see I didn't do it? But you keep on bothering me, ever since I've been on probation."

"You wanted to teach us a lesson?"

"I just wanted you to realize you're wasting your time with me. I'm reformed, I'm not a criminal. I'm a deliveryman for a company, that's their number, you can call them if you like."

Garzón stood up. I glanced at him and shook my head.

"We're not calling anybody. All we're going to do is stay like this. What were you sentenced for, what did you do?"

He lowered his head.

"I fondled a girl as she was leaving school," he mumbled.

"What? I don't hear you!"

"Let me put my clothes on!"

"No."

"Please!"

"Stay where you are."

Garzón got to his feet and asked for permission to leave. I gave it and bolted the door behind him. The guy was so worked up and distracted I thought he would burst into tears. But he didn't, he carried on with bulging eyes and ears flushed with humiliation. I forced myself to endure another twenty minutes in the same position, looking at him all the time. Then I stood up.

"Get dressed, you creep. Rape's not a laughing matter. Now bugger off and keep your mouth shut, or I'll arrest you."

Before leaving, I asked him again:

"Was it you?"

And he limply replied:

"I swear it wasn't, I swear it."

Garzón was waiting for me in the corridor. I smiled at him as if nothing had happened.

"If you don't mind, we'll take a break and have some coffee."

He followed me down the corridor, walking two steps behind me. We crossed the street and entered the bar. He had kept very quiet but, as soon as he'd taken a sip, he couldn't help exclaiming with a tense smile:

"My word, inspector, you managed to surprise me! I'd seen you acting hard, but today's method was pretty unusual."

I ignored his comment as if I hadn't heard it.

"What do you think about the watch, Garzón? It seems to me an interesting possibility. Here you have an object that you don't hold but can wear and apply to the skin, exactly as happened. Perhaps there's a watch on the market that's fringed with barbs, used in some sport or for hunting, anything! We need to pursue this line, that wretch may have given us something."

"You do know that if someone had come in while we were questioning him, we'd have been done for."

"Come off it, sergeant, you were so upset you didn't even realize I bolted the door."

"Me, upset?"

"I believe so."

We looked each other in the face. He still wore that vibrant, metallic smile.

"To tell the truth, Petra, you may be right, I was a little upset. Each person has a different way of going about questioning but if I'm honest, this time I think you went too far."

"Why?"

"What can I say, inspector? A man exposed naked like that . . . it goes against the detainee's rights."

"And smacking him doesn't?"

"At least it doesn't offend his dignity."

"I didn't know you were so concerned about dignity."

"Well, I am."

"And is it not that your male pride is jointly wounded?"

His smile dissipated.

"Absolutely not! But now that you mention it, I think what you did in there is take advantage of the fact that you're a woman."

A cloud of anger descended on me. I let out a theatrical cackle and raised my voice:

"Well, fuck me, Garzón! So I've spent my entire life putting up with historical affronts and it turns out I take advantage of being a woman."

"I don't know what you're talking about."

"Yes, you do. Would it have been better if a girl had been questioned? How often have you seen the dignity of women detainees being violated? How often have you heard them being taunted with jests, double entendres, insults and signs? More than once. Do you think I accept the police force is a kind of summer camp in which everybody has a stake in dignity? You've seen or even done these things very often, sergeant, I'm sure of it, it's just you thought it was so normal you didn't even notice. Do you know what? If there's any chance of taking advantage of my gender, I intend to do it!"

The bar was so noisy that, fortunately, no one was looking at us. Garzón whispered a hurried apology and left. He was red with indignation, so angry he didn't pay the bill, which he always insisted on doing. As he was going outside, I shouted to him:

"Look into the watches!"

"As you wish," I think he grumbled. So, we'd just about committed every mistake in the book and the battle of the sexes was in full swing. Is everything that takes place inevitable? And if that situation was avoidable, was I the one responsible for avoiding it? I probably was, after all I was his superior. On the other hand, I couldn't allow him to step out of line even once. It was fairly predictable what would happen next: Garzón would go to the chief inspector and ask to be replaced. This would perfectly suit our boss, who could then get rid of us both. It was a shame, especially because of Garzón, who wasn't such a bad guy. Original, contradictory, with all that business of reviving geraniums and underwriting the social contract.

A guard suddenly came in and headed towards me.

"Inspector, there's a man at the station asking for you."

"Do you know what he wants?"

"It's about the rapes."

"I'll be right there. Fancy a coffee?"

He smiled pleasantly:

"No, thank you, I took some refreshment when I reported for duty."

I loved the guards' official language, as rigid and studied as if it had come out of some ancient document: "murder victims who've pernoctated in their residence," "ocular inspection," like a sheaf filled with signatures and stamps.

"He's expecting you in the lobby."

Anyone with greater understanding or experience would have known straight away it was a journalist, I had to see him for my suspicions to be aroused. He worked on a TV show that looked into police affairs. No specialty was beneath them— disappearances, homicides, thefts—but rapes were the jewel in the crown, something that could move the audience. His boss, director and presenter of the beast, was my age and was considered quite beautiful. I had seen her once or twice. They were clearly planning a whole series of programs devoted to the rapes and were after information, collaboration. The envoy was taken aback when I said I wouldn't help them.

"This is Ana Lozano's show. We're at the top of the ratings."

"Sorry."

"Our programs influence public opinion."

"Sure."

"The police always lend us a hand."

"Listen, this is a complicated case, delicate too. We can't start slipping you information or worrying about details you might give out."

"I warn you that this series of reports will go ahead with or without your participation. What's more, if we don't get inside information, we may miss something or cover it wrongly."

"If you say anything out of line, I'll have you up on charges."

He shrugged his shoulders, smiled. He wasn't the slightest bit offended, this was his professional routine.

"All right then, I'll be off. By the way, do you know anything about the rapist?"

I gave him a smile:

"Have one on me."

I left him there coolly taking in my brazen reply, which oozed omnipotence and bravado. Perhaps I was starting to like being in command. It felt good and was slightly addictive. You could say things that, in another context, would have sounded ridiculous. It was like adding another incentive to the romp of destiny. Was the sergeant right? Had I gone too far, making that guy take his clothes off? I felt no remorse, I wasn't using force, only the subtlety of inverting the terms of a given situation. Garzón had given a good diagnosis: I was taking advantage of the fact I was a woman. The scene was set: prejudices, conventionalities . . . To turn it around, all that was needed was a little power. And that was usually the part that was missing, a pinch of power in feminine hands. But now I had it and, if till that moment it had been merely an instrument I didn't know how to play, from that day on I became interested in deciphering the score and even entertained the possibility of producing hitherto unknown notes on the harp, which, if handled with wisdom, could manage to emit fabulous tones.

5

As was to be expected, there were no watches on the market with blades or needles round the edge. No one had ever heard of such a thing. Following our instinct, we deduced it may have been a watch designed for mountain climbers or divers . . . but no. It immediately looked like another one of our failures, though actually it was better this way. Had the watch been mass-produced, anyone could have owned it. But now the weapon retained all the possibilities offered by its unusualness. And I refused to reject the hypothesis of the watch, it seemed too plausible to leave aside. However, the path was again blocked and I didn't know which way to turn. I suggested to Garzón that we bring the three girls together. They might provoke in each other the surfacing of buried memories, compare gestures, specify, at least it had to be illuminating. Garzón, who mysteriously had not asked to be relieved, thought it was a good idea and helped me to set up the meeting.

He located the victims and tried to coincide their visits. Every time we called them in for something, we had to expect an emphatic no or else excuses not to collaborate. It clearly wasn't much fun going over the past, reliving sensations. I supposed none of them had any faith that our investigations would lead to a rapid solution. But remarkably nor were they motivated by a desire for revenge, the possibility of seeing the culprit behind bars did not elicit in them a positive response. Appealing to their sense of solidarity—"Let's lock him up so he doesn't attack anyone else"—was also difficult. They had suffered terribly, been profoundly humiliated, and in order to show some solidarity it's necessary to have your dignity intact. Humiliation isolates the individual to a surprising degree, it's the root cause of inner conflict. Garzón took care of the preliminaries, so I didn't have to see the first long faces. I sincerely believed that bringing the girls together would serve a purpose, otherwise I wouldn't have done it, since the mere thought of seeing them in the same room, heaping public shame on their defenseless situation, depressed me.

I dropped by the gym on my way to the station. I needed to sweat and lower the tension. A bundle of manacled demons had taken refuge inside me and had to be released. As I thought about the questioning that awaited me, the dumbbells became lighter than ever. I stretched my muscles, got tired. As I came out of the restorative shower, one of those young gymnasts approached me. I saw that a small group was watching me with curiosity.

"Are you a cop?" she asked immediately.

I froze. I'd never mentioned anything to them about my profession. Saying you're a cop is usually enough for a halo of mistrust to form around you. It's worse if you go on to say you deal only with documentation, they then think you prefer not to tell the truth, you're a member of the secret police and take part in unspeakable underground activity.

"How did you find out?"

"Your name's in this paper and since there aren't many women called Petra Delicado . . . "

"Can I see it?"

The newspaper was folded on the right page. I deduced there had been a load of comments prior to her question. The other girls waited expectantly, their cosmetic movements suspended, dependent on me.

Inspector Petra Delicado belongs to the Department of Documentation, which she has never left since she joined the police. Sergeant Garzón serves as a kind of movable chip between forces and even police stations. One has to question whether either of them has the experience the case requires. One has to wonder whether they are not about to be relieved of a mission that is clearly too much for them. The case of "the flower rapist" has gotten extraordinarily complicated and raises the specter of social unrest. Many parents are beginning to ask themselves, "Are our daughters not in constant danger just by being out in the street?"

Who had written this? It didn't matter, the arm of the press is much wider and longer than the arm of the law. The net formed by journalists is so dense even plankton couldn't get through. My visitor the other day had left me a clear message I was unable to interpret:

Collaborate, and you may be fucked. Don't collaborate, and you can be sure we'll all go after you.

The chief inspector would be happy to read this—and he would. In a matter of minutes it would reach his hands if it hadn't already. I looked up and there were my once jovial companions watching me with fear in their eyes. I was a cop, a bad one at that, I was involved in horrible things, I walked on the dark side of life. They would never view me as before, hum alongside me sans clothes in a spirit of comradeship. I'd frightened them off like owls in an attic.

"Do you think you'll find the culprit?" asked one of them.

"Of course we will."

A wave of unexpected fury exploded from her young face, which was red from exercise.

"For rapists, castration!" she said for the sake of it and went to rejoin the group.

"Don't you worry, I won't just castrate him, I'll send you his balls wrapped in cellophane."

They were a little annoyed, not sure how to react. I collected my things in a black mood and left. Stupid girls, happy in their simplicity! Well, I'd lost a good place in which to merge with the outer magma. I'd have to change my gym, supposing there was still one left where Petra Delicado could carry on being a normal, anonymous citizen.

When I arrived at the station, I was so irritated I passed in front of Garzón without seeing him. He called to me.

"Have you read what's in the paper?" I spat at him.

"No."

"We get slaughtered."

"Right."

"You were expecting it?"

"Ever since you told me about your interview with that journalist, I thought something like this would happen."

"Really, Garzón, I don't understand how you manage to be so insensitive. You don't feel or suffer. You've seen it all before, haven't you?"

"No, there weren't a lot of journalists in Salamanca."

"So?"

"Why are you getting so worked up? People enjoy scandals."

"Till now I've done my job in total anonymity. It horrifies me just to think there's someone poking their nose in my business, harassing me, wanting to know."

"It's normal."

He was wearing a tailored gray suit with thin stripes, but could have had on the toga of the Stoics. Lucky him! He seemed impervious to any downpour. Nothing checked him or got him going except his fits of hatred towards me. The rest of the time, he was happily deadlocked, above pain or joy, even above opinion.

"To be a good cop, you have to avoid the passions," he pronounced.

"Are you a good cop?"

"I've stuck at it for thirty years."

"Do you know what I think, Garzón? I've had about all I can take of this case. If they dropped us now, it wouldn't be so bad. We're completely in the dark, no clues, no intuitions, not a blasted glimmer of light. And, on top of that, surrounded by journalists."

He put on a blank face. I started again.

"Yes, I know, don't tell me. You'll do as you're told."

"That's what I'll do."

Such demonstrations of impatience merely served to turn the sergeant further against me. I tended to forget he wasn't my ally. We weren't even in the same boat, I was his boss and a woman. I was on my own in this stupid investigation.

"Have all the girls arrived?"

"They're in the meeting room, the three of them."

"Well, let's go and see if we can get any damn idea how to proceed."

My impression that bringing the victims together had not been a mistake was confirmed. In the first place, I could clearly perceive they were of a similar physical type. While they were not absolutely identical, no one could deny they produced the same sensation of total fragility. Thin, frail, with eyes like a guide dog's, attentive but uninterested, it was as if a perpetual drizzle fell on them, wetting them through. It was obvious they would never act in self-defense. Their complete helplessness was imprinted on their bodies and prevented them from reacting by opening an umbrella or emigrating to drier lands.

I greeted them on entering. Paradoxically with the life that had befallen them, they had all received beautiful names that resounded with luxury and seduction. The cook's daughter was called Salomé, the hairdresser Patricia and the student of

design and dress-making Sonia. They sat apart to avoid forming a homogeneous group. They didn't look each other in the
face, dodged any eye contact. Nothing in common with other
victims of shared misfortunes such as fires or floods. It wasn't
going to be easy to get them to talk.

"Perhaps you won't need to repeat your statements, but
there are some things I would like to ask you. With the three
of you together, we may be able to form a clearer picture."

No reply.

"Have you understood?"

Still no reply.

"Does anyone speak?"

Patricia raised her voice a fraction.

"We already told you lots of times."

I adopted a more maternal tone.

"It's not a question of remembering bad things just because.
We're trying to catch this guy and any detail's going to help us."

Detail? They hadn't offered practically any. I glanced at
Garzón, who was smoking like a chimney. I hoped he at least
appreciated my softer approach during questioning.

"I know what we'll do. I'll take us through and if there's
anything you'd like to rectify or expand on, you stop me."

I had the impression I was lecturing a group of Koreans
without the services of an interpreter. I began.

"It was always at night. There was little light. His face was
covered with a ski mask. He barely said anything and, when he
did, it was in whispers. All right so far?"

They each looked the other way.

"While you couldn't see his face or hear his voice clearly,
you all thought it was a young, athletic man with no physical
defects. Yes?"

Silence reigned. I armed myself with patience to continue.

"He didn't use violence."

Patricia spoke very softly:

"He jostled me."

Encouraged by this first intervention, Sonia said:

"He gave me a shove and pulled my sleeve."

I held up my hands:

"You mean that, while he didn't beat you up, he treated you roughly."

Both heads gained momentum to say yes.

"Good, now I want the three of you to think hard . . . "

They all looked away. "The three of them" was a collective they found difficult to accept.

" . . . when he marked you with those points, what movements did he make?"

They were momentarily paralyzed. Patricia shyly pointed at Garzón.

"Can he leave?"

Although I had avoided mentioning the precise fact of sexual aggression, the mark functioned like a symbol, more degrading even than the rape itself. It united them, turned them into a kind of cattle ready to be sacrificed. Garzón imperceptibly snorted behind his mustache. He moved his abundant bulk from one foot to the other, waited.

"Would you mind stepping outside, sergeant?"

Perhaps I shouldn't have passed on the order, I was aware of notching up yet another grievance that would go against me. Having been unusually harsh in all the interviews, I was now yielding to the affectations of a girl who really had no reasons for such a demand.

"Of course," he grumbled.

Nothing changed after he left, the same refusal to speak, the same guilty shame.

"What then?"

The hairdresser stood up.

"This is how he did it."

She hesitated in her choice of who among the others should

act as her dummy. Salomé held back, it was Sonia who proffered her arm. Patricia took it in her right hand, immobilized
it by force and pushed down with the back of her left hand.

"Now you do it, Sonia."

Sonia swapped places with her partner and reproduced
almost exactly the same maneuver.

"Great. Do you want to have a go, Salomé?"

The cook's daughter was as distressed as if she were really
going to suffer a second attack. She bowed her head so that it
was difficult to understand her.

"He did the same to me," she murmured.

"I need you to act it out."

She stood up, carrying a dead weight. She had on an oversized T-shirt and faded jeans. Instead of turning to the other
girls, she came towards where I was. She took one of my
arms, brought hers close and applied surprising force. She
then lifted her face and fixed me with a look of fury. I felt the
hatred flowing from her body. My arm smarted freudianly. I
pulled away.

"That's enough."

I tried to calm myself before talking.

"So he was wearing something on his arm and had to push
down quite hard for it to stick in."

They nodded.

"Listen carefully. Would you say he was wearing a watch, a
watch around his wrist?"

They thought for a moment.

"I'm not sure," said Patricia.

Sonia intervened:

"It's possible, but it could also have been a bracelet or
something tied with strings."

Salomé remained silent.

"What do you think?" I asked her.

"I only know it hurt a lot," she replied.

"Finally, and this is no joke, would you say the three of you were attacked by the same guy?"

They all answered in the affirmative. I managed to force a smile.

"That's it, you can go now."

They stormed out of the room, desperate to leave, and didn't say goodbye, nor did I.

Garzón came in, preceded by a fanfare of vengeance. But I decided not to apologize.

"How was it?" he asked.

"Nothing amazing, but at least we can be sure it's the same guy."

It was his turn to get up my nose.

"I thought we already knew that."

"Well, no, it could have been a gang, a group of undesirables."

He looked as if a deep respect for hierarchy prevented him from laughing out loud. His Chicano mustache fluffed up with contempt.

"What's more, I now know exactly how he performed the maneuver of marking the girls."

"Fine, tell me where we go from here."

"Do you know if the social worker's at the station?"

These inopportune questions succeeded in returning him to his official role.

"I'll go and see."

"I want to be sure we know everything about the act of aggression."

Poor Garzón, he left, having clicked his heels. A sense of duty prevailed in him. He clearly saw I was out of my depth, making vain attempts to stay afloat, but he still carried out my orders as if they were the Pope's. He came back after a short while with the social worker.

She was very direct.

"What do you want to know?" she asked.

"Tell me something about the girls, what are they like?"

She sat down and crossed her legs. Her sturdy heels made a noise even when she wasn't walking.

"The girls? Well, you can guess, working-class. Little money, little intelligence, little education. They work their shifts and spend the rest of their time in bars."

"Do you think someone close to them could have done it?"

"What can I say! In these situations, you can't be sure of anything. It's as if everyone's permanently on the verge of crime. They play pool, on machines, may or may not be offered drugs. If they don't get hooked on anything, they usually marry a mechanic or wash stairs . . . you know."

"Do any of them move in circles of drug addiction?"

"No, I don't think so."

"You were the first to talk to them after the event. Did anything strike you in their reactions?"

She took hold of a file she had brought with her.

"Let's see . . . That Sonia was very worried about her boyfriend, a guy who washes cars, since the bastard went and marked them into the bargain . . . Patricia was the angriest, she said she'd have liked to kill him, but she soon calmed down. The other one, Salomé . . . she's a strange girl, doesn't speak much, seems to swallow everything. I guess she was a virgin."

"And the others not?"

"I don't think so. Listen, these girls know a fair amount about life, don't think of them as traumatized children. Their conditions are pretty harsh, this is just another blow."

I stared in amazement at that face reflecting insensitivity.

"Do you mean it doesn't really matter they've been raped?"

She gave an obvious start and looked at the sergeant as a witness to the provocation.

"I didn't say anything of the sort. What are you insinuating?"

"You can go now, that's all I wanted to know."

She pursed her lips as if she had to stop herself from spitting on me. She said goodbye, her voice stentorian and left, slamming the door. I turned to Garzón.

"Did you see that? She's supposed to work here in order to give the victims support."

Garzón remained expressionless, an Englishman at tea. He seemed unwilling to agree with me or share in the scandal.

"How can she do anything to help them if she only thinks of them as local prostitutes?"

"Everyone has their own way of performing their duty."

Blasted Garzón! Ever ready to return the ball, to slip in some insinuation, keeping the barrier between the two of us raised high.

"I'm going home, sergeant. Call me if anything turns up."

Not even Chopin could improve my mood. I sat down in an armchair and put my feet up, but I was uncomfortable and opted to go out into the garden. The geraniums appeared as stiff as always, only now they had developed a patina of earth that made them look awful. I decided to make myself something to eat; they say that cooking relaxes, and it may be true because the sight of my new kitchen reassured me. It looked great, spacious, fitted with simple cupboards, a large window. I lovingly drew the curtains I myself had chosen on the outside world full of prejudices, stupidity, social workers, sergeants . . . Perhaps I should resign. Go to my boss and tell him, "I'm sorry but I can't take any more." Be honest, recognize that I was up the creek without a paddle. I broke a couple of eggs and began to beat them, not knowing what I would do with them. The phone rang. It was Hugo.

"The notary will be waiting for us to sign at four. We could have lunch together."

"I'm sorry but I'm making a soufflé."

"A soufflé? Have you gotten remarried?"

"No, but I take care of myself, go to the gym, have baths with salts, make fruit salads."

"And soufflés."

"That's right, and soufflés."

"Then we can meet a little before in a café, I've something to tell you."

I agreed like an idiot and we arranged to meet. I'd gone and done it again: fear his opinion, unnecessarily prove to him I was respectable, careful, reasonable, conventional. I'd never manage to avoid feeling small before him. Hugo was the measure of all things and it wouldn't be easy to remove his biblical figure from my life, to be myself, to stop thinking that, deep down, he was always right.

I reached the café at the agreed time. I was about to make a real soufflé so as not to appear before him having lied. Fortunately I controlled myself and stuck to an omelet. Hugo looked extremely refined, a real gentleman. He couldn't hide a certain tension in his face when he saw me: his civilized Europeanism still retained traces of Calderon.

"I'm sorry to have made you come, but I'd like to sort this all out before getting married. It wouldn't be right to have properties with two women at the same time, now would it?"

"No. What do I have to sign?"

"The private contract of sale. The deed will follow. I'll then give you a check for your share."

"All right."

"You said you could do with the money."

"Yes."

"Financial problems?"

"No problems. But, as you know, the police don't earn very much."

"If only you hadn't abandoned the practice . . . "

I tried to be suave:

"Hugo, please."

"It was a guaranteed income."

"I know."

"And a somewhat more dignified job for a woman."

Just the right time to tell him where to get off, but I couldn't do it, so I let it go.

"I've read the papers."

"Right."

"Depressing. They'll crucify you. Do you realize what you've gotten into? A serial rape case you won't get away from without a lot of fuss. The press will hound you."

"I can't choose the cases, they give them to me."

"Nonsense, Petra, no one wants to get their hands dirty, so they've passed it on to you. Is that what you expected when you joined the force?"

"The thing is . . . "

"To have to spend the whole day with a fat cop, going in and out of singles bars and the like. You're risking your dignity. They've found out you're in Documentation, the journalists will investigate the rest of your life, dig down deep, now it's your inexperience, tomorrow something else will come out."

For example, the fact we'd been married! My God, I could clearly see what he was up to, but that strange weight of ancestral guilt stopped me answering back. He feared his implication in my disastrous life, his name next to mine. It would have been the limit to be affected by my stupid decisions that he had always condemned. Cheated on and beaten. Abandoned and mocked.

"Accompanied all the time by that deputy superintendent or whatever he is, looking like a tango singer. It's not a job for you."

"It's just temporary."

"Long enough for your reputation to be ruined. Listen, I have friends, I think I could find you something in a practice. Not mine, of course, but there are others you could slot into, return to the law, straighten out your life. Haven't these years done enough to quench your thirst for adventure and change? You tried a second crazy, mistaken marriage, you can't now allow your profession to go to the dogs."

"It's just that . . . "

"Or at least ask to be taken off the case, say you don't feel qualified, go back to the Department of Documentation. I doubt they'd turn you down, it's only reasonable."

"I'll think about it. I promise you I'll think about it."

He scrutinized me, trying to work out if he'd convinced me or if it was an excuse. He must have thought it was a good start for now, he'd soon have time to finish off the job when he saw me again and handed over the blasted check. He rose with a marquis's elegance, took my hand and left without so much as a smile.

On returning home, I gave the door a tremendous slam, which echoed in the loneliness. I didn't switch on the light. Was this a woman's destiny? Did husbands, friends, lovers who once passed through your life, never leave? I hadn't managed to shake off Pepe after a year and a half's separation, now Hugo appeared like a sepulchral goblin. Were these the stages of a woman's existence: first husband, second husband . . . ? Were they not like those of other mortals: birth, dentition, puberty . . . ? Stuck always in the past. Hugo must be feeling the same: "What other crazy ideas will she come up with to compromise my name?" And yet he was right, I wasn't qualified for this kind of case, I didn't know what to do, not even the tango singer was on my side. The reasonable thing would have been to resign. Hugo's advice was always reasonable. It gave me the chance to start anew. Only that I didn't want to start again, I wanted to draw to a halt, leave my biography hanging by a thread without milestones or anniversaries, stuck in a hole. I left acts to those who still had momentum, I settled for the excipient of life's drug: walks, books, the decoration of my new home, films, cups of tea . . .

The phone rang in the dark, I reached out for it with difficulty, I hadn't even taken off my coat.

"Yes?"

"Petra, I'm sorry to bother you, it's just that . . . "

"Don't worry, Garzón, what is it?"

"It's about the rapist."

"Yes?"

"He's committed another rape."

"What?"

"You heard me."

"How did it happen?"

"Not on the phone. You'd better come to the station, I'm
already here."

Blasted Garzón! What was he doing at the station, did he
live there? And why couldn't he speak over the phone? Was he
thinking of journalists or had he confused the police and spy
genres? I rubbed my face, trying to get a reaction, but couldn't
wake myself up, this was a bad dream, a nightmare. What kind
of son of a bitch managed to keep up such a frenetic activity of
rapes and markings? Did he want to be noticed, to have all the
news media after him, to confound the police? He was clearly
crazy. I left the house in darkness, I hadn't even been able to
look at it.

The rapist's latest deed debunked Garzón's social theories.
The girl this time came from a rich family. The act had been
committed at dusk in the upper part of the city, in a swish
neighborhood. The requirements of the other attacks had been
fulfilled one by one: penetration, no accidental clue, masked
face, young, athletic man and no violent aggression except for
the mark on the arm, which was identical to before. The girl
was returning home from her tennis lesson when he surprised
her, pinned her to the wall next to a garage and forced her. No
witnesses. We couldn't question her, she had suffered an attack
of nerves and was in the hospital. We couldn't be with her until

they'd managed to sedate her and get her over the shock. I wanted to see her, to find out if her physical type coincided with that of the other victims. I was virtually convinced the motive was psychological, the suggestion of other motives began to look absurd given the rate of assaults.

The girl's father, however, was there. He was an important architect, a guy barely in his forties and seemingly endowed with boundless energy. When I entered the office and saw him, I understood he blamed the police for all his personal misfortunes. His manner was that of someone lodging a complaint. He was completely out of his mind, pacing up and down and talking a mile a minute. Garzón told me he had asked to see the chief inspector. He started giving off sparks as soon as he saw me.

"Listen here, inspector, till now you've been plodding along at your own pace. Well, not anymore. I want you investigating 24/7, I want special teams. I'm going to have a meeting with all your bosses and I warn you I plan to reach the Department of the Interior."

I looked at him without any irony, wondering how I could get through to him.

"Needless to say, the first thing I'm going to do is have you two taken off the case."

Garzón was silent and impenetrable.

"May I ask why?"

"Don't you think I read the papers? Do you take me for an idiot? I know you're not qualified, the inept way you're leading the investigation is shameful."

"Do you believe everything you read? Are you planning to provide the press with information?"

"If they so much as publish my name or anything about my daughter's rape, I'll sue them."

"Well then, if you don't trust journalists, why do you pay attention to what they write about us?"

"I'm not in the mood for clever games. There's a rapist on

the loose, that may seem normal to you, but it so happens that son of a bitch has attacked my daughter and he's going to pay for it, right now, understand? Right fucking now!"

Garzón stretched a hand towards him.

"Please calm down."

"Don't tell me what to do! I don't even need to read the papers, I only have to look at you, a woman and a pensioner, is that all the police has to offer the citizen?"

I saw Garzón's jaw contract. Fortunately a guard came in at that moment.

"Inspector Delicado, the chief inspector says he'll see Mr. Masderius now if you don't mind interrupting the session."

"It's already interrupted," hissed Masderius.

He left in a fury, looking at Garzón and me as if we were two snails on a lettuce leaf, ready to be ejected once and for all from the salad.

Garzón scratched his mustache.

"He's quite nervous," he said.

"Meaning his behavior is justified?" I asked.

"Well, if a daughter of mine had been raped . . . "

"Honor, right, Garzón? There's no greater affront to a man."

"I prefer not to judge."

"I don't like the chief inspector seeing him. Did you notice? He never normally sees anyone, especially relatives."

"Right."

"What hospital's the girl in?"

"Sagrada Familia."

"Then let's pay her a visit."

"They won't let us question her."

"We'll try."

In the car, Garzón appeared worried. Four victims of the same rapist was enough to make anyone think. And we didn't have the slightest clue, not a hint. We both realized we were sitting on a time bomb. I stared at him, actually he didn't look like a tango singer, Hugo was wrong, he looked more like a bear-tamer, a Hungarian visiting the city, hoping to set up shop in the middle of the street.

"Well, the motive of social difference is out, isn't it, sergeant?"

"Don't be so sure."

"I want to see that girl, you know. I'm convinced she'll have a helpless appearance, small bones, little weight."

"Do you think the rapist's a weak man despite his size?"

"It's not that. For me it's psychological, a timid guy who only takes on small women or is obsessed by them. Their fragile appearance is the victims' only point in common. When you push there, something gives."

"That's not going to help us very much."

"It always helps if you know what you're looking for. Later, he'll explain."

"He?"

"The rapist, when we arrest him."

"I thought you were waiting to be taken off this case."

I didn't reply. In the hospital corridor, Mrs. Masderius was standing in front of her daughter's room. She was wearing a white tracksuit under her fur coat, sports shoes. Her blond hair was disarranged in beautiful waves, she looked dismayed. As soon as she saw us, her face became contorted.

"You mustn't disturb her," she said.

"When do you think she'll be in a position to speak?"

"My daughter will say what she has to say when a judge tells her to do so. And preferably she won't speak at all, either to journalists or to the police."

"Madam, this is an obligatory step, we must take a statement."

She anxiously shielded her eyes and repeated the lesson she had learned.

"You must leave her alone."

"Mrs. Masderius, you know there's an investigation under way. It would help us to see your daughter even for a minute.

This guy's raped other girls, we have to catch him as soon as possible."

She wavered. Trapped inside her, common sense struggled to gain the upper hand.

"Let us in for a moment. We won't talk to her, you have my word, we'll leave as soon as we've seen her."

"My husband . . . " she began. Her eyes filled with tears, her features softened. "You can go in," she said, and went to sit on a bench. She dropped the weight of her body and stared into space, her hands lying lifeless in her lap.

The room was immersed in the hospital's cocoon-like penumbra. The girl was confined to bed, probably under the influence of sleeping pills. Her body was little more than a horizontal line covered by a sheet. Her face, which in sleep had frozen in a wince of anguish, had slight, blurred features. She had the same blond hair as her mother, which created a halo on the pillow.

"She looks dead," whispered Garzón.

"You see? Just as I expected, she's very thin."

Her forearm was bandaged. I thought that the pathetic flower, still painful, would be throbbing underneath.

"They've stuffed her with tranquillizers."

"Yes," I said, "but when she wakes up, she'll remember it all and only have the hope it's been a bad dream."

Garzón stirred nervously.

"I tell you, Petra, I've had about enough of this guy. When we lay hands on him, the first thing I'm going to do is give him a good hiding."

It was the first time I had seen him upset, letting his emotions get the better of him.

"Calm down, sergeant, we mustn't lose our cool."

Someone opened the door behind us and startled us. It was a young doctor with spiky hair and enormous glasses.

"They told me I'd find you here."

"We're in charge of the police investigation."

"I know, but we've given the girl sedatives, so you see she can't tell you anything."

"When do you think she may be able to speak?"

"I don't know, before long. But as soon as she wakes up, we're taking her in for surgery."

"Surgery?"

"Cosmetic surgery to remove the mark on her arm."

"So soon?"

"It's what her parents want. It may have been better to wait for her to recover psychologically, but they're keen to get on."

"Erase what we don't like—right?—as if it had never happened."

He shrugged his shoulders, adopted a philosophical expression.

"Well, it's a fairly minor operation, so it doesn't really matter when we do it, from a technical point of view, I mean."

The three of us turned towards the bed. The sleeping beauty hadn't moved, couldn't hear us. Others determined her life, she was just a frail body in the hands of chemistry. The doctor turned to me.

"We've something for you, I was going to send it to the station, but since you're here . . . Why don't you wait for me in my office? I'll be there as soon as I've finished my rounds. The ward sister will show you."

Mrs. Masderius was still in the corridor. She didn't even look up as we passed. Her expression frightened me, it was like that of someone lost in a maze without doors or windows, unable to escape. I said this to Garzón in the office.

"Did you notice the mother's face? I reckon she needs psychiatric help."

"It's always the same, the working classes are better able to cope with misfortune. The pathologist in Salamanca once told me this. If a mentally handicapped child is born into a well-off family, the event is turned into a drama, a tragedy, a cause for concealment. But if it's a simple working-class home, the child is immediately accepted, kept clean, looked after, shown to everybody for them to see how affectionate and even pretty the child is."

Amazing! This was the most Garzón had spoken since the day we met. The class struggle seemed to be the only theme that made him talkative and passionate.

The doctor finally arrived. He must have been a year or two older than Pepe, people in positions of importance were always young.

"I hope you haven't had to wait too long."

"I'm always at my ease in medical surroundings," said Garzón.

"That's because you're in good health."

They both laughed. Well, blow me down, my colleague had not only begun to emerge from his mutism, he even knew how to have some fun.

"I called you because I've something to show you. Let's see . . . " he searched in a drawer, "we removed it from Cristina's arm when she first came in . . . here it is."

He opened a small box of transparent plastic filled with cotton. He took some tweezers, rummaged around and produced a tiny object we had to lean forward to see.

"Can you make it out? It looks like the minute tooth of a silver comb. It was lodged in the wound, deep in one of the orifices. It obviously broke off and, when the other teeth were drawn out, it stayed where it was. There was some swelling around it, but the tissues didn't reject it."

We were ecstatic before it, our eyes out on stalks. I couldn't move, I had the impression if I breathed too heavily, the only concrete object we possessed would disintegrate.

"Do you think it'll help?"

"Are you serious? You bet it will! This is the first piece of evidence we have. Has anyone touched it?"

"No, I took it out using the tweezers and put it in this box. I don't know much about legal medicine, but I reckon it's going to be difficult to find traces or remains on such a small object, especially when it's been buried in a human body. I suppose Cristina's blood and body fluids are always going to overwhelm anything else. But don't pay too much attention to me."

"We'll have it analyzed."

"I hope it helps, this guy's going too far."

"We know."

He made us sign in a register to acknowledge receipt of medical evidence. He said goodbye with the same eclectic style he'd used throughout. I carried the box in my pocket, gripped it tightly, it was like a talisman that would open sinister doors leading us to the ogre's chamber.

"Do you fancy a drink, Garzón, to celebrate our first piece of evidence?"

"No, thanks. If you give me that tooth, I'll take it straight to forensic."

"How about afterwards, will you fancy a drink then?"

"No, thanks. Afterwards I'm going home to bed. See you tomorrow, inspector."

I placed the magic box in his fleshy hand. Without a single smile, he left. Silly old oaf, I thought, but then I realized I also was exhausted, disheveled and in need of a shower, and I headed in the direction of solitude.

6

Pepe turned up at eight in the morning. I had just gotten up and had on a bathrobe. I thought, if he has to honor me with his visits, he could at least warn me; the telephone is a great invention, but Pepe functioned on the margins of conventionality. He greeted me as if we'd met on a bus. I, however, wasn't ready yet for any public contact. My skin exuded the aroma of sleep and he no longer had rights over me, so I should have gotten angry and kicked him out, but I didn't. The opposite, in fact, I showed him in. He didn't notice the disturbance his presence caused me, nor was he shocked to see me in my nightdress, all he did was stare at my bare feet on the floor tiles and exclaim "You'll catch a cold if you don't put something on!" He continued, "Shall I prepare breakfast while you get dressed?"

By "breakfast" Pepe meant no more than a cup of black coffee, which he prepared as best he could in a kitchen he didn't know; so I made toast, rummaged around in the cupboard for biscuits, warmed some milk and pulled out butter and jam. Pepe fell to swallowing without hesitation, concentrating on what he was doing, not lifting his eyes from the plate. I guessed he hadn't had a decent breakfast in months.

"You're hungry, right?"

"A bit, but I didn't just come to eat. I've something to tell you."

I hoped it wasn't one of his strange investigative deductions or an offer of help for my new home.

"Last night a woman came into the bar, more or less your age. She wanted to know things about you."

"Things?"

"Things in general. Whether it was true we'd been married, how long you'd been in the police, what you'd studied, things . . . "

"So the journalist found you!"

"Then, amidst various stupid remarks, she asked if you had any clues, any leads in the case."

"I hope you didn't tell her anything."

"But I don't know anything."

I finished breakfast in a foul mood. It was obvious that avoiding contact with the press was no guarantee of a quiet life. Pepe bit into a piece of toast and gooseberry jam.

"So do you have any clues or not?"

"Well, nothing substantial."

"I reckon it's a sect, one of those weird sects that go about celebrating sacrifices and bloody liturgies. No one's interested, but the world is full of sects, there are loads of crazy guys, seriously, I'm always telling Fermín."

"Who's Fermín?"

"What do you mean, who's Fermín? Your partner, Sergeant Garzón."

I had to hold my eyes in their sockets.

"Garzón? And when did you see Garzón?"

"Loads of times. He comes to the bar, has a drink or dinner. He loves Hamed's couscous."

"But that's outrageous!"

"What is?"

"He never told me."

"Why should he? He's just a customer, that's all."

I fell silent.

"Pepe, thanks for the information. Now you'd better go."

"What, already? Can't I smoke a cigarette?"

"No. I have to leave at once."

"I thought you'd come to this house for some tranquility."

"That's none of your business. If that journalist comes back, tell her . . . "

"If she asks for a coffee, she'll be a customer and I'll have to treat her well."

"All right, Pepe, do whatever you want."

"It's my duty."

I pushed him in the direction of the door and slammed it shut behind me. We each got into our car. I saw him disappear into his clapped-out Dyane. It was the perfect vehicle for him: slow, out of date, with plenty of room inside for transporting his cats. I must have been out of my mind marrying a man capable of driving something like that. I felt my face had become flushed, my pulse had quickened. The revelations about journalists on my tail and Garzón in open friendship with Pepe were too much for a day that was only just beginning.

As soon as I reached the station, I went looking for the sergeant. He was in the boardroom, hieratic and imposing like a Chaldean statue.

"When the hell are they going to give you somewhere permanent to sit, Garzón?"

He was astonished at my outburst.

"I suppose I'll be on the move for as long as I'm helping the Civil Guard," he said, not knowing what to hold on to.

"Still on about smuggling?"

"That's right."

"Always after an informer?"

He was becoming increasingly perturbed.

"As you can see."

"It's strange that, having just arrived in Barcelona, you should know so many informers."

"I don't know them, I'm given a list and get in touch with them. I think I explained it to you."

"Yes, you may have. All the same, you're good at connecting with people."

"Possibly."

I couldn't take any more.

"Listen, Garzón, I may be interfering in your private life, but the fact is there's something that intrigues me and I'd like to ask you."

His gaze danced nervously over my face.

"Go ahead."

"Is it true you often visit Pepe's bar?"

"The Ephemerides? Yes, I do, I like the food and the atmosphere. Why?"

"Well, you never mentioned it to me."

"I didn't think it was necessary."

"Well, of course not! The reason I bring it up is that a journalist's been there, asking Pepe questions about our case. He thinks they managed to find the Ephemerides by following you."

He winced but concealed it quickly. He lit a cigarette as coolly as he could manage.

"It's obvious the journalists won't leave us alone. They could follow us anywhere . . . In any case, we can't be conditioned by their movements. It may be more prudent to offer them a few scraps of information, they might leave us alone."

"No way!"

"My experience tells me . . . "

"Not while I'm in charge of this investigation. Their reports are an affront to human dignity. I forbid you to give them a single detail. I hope I won't have to repeat myself."

He swallowed a rather bitter pill. His eyes were too meek to express hatred, but I knew I'd done the worst thing, remind him of my authority.

A guard came in:

"Inspector, you're needed on the phone."

An opportune moment to break up this awkward situation. I made my excuses. It was the forensic specialist.

"We've examined the barb from Cristina's body, Inspector Delicado. I'll send you the report right away."

"Tell me something now."

He cleared his throat.

"In short, externally the barb is devoid of interest. There are no traces, no marks, no prints. But I can tell you what it's made of. It's pure silver, without alloys, and it's been coated in rhodium."

"Rhodium?"

"A material that makes silver shine, used in jewelry, I'm told. That's all, do you think it'll help?"

"I guess so. We didn't have anything before and now we've something . . . "

I don't know if I believed what I was saying. A material used in jewelry is not one of those spectacular clues that set you on the right track, but who knows? Perhaps this material had special characteristics that led unequivocally in a certain direction, belonged to a guild of craftsmen or was used in one particular place. It was a starting point at least . . . The investigative method had its charm, it was like an empirical science, first your intuition flowed, later the evidence served to prove or disprove your theory. I felt a sudden thirst for knowledge.

Garzón was waiting for me outside the office. I thought the time had come for an open declaration of hostilities. I expected some kind of deflagration, but no, he wasn't waiting there to send me to hell. While he was still revving like an out-of-gear vehicle, he simply announced:

"The chief inspector wishes to see us both."

I was wrong, I was prepared for a tactical skirmish with my allies and my avowed enemy was declaring nuclear war.

"Do you know what he wants?"

"No."

"Well, it's not difficult to guess."

"I never guess, inspector. I go where I'm told, obey the orders I'm given and don't ask questions, as you well know."

Musket in hand, ready to shoot me. Now, in the boss's office, he'd make the most of this golden opportunity to turn against me.

The chief inspector's furtive sideways glances and his delay before talking to us combined with his open smile convinced me of the reasons for our being there. He must have thought it was pointless beating about the bush because he immediately said:

"I've summoned you to tell you that you can both go back to your usual posts."

Despite his efficient style, Garzón misunderstood him:

"In Salamanca?" he asked.

This momentary confusion enabled our boss to reduce the tension. He guffawed while raising his hands:

"No, sergeant, God help me! You're fine where you are. What I mean is you're both needed back in your positions, Inspector Delicado in Documentation and you . . . "

"Sorry, I wasn't paying attention."

Garzón laughed for no reason.

"We're not needed anymore in the rape case?" I asked.

"Well, the general opinion is you've fulfilled your duty and now you're much more useful in your posts."

"What about the case?" I insisted.

"Another inspector will take it on."

"One who so far has been busy with more important things?"

He stopped smiling, but exercised control, his manner tolerant:

"You see, from a more elevated position you get a much better idea of how the machine works. Sometimes people are needed here, sometimes there . . . What really matters is that the machine as a whole carries on functioning. I don't think it's difficult to understand."

"Isn't it closer to the truth that there's been pressure?"

"I'm not sure what you mean."

"Sir, you know the journalists have been kicking up a fuss, trying to turn public opinion against us. What's more, the latest victim's father swore he would use his influence. Are we to conclude that he has?"

"The commissioner of police has decided to relieve you, let's get that clear, and you've been slow enough in your investigation for no justification to be needed in taking it off you."

"What were our mistakes?" I asked.

The chief inspector was already squirming in his seat.

"I can't give you concrete examples, but the case is still unsolved."

"Come off it, sir! You're well aware that in Spain only a tiny percentage of reported rapes are ever solved. How can we be expected to do more right at the beginning?"

"Inspector Delicado, please! I cannot permit myself the luxury of discussing this with you, it's quite unorthodox. If you have an official complaint, make it, otherwise leave."

"Well, yes, sir, take everything I'm going to say as an official complaint, and I'd like to point out I'm talking only for myself here and not for Sergeant Garzón. I have to say I consider myself the victim of a frivolous exercise of power. You can't ask a professional to take on a case just because there's a temporary vacancy and you want to avoid outside interference. Also, you can't take a professional off a case just because there's a smear campaign or someone who's directly involved in the case decides to become hysterical. With all respect, sir, I wish to indicate I'm convinced I've been treated unjustly because I'm a woman, an irrelevant group in the force who can be sidelined or ignored without fear of consequences. I protest against this decision, I believe it sets a dangerous precedent and the credibility of police independence in the face of social vicissitudes has been seriously damaged. I protest with respect, sir."

"You're within your rights. Put it down in writing, and now leave."

I did so with all the delicacy of movement I could muster, I wanted none of this to be considered a fit of bad temper. Garzón remained silently in the office. I couldn't see what expression he wore because I never looked at him.

I headed for the bar. Can you believe it?—I thought—I've spent the last few weeks hoping to be relieved of all this dirty business and now decide to assert my claim to it by getting on my high horse. I leaned on the counter. A childish tantrum, an outburst, an idiocy I would no doubt pay for. I ordered a white wine. The waiters' attention was distracted by the television. Why had I acted in this way? It was obvious really, out of vanity. That damn rapist could have been attacking girls for months in front of my nose, and what would I have done? Nothing, watch them go by in an infamous procession, vestal virgins queuing up in front of the sacrificial altar. Hope for a clue, carry out a small test, no impulse to catch the culprit, and all this with a pinch of everyday burlesque: stop to eat, spat with the sergeant . . . But now someone had dared to undermine my sacrosanct ego and I pounced like a cat, thought I had been snatched from an investigation when about to make essential discoveries. Come on! The motives that move a human being are rarely complex: self-esteem, hunger, thirst, sleep, cold . . . a frighteningly close communion with animals. I suddenly realized Garzón had sat down beside me with his elbows on the bar. I greeted him with an imprecise gesture and carried on drinking. He had now become an uncomfortable witness of my stupidity. I was overcome by waves of his aftershave, Dandy Man, which was thick and heavy like grandma's soup.

"I backed you up," he blurted out.

I remained silent.

"When you left, I told the chief inspector that I stood by you."

"Could you say that again?"

"You heard me."

"That was a stupid thing to do."

"Maybe."

I took a long pull on my drink.

"Listen, sergeant, I'm not at all sure I acted correctly."

"Well, I liked it, especially that bit about a frivolous exercise of power. It was exactly the right thing to say. You were great."

"It was an outburst that served no purpose, I might even receive a warning."

"That's another story, the point is you were great, controlled, reasoned, eloquent . . . you showed balls in there, if you don't mind me saying."

He can't have been saying anything he didn't feel because he didn't even dare look at me, maintaining his sideways position like an Egyptian painting.

"I still think you openly take advantage of the fact you're a woman but—who knows?—maybe it's good to use the weapons you have."

We remained silent for a moment, then he continued:

"I wish you'd seen the chief inspector's face when you left! He'd been through an ordeal."

I smiled:

"What did he tell you about me, that I'm a rich kid turned cop?"

"Something like that."

"I guessed as much."

"Maybe, having heard you, he's changed his mind."

"I don't think so! And even if he had, it's a bit late now. We've been taken off the case."

"That bothers you, doesn't it?"

"I like to finish what I start."

"Me too."

"Not much we can do about it."

Few people were left in the bar. Garzón downed his brandy.

"Petra, I have the impression I've not been very nice to you."

"Oh, forget it!"

"What do you say we have another drink somewhere else?"

"Don't feel you have to."

"To round off our collaboration in a civilized way."

"All right then, let's go."

We walked down the Ramblas. It was bitterly cold, but my own private Hercule Poirot didn't seem to notice. He carried his wrinkled raincoat under his arm and looked as lissome as ever. He was content. What had caused such a metamorphosis? Could this have been the first time he'd seen an order questioned? It probably was. In his long career, he'd have witnessed a few rebellions by marginalized types, the odd back answer, perhaps even a subordinate's violent reaction against his superior, but my sensible, rhetorical claims were clearly new to him, full of formal gloss. Even better, now he'd retain a good memory of me after all our quarrels, the feminist struggle could chalk one up to me. Fifty-something years of following orders must have produced a terrible pain in the kidneys, but Garzón had worn them well. However, vital reassessments at the end of the road have a much more lethal effect than all the cigarettes, pig fat and coffee. That's what people really die of, the shock of asking themselves one day if their lifelong position has been worth it or not. I hoped this wasn't the sergeant's case and that his feeling of solidarity with me was merely an anecdote, a prank, a small, insignificant ripple.

"Do you know we even had a lead?"

He didn't understand me. I told him about the conversation with the forensic specialist and the silver barb coated in that unusual material.

"It's always the same!" he cried out. "When you finally get on the right road, things fall apart."

"What do you mean?"

"I was just philosophizing."

"Right."

"You think it's strange for an overweight sergeant to philosophize, don't you?"

"Not at all!"

"Well, that's how it is. You say to yourself, O.K., now things are heading in the right direction, I'll just be quiet and stay where I am, when suddenly circumstances take a turn for the worse, everything collapses and you have to start all over again."

"Not in my case."

"No?"

We stopped in front of the Café de la Ópera.

"Do you want to go in here?"

We looked for a table among groups of pseudo-Bohemian youngsters and the odd tourist. Garzón stared at the dirt-encrusted stucco ceilings, the withered lamps, the mirrors that had shined once upon a time.

"Do you like it? It's like a relic of the past, but don't be deceived, it's not very authentic, in fact it's not at all unconventional, the clientele's loaded."

Garzón scratched his mustache.

"I have to say I love this luxury from the last century. As soon as I arrived in Barcelona, I stood at the door of the Lyceum just to have a look. Modern luxury's different, not so dependent on detail, more comfortable, not so frivolous."

I observed him with curiosity. He was the most contradictory guy I'd ever met. Till now he'd seemed concerned about social problems and here he was going out of his way to praise the bourgeois spirit.

"I'd give anything to go and see an opera there, *Madame*

Butterfly, for example. That beautiful, desperate Japanese woman letting down her hair, the little bridges of oriental gardens . . . "

I burst out laughing. A truly eccentric man. Was it only the heroic altercation with the chief inspector that had brought about this change? I hoped not. He'd probably liked me right from the start. He must have been tired of acting all dignified with me, of being the dominant sex's official representative. This resurgence was interesting. When the iron gates of his striped shirt clanked open, there appeared a dreamy, sensitive man. But, as he'd said, circumstances cut life short and you had to start over. However many treasures were stored up inside that strange policeman, they were no longer meant for me. Once we abandoned the case, most probably we'd never meet again.

"How is it in your case?"

"What?"

"You were going to tell me in the street, the way your life works, remember?"

I smiled. It had been some time since anyone had expressed interest in my way of thinking, that belonged to another era, youth, the fever of conversation. Garzón was hanging on my words. He looked like a Roman senator from a southern province. I could see his incipient occipital bald patch reflected in the mirror.

"Oh, I don't know . . . You said in your life everything is going well and suddenly there's an unexpected change that leads to destruction. For me it's the reverse, my life's never going well. As soon as I reach a static point where things begin to repeat themselves, I want to change. Not in a conscious, measured way but by means of a great show of passion. So I change profession, husband, home . . . It's like a kind of permanent restlessness, I need to give the building a good whack, knock it over, an unexpected decision, a break."

A group of students next to us burst out laughing, but Garzón didn't hear them, he was absorbed, hypnotized.

"Then that means . . . you control your own life."

"No, no, I wish! That means I'm constantly paralyzed by a sense of dissatisfaction, I wreck what's good in my life, let the deeper elements of my personality run riot."

"Hang on, inspector, I'm not as cultured as you are, you've lost me."

"Don't talk nonsense, what I mean is when I've something firm, solid, valuable, there's an uncontrolled impulse in me that makes me look elsewhere, stray into unknown, dangerous territory. This is what caused me one day to stop being a lawyer and become a cop, to get divorced, to get remarried . . ."

"And to get divorced again."

"Exactly. That's not what I would call self-control."

"But you do what you feel like."

Strange people were still walking down the Ramblas. We remained silent for a long while. Garzón had smoke coming out of his head from so much thinking, he was reaching a climax of contemplation. He shook his head sadly.

"What a world we live in, inspector!"

"Yes."

I was famished, having drunk on an empty stomach, and suggested eating. His counter-proposal took me by surprise, he suggested paying a visit to the Ephemerides. I knew it would be too much for me, but accepted.

Pepe didn't flinch when he saw us. The bar was fairly busy, full of youngsters drinking beer with ease. Someone had stuck a sign to the wall saying, *I too cast aside the first stone.* Hamed gave us his finest smile.

"What's on today's menu?" inquired Garzón like a real regular.

"Bean stew with yogurt."

"Fancy it, inspector?"

"Why not?"

Pepe opened bottles and served beans with calm gestures. I had to admit everything there was very well organized. Hamed brought us two steaming plates. I turned to my investigative partner.

"Why do you like coming here?"

He was spooning down the food as if some stray dogs were about to deprive him of it.

"I don't know, it's lively, nobody looks at you, there are young people. Pepe and I have interesting conversations. His viewpoint is quite unusual."

"Yes, I know him well, you don't have to explain."

"And I've discovered Arabic cooking, that's another reason."

He asked for seconds and we continued in open harmony, eating and drinking wine as if we'd done nothing else all our lives and this were the height of happiness. Once all the dinners had been served, Pepe and Hamed joined us for a chat.

"Have you found the culprit yet?" they asked.

"I'm afraid not."

Pepe gave his opinion:

"I'm increasingly convinced it's an initiation rite. Some guy who's been good all his life and has now decided to give evil a try. I don't think there's anything personal in his motives, he's moved by intellectual convictions and the desire to experiment."

"That's ridiculous!" I replied.

Garzón laughed.

Pepe's theories were always otherworldly and out of touch with reality. How often during our marriage had he driven me crazy with his far-fetched ideas! Everything that, when I first met him, struck me as original was later tinged with an air of fantasy I couldn't stomach.

"We're no more than transcendent animals, there'll never be a universe free of evil," said Hamed.

"Well, there's no point in speculating now," I said. "We've just been taken off the case."

"No way! Why?"

"Because Petra's a woman," said Garzón, and I heard the little bell of irony tinkle inside his words.

"Doesn't seem like enough of a reason to me."

"But it doesn't strike you as completely unreasonable either," I retorted.

"Deep down, since you were assigned the case, I've always thought that getting a woman to investigate rapes is like asking a black man to judge apartheid. Too much personal involvement."

They were waiting for me to jump, so I felt I had to.

"Of course you're right, Pepe, to be fair you'd have to catch the rapist in the act and before putting on the handcuffs, ask him, 'But perhaps your intentions were good?'"

They laughed, Garzón most of all. He must have felt relieved for once not to be the target of my feminist invective. Pepe patted me on the head.

"Isn't she a passionate woman?"

Like a father proud of his daughter. We had tried this game before: I, a child under his protection, he, firm and steady. We attempted to subvert the equation of our ages through role-play. But this wile also didn't work. Garzón intervened:

"Although I have to admit we were going nowhere, everything seems to indicate they'd have taken us off the case anyway. Especially since it's received a lot of coverage in the press. But Petra's made a verbal protest and is now going to make one in writing that I will sign as well."

"I don't know if it's worth it. I can't be bothered!"

Pepe served us some coffee and a jelly-filled pastry.

"If this were an American movie, you'd start investigating for yourselves till you caught the guy."

"I hate American movies," said Hamed. "They're always racist. And the action's too fast for me to follow."

I thought they could spend the whole night like this, chatting, laughing, talking nonsense. Now I understood why Garzón went there, what he did. Nothing basically, vegetate in a friendly atmosphere, come out with inconsequential reasonings, crack jokes.

I left at two in the morning, having had various drinks on the house. Garzón stayed behind, waving goodbye from his seat. There was a kind of mist, low clouds. I started my car. At that time, there was almost no one about. So that was that, it was over. An unsolved case had been taken off our hands. We had spent a short part of our lives facing a terrible reality and had been unable to do anything about it. We were ridiculous, useless, pathetic: an overweight sergeant and a forty-something advocate of women's rights. Comical!

The following week, I went back to my usual position in the Department of Documentation. Working on this case had been like eating a little manna, now everything seemed tasteless by comparison. There was a hugely exciting element to investigative work, it would have been foolish to deny it. It was like traveling by train, while your body remained stationary, the things around you advanced, all the parties concerned carried on operating. You stayed where you were, thinking, ordering events, eyes wide open so as not to miss your station. It was enthralling to have such direct contact with reality, to witness the moral misery, the corruption, the horror. I would never have believed myself capable of putting up with it, but it was incredibly easy, you didn't judge, you didn't get involved, you blunted your sensitivity and ended up believing Providence had set you there to undo wrongs and fight for justice. In reality, however, it wasn't like this at all—even if you managed to catch the culprit, you could only aspire to send each one back to his hole: the victims to their traumas and the criminals to prison. That said, the cocktail of righteous struggle and power acted like a real narcotic I wouldn't taste again.

After a few days, I had made progress in attaining the peace I once desired. I came home early, prepared dinner, had coffee with friends and took care not to find out who had taken over the investigation: I preferred not to know. One Friday evening, in my wish to be perfect, I even started putting my books on the shelves. Like all long-deferred tasks, it seemed to me unbearable and I stopped to drink some tea. I sat down with the cup in my hand, lit a cigarette, inhaled, looked around. The geraniums smeared with earth were still asleep. Suddenly the phone rang. It was Garzón.

"Switch the TV on immediately, channel three."

He didn't say another word and hung up. To begin with, I thought nothing, but, as I approached the set, it occurred to me they were breaking the news of the rapist's arrest. It wasn't that, I instantly recognized Patricia's features on the screen. She spoke straight at the camera with confidence, like a consummate professional actress.

"It was terrible," she said.

The camera moved back and I saw that Sonia and Salomé were sitting next to her on identical chairs. Opposite them, revealing only her studied profile, was the journalist I was supposed to talk to.

"Are you resentful towards him?" she asked.

"No," replied Sonia.

"What do you want for him?"

"We only want him to be caught, so other girls like us don't have to worry when they're out in the street."

So they'd prepared for them a careful script, not a word out of context, not one outside the burning drama. The phone rang again. It was Pepe.

"On TV . . ."

"I know, channel three."

I hung up.

"Did you have a good relationship with the police?"

"The boss was a woman," intoned Patricia with an angelic expression.

"Then she'll have been highly sympathetic towards you."

"Not a bit! She shouted at my mother."

"Shouted at her? For what reason?"

This blasted newscaster was prepared to blow it out of all proportion.

"Because she was crying."

"No way!"

"Yeah, and she tortured us psychologically."

I swallowed twice.

"How come? What did she do?"

"She brought us together and asked us all the same things. We felt ashamed and were forced to relive what had happened."

The journalist then interrupted the conversation and turned around to face the camera. The girls remained in the background, looking gray. Only Salomé hadn't said anything, I could see she was sullen and grim.

"There you have it. I should make clear that the cops the girls refer to have already been taken off the case. All the same, they still have the hope that . . . "

I leaped up and switched off the television. I grabbed a sheet of paper and began to write:

To the Commissioner of Police, Barcelona Police Headquarters.

Dear Sir,

Having seen my honor brought into disrepute and with unfounded doubts cast on my professional behavior, I am obliged to point out that a public threat hangs over the small but important female section of the police force you direct. Knowing your sense of justice, may I be so bold as to request . . .

Garzón called again.

"Did you see that, Petra?"

"Yes."

"Unbelievable, right?"

"Forget it, sergeant, don't worry about it."

"I bet they were paid to take part in that disgusting comedy. Do you think the culprit will have seen it?"

"Possibly, and I wonder what the consequences might be."

"Well, I suppose that's no longer any of our business."

"We'll see about that."

"What do you mean?"

"Oh, nothing. I'm tired, excuse me, I think I'll have to go to bed."

"Lucky you that you can sleep."

"Why, can't you?"

"I don't think so."

"Well, try at least."

. . . that the decision of our superiors to take us off the case be reconsidered. This would show to what extent the police can allow themselves to be influenced by information given out by journalists, setting a dangerous precedent . . .

The phone rang again. It was Pepe, ill-timed as always.

"Did you see what horrible stuff?"

"Yes, I saw it."

"I suppose you must be . . . "

"Listen, Pepe, what I am is dog-tired, so let's leave such a disagreeable topic for another day, O.K.?"

I didn't even give him time to answer. Poor Pepe, in the end he was always having to wrestle with my bad side.

7

Forty-eight hours after I sent that letter, we were back on the case. The order came directly from the commissioner of police, an executive post that makes important decisions but doesn't get involved in the details. For this reason, I then had to negotiate with the chief inspector. I wanted everything to stay the same, to be in charge of the investigation with only Sergeant Garzón under my command. This is how it was. It would have been puerile to believe that my letter was entirely responsible for this new situation. Lots of internal wrangles must have sprung up as a result of our dismissal. The image of the police yielding to pressure from the press was unsettling. The three victims appearing on TV and the insidious interview they were subjected to must have had something to do with the official change of policy. To have confirmed the dismissal would have been to admit that our superiors had been frivolous in choosing Garzón and me to start with. Then there was the gender issue, of particular interest in a rape case. Was the police force sexist? Were women in the police force being assigned insignificant tasks in spite of their qualifications? Too much for public consumption even if—or precisely because—it was true.

Garzón was very happy to learn about our reinstatement. When I mentioned the letter, his mouth dropped open.

"Why didn't you tell me?"

"Well, if nothing had come of it, you'd never have found out."

"You're amazing!" he exclaimed.

He then launched into a series of complex observations concerning women's behavior, never direct but always effective, getting so entangled in his reasonings I had to cut him short before what had started as a compliment turned into an insult. At the end of his oration, he gave a vociferous rendition of "Begin the Beguine." Anyone would think we were getting ready to go to a party instead of preparing to catch a rapist. I resigned myself to his happiness, I'd never seen him so euphoric.

For the moment, we had to pick up the case where our temporary replacements had left off. To my surprise (deep down I'd always believed others were better), things hadn't advanced one jot. They'd spent the whole week coming to grips with the situation. So we had to start where we'd finished—with the silver barb. This was the thread that needed pulling. I asked Garzón to find out the name of a jeweler who normally acted as an informer, a go-between, or who at least was trusted by the police. While he went about this, I decided to see what events had occurred in our absence. Nothing substantial beyond attendant circumstances—a certain aggression on the part of the latest victim's father, something I expected, and a juicy bit of information: the girls had received 600 euros for appearing on television. Each! In their private economies, this sum represented many hours' work, so they'd go back in front of the cameras whenever they were asked. I had to get the judge to impose a ban on reporting the case. I was convinced that, if the rapes were the work of a solitary individual seeking notoriety, the girls' star performances would only serve to flatter his ego and worsen the situation. It was difficult, however, to impose a ban when there were no defendants or suspects in the case, no natural person against whom to institute legal proceedings. Furthermore, the victims could presumably do whatever they liked with their lives. Till the scandal surrounding the case died down, any vulture could pleasurably descend on the slightest strip of rotting flesh. In a desperate attempt to avert the degenerative process the girls' declarations could set off, I decided to pay them a visit and persuade them not to give any more interviews. I didn't want to pass moral judgment on the act of taking part in such journalism. I didn't feel I had a right to criticize them, their behavior was understandable, perhaps for the first time in their short, insipid lives they had profited from evil. It would have been hypocritical to judge. The only tactic I considered valid to stop them selling their misfortunes was to make them afraid, not very honest but effective, I hoped. I noted it down in the new diary I had bought specially for the case, which demonstrated my renewed investigative vigor.

At seven in the evening of that rainy day, Garzón walked into the office. He'd done what I'd asked, in half an hour we had an appointment with a jeweler. He could only see us at the end of his working day. He was an important jeweler in Barcelona, supplier to the upper classes, and had no interest in his distinguished clients finding out he occasionally collaborated with the police. But he did, and he charged a lot for it. He usually gave his attention to stolen goods. He wasn't greatly amused to be involved in a more "gory" case and received us coldly. We arrived at his shop under the same umbrella. It was an elegant, luxurious place, almost without thinking I looked at myself and my old shoes, which were leaking. I then glanced at Garzón wearing a light raincoat and crimson tie, I thought he only needed a sign on his back saying "COP." The jeweler experienced first displeasure, then curiosity, and finally his eyes revealed a certain irony. Like everyone else, he obviously watched the news on TV and identified us as the two useless cops being talked about. We showed him the barb. He studied it through a magnifying glass.

"I don't know what to say, it's a silver barb coated in rhodium."

"Tell us about that material."

"Rhodium? There's not much to tell. A few years ago, it was used a fair amount in silver jewelry. It shines a lot, brings out the dull color of silver, the effect is dramatic. But then it was discovered to cause skin allergies in lots of women, strangely enough. Little by little, it fell into disuse."

"Aside from the shine, what other properties does it have?"

"None that I know of."

"Could it be said to strengthen the hardness of silver?"

"Well, a coating of any material would do that."

Garzón was about as attentive as a schoolboy. I continued: "You said it's fallen out of use."

"That's right."

"Could you tell us if there's someone in the trade who still uses it?"

He snorted:

"There could be many people, or no one at all, I don't know!"

"But if the material is dated, out of circulation, don't you think there could be a small or old-fashioned workshop, someone slightly removed from novelties, where it's still used?"

"Possibly."

"Can you think of someone?"

"Goodness gracious, do you know what you're asking? There are loads of small, old-fashioned workshops in Barcelona."

"I'm not asking you to answer now. Take your time. Perhaps you could put together a list we could work from."

"It'd be a long list."

"Please make it."

"O.K., I will, but I don't think it'll help you. There are small workshops scattered all over the city. There are even craftsmen who work in a back room without a license, doing odd jobs, repairs for relatives and friends. They're impossible to keep track of, as you can imagine."

"We've reason to believe the man we're after won't have gone to someone he knows. It's more likely he would have preferred the anonymity of a public place."

"This list will involve a lot of work on my part and I still think it may not help."

"That's our business," intervened the sergeant.

I was happy, it was just the right thing to say. Garzón knew the standard expressions, the ideal catch-phrases, and exactly when to insert them. What's more, the appearance he gave of an owl deep in thought made the questioning seem plausible in a way I could never have managed. We re-emerged into the damp night.

"What a guy!"

"Everyone who collaborates with the police is a bit of a jerk."

"How can you say that, Fermín?"

"What did you call me?"

"Fermín is your name, isn't it?"

"Yes, but it's the first time you've used it."

"I thought you didn't mind."

"I don't. It's just that a little personalization doesn't go amiss from time to time, it lightens the load."

"Would you like us to switch to *tu* when we're talking?"

"No, not that, you're an inspector and I'm a sergeant. It wouldn't be right."

I laughed. This sergeant was an oddball or was caught up in the ironic process of rejecting the transcendental. He no longer resembled that leathery individual at the beginning who seemed to have the tables of the law stuffed up his shirt for safekeeping.

"Do you fancy a drink?"

"Not now, I'm tired."

"Do you go to sleep so early?"

"I'll read for a while."

"Well, I think I'll drop by the Ephemerides."

"What do you get out of going there?"

He lifted the lapels on his raincoat and hesitated to answer. In the end, he leveled with me:

"You may not have noticed, but the vast majority of people always talk about the same things in the same way, using the same words even. I'm fifty-seven. That's a lot of hours' conversation. I've had it up to here, that's all! With those guys, I never know what topic they're going to propose. We talk about agriculture, about Abyssinian tribes, the Bible. Did you know Hamed is very familiar with the Bible? He's a kind of renegade, he says he finds it much more interesting than the Koran."

He looked at me suddenly:

"Do you understand what I'm saying?"

"I think so," I replied.

"That's why I go there."

I nodded, smiling. He said goodbye. I watched him leave. His resemblance to a barrel of whisky gave him a congenial air. Maybe at some point in the future one of his tobacco smugglers would shoot him and he would die. Then nothing would change and probably no one would remember him. Or perhaps some customer of the Ephemerides would dedicate a strange obituary, a lapidary phrase or a biblical verse to him. This must have been what gave him the strength to go on.

The following morning, I woke up early because I had lots to do. I went to visit all the doctors who had cured the girls of the mark on their arms. In no case had there been symptoms of allergy. I was aware that these visits didn't clarify much and I was stuck in the middle of a haystack without even being sure the needle was in it. In the final clinic, I came across Mr. Masderius.

"What are you doing here?" he spat at me.

"We still haven't been able to question your daughter."

"There's no hurry, she's recovering."

He despised me as if I were the rapist.

"Listen, Mr. Masderius, if we meet like this it's because I'm investigating and that should please you."

"Investigate as much as you like, but away from my daughter."

"You know that's impossible, your daughter has to appear officially."

"And she will. But in the meantime I don't want you near her, reminding her of what's happened."

"You can't just erase things."

"Did I ask for your opinion? You have your fucking case back, you can go and have fun, appear in the papers, devote yourself to your damn profession or get hanged, as far as I'm concerned."

"Next week your daughter will be summoned to make a statement."

"She's recovering from a cosmetic operation."

"You should have sought permission from the police to carry out that operation, you've destroyed relevant evidence."

He turned red. We were near the reception and the receptionist looked at us in alarm. He raised his voice still further:

"You have no rights over my daughter's body!"

"Nor do you!"

The receptionist approached, concealing her horror.

"Please, Mr. Masderius, your bill is ready, why don't you come with me?"

He controlled himself. I must have been flushed as well and felt a warmth rising in my chest.

"It was my pleasure," said Masderius as he stuck invisible claws of his hatred into my neck.

I reached the parking lot, breathing heavily. It would take me some time to get used to this confrontational man. It's one thing to pretend you're angry, to brag while being in control, quite another to be overcome with anger. Something was very

clear to me: a cop isn't Father Christmas. He's unloved by victims, witnesses, superiors, journalists, society . . . Every cop
would do well to buy himself a dog to assure himself of a little
affection.

Garzón was waiting for me at the station with Sonia and
Patricia. Salomé's mother had been unwilling to let her come,
if we wished to talk to her we had to go to her house. I was still
reeling from the encounter with Masderius, but tried not to
lose my nerve and smiled at the girls.

"You look good on television," I hit the ground running.

They glanced at each other with distrust. Their public performance must have created a bond between them. They fixed
their eyes on me with contempt. They'd also been taught we
were their enemies. I had no alternative but to dive straight in
and forget the friendly overtures.

"I've nothing against you making statements to journalists.
I understand your case raises issues that need to be
denounced. But I do want you to realize that all this business
on TV could arouse the rapist, provoke him into attacking
another girl."

They wouldn't look at me. Sonia kicked the air with her legs
crossed.

"It would also be better for you not to appear on that program again. People now are treating you like heroes, but they'll
soon grow tired, forget all about you, you'll have been a subject for gossip and will find it more difficult to go back to your
normal lives."

Patricia dared to speak:

"You don't want us to go back on that program for people
not to know what a mess you're making of the investigation."

"Is that what the journalist told you?"

"Besides," continued Sonia, "how much did the police pay
us for our statements?"

"My God!"

I wrung my hands and would have torn out my hair. Just great! How much do we get paid for telling the truth, for showing solidarity, how much for our vote? Everything was reduced to a simple transaction, name your price and then we'll see. I was close to desperation. Garzón nodded for me to let him intervene.

"You might also find the rapist gets fed up and decides to have it out with any of you three."

They looked at him as if he were mad. It was pointless, every attempt was destined to fail, they were equipped like the top British spy for a mission in Moscow. They'd been alerted to any tactic we might use to persuade them, including fear. That journalist was thorough. Besides, they had their thirty coins, and if Judas decides to hand himself over, who can stop him? We had to let them go.

We went around to Salomé's house, where things were even more explosive. Her mother was present; when she found out we wanted to question her daughter, she took time off work to be with her. She kept on interrupting, she was furious. Taking part in that program was a gesture of denunciation for the common good, this is what she said. Salomé didn't open her mouth. At such times, she hated her mother as much as she might hate me or the rapist. The concentration of hatred in her eyes was so intense it was scary. I realized she'd appear on TV as often as they liked, her will asleep as if she were a zombie, with only that indication of life in her eyes, pure hatred, sometimes contained, others in full flow.

We emerged into the street. There was lots going on. People were closing their workshops, the shops stayed open a little longer. Small, narrow, wretched bars with two or three customers sitting at the counter, talking at once. Children in tracksuits. Women in a hurry.

"Do you fancy a beer?"

We went into a Galician bar. I sat down on a stool as if it

were the most comfortable armchair, dejected, close to moral collapse. It all struck me as so obvious now, a rape was a case to be forgotten or to make money out of. We wouldn't get any cooperation from the victims. It would always be a family affair and the rape victim was its weakest point, through which the stain could spread to the family name. So it had to be neutralized, forbidden to speak or told to follow a script thanks to which it was still possible to reap some material benefit. Everything was going to be much harder than I imagined, the implications stuck to the fingertips like fresh cobwebs. Who was really interested in catching the rapist? My colleague sipped Ribeiro wine, unaware of the quagmire I was in. I asked him:

"Do you really think he could attack any of these girls again?"

"It's not likely."

"Have you seen how the parents take the lead?"

He turned to face me. I was asking too many questions whose response was obvious.

"You've formed a negative impression of this, haven't you, Petra?"

"It's horrible, family's a horrible invention, Garzón. Some want to erase all evidence of what's happened as the only cure while others exhibit the girls like they're part of a freak show. I wonder if they're not as much to blame as that blasted rapist."

"But aside from their miserable families, no one else cares."

I breathed out wearily.

"Maybe you're right."

"Still, I'm glad you're depressed, it means you're in the right frame of mind for what I have to tell you."

This put me on my guard. Garzón calmed me down, lazily gesturing with his large hands.

"Don't worry, it's just the list of jewelers and silversmiths."

"How many?"

"About a hundred."

"A hundred craftsmen working with rhodium, didn't the guy say it had fallen into disuse?"

"The bastard's listed every possible option."

"My God!"

"It's not a problem, we'll comb through them all."

"We don't even know what we're looking for."

"Sherlock Holmes had more fog to deal with!"

"Nothing gets you down, does it? And what if the rapist starts again?"

"No, right now he's having fun watching television, reading the papers, contemplating the outcome of his endeavors. I'm pretty sure he'll lie low for a while."

"I hope so."

"By the way, are you hungry? I suggest we eat together."

"I don't know if I'm in the mood."

"Better. That means if it's a bad mood, you'll get over it."

We went to the Egipto, full of young people and happy couples. I wasn't hungry, but Garzón was, ever ready for any kind of gastronomical adventure, so long as it was plentiful. Besides, I hadn't asked to be put back on the case just to fall into a deep depression. I tried to be smiley and cheerful. My problem was that I had what the French call "a simple heart." I wanted things to be monochromatic, to be obvious, flooded by the same ray of light. Culprits, guilty; victims, innocent; society, expectant and vengeful in the face of evil; the police, protected and supported as a moral guarantee against chaos. I wasn't prepared for the general sense of hostility that came bouncing back from all directions like a tennis ball off a wall.

"The lentils are pretty good, aren't they?"

For Garzón, however, none of this was new, he was used to dealing with victims and executioners, he knew that crime is a sticky substance that stains you as soon as you brush against it.

"A little chili sauce wouldn't hurt."

Now we were getting down to the nitty-gritty: fathers in denial, dominant mothers, common victims, the power of money . . . Of course, no doubt Robin Hood had to face up to the odd loutish woodcutter from time to time. Our task was not to do good, but to fulfill our duty, a duty that was laid out in icy orders. I suddenly felt like giving up the case, but then I thought this decision may not go down very well with our superiors. Garzón was finishing off the lentils, scraping the plate. He derived some of his existential strength from food, you only had to see him eat.

"I'm confused, I don't know what attitude to adopt."

"Act aggressive like you did before."

"I thought you didn't like it."

"In one or two interviews you may have gone overboard."

"You have to be forceful if you're a woman, otherwise you'll never get anyone to take you seriously."

"Don't start again with the use of your techniques as a woman!"

"Listen, Fermín, I'd hate to come across as an intellectual pedant but tell me, are you familiar with Darwin's theory of evolution?"

"I am."

"And do you agree with it?"

"It appears to be watertight."

"Let's say Nature, over time, equips creatures with the weapons they need to survive. Then why the hell am I going to renounce my sensitive antennae or extra female leg?"

He found it funny, he laughed, shaking his urban Buddha's belly. We then fell silent for a while as he went into ecstasy in front of a beefsteak. I imagined in the boarding house where he lived the meals were insufferable. When he finally managed to stop eating, he wiped his mustache a thousand times with the napkin and blurted out:

"Why did you get divorced?"

He had caught me by surprise, I never thought he'd go for the personal approach. I flicked a few crumbs of bread across the table.

"When, the first or second time?"

"Both."

I cackled uneasily. I hoped he'd give me the polite option of not answering, but he carried on looking at me, waiting for reasons with the ease of manner only a man who's eaten sumptuously can have.

"You'd better ask me why I got married, it's less complicated."

"O.K. then, why did you get married?"

Blasted Garzón! He really was interested. I clung to my cigarette like someone waiting outside the hall to take an exam.

"Well, the first time . . . Oh, you know why people get married the first time!"

"I don't follow you."

"I mean we were both young, proficient in our studies, not bad-looking . . . We met at university and graduated together. We decided to set up in legal practice with two other partners and, against all expectations, it went really well. Then, little by little, Hugo began to assume the leading role and I became his assistant. A secure job but without prominence and with my husband for a boss. So you see, it was never going to last, was it?"

"I suppose not. And then what happened?"

"Then? We were married for fourteen years, Fermín! What can I say?"

"Where else did it fail?"

"Fourteen years isn't so bad, breaking up after so long isn't exactly a failure."

"Marriage is for life."

"Yes, I know."

"Was your husband unfaithful?"

"Hugo? No! To tell the truth, things don't just happen. For

a cannon to fire, you first have to load it with a cannonball. We worked a lot, Hugo's what you'd call an upright, moderate, discreet man. He wielded great influence over me, let's just say I saw the world through his eyes both personally and professionally. So much so that in the end I felt I'd been annulled, I was tired of always doing what was reasonable and virtuous, of being the second in command. So one fine day I up and left. I decided to abandon both the law and him. But take note: I up and left, I never had it in me to confront my husband and tell him what I really thought either at home or in the office, maybe because I knew he was right. I still haven't gotten over the trauma. When I'm with him, I never contradict him."

"I see," was the only remark my confidant made, but not because he was detached, he was listening to me with real unction.

"And with Pepe what happened?"

"Do you want to know everything about me?"

"I'm sorry, I'm normally more discreet but I've never been divorced, so I'm curious."

"Don't worry, you do well to ask. Besides, with Pepe it was much simpler. I met him by chance and he was so charming! Prudence went out the window with him and so did convention. He didn't care if he was taking part in a military parade or a procession. I thought this time I'd be the one who wore the trousers and we had no work ties."

"But you were wrong."

"No, I wasn't. We got married and, in effect, I was the one wearing the trousers. But I went from having a father-husband to having a husband-son. I felt tenderness and pity for him, he seemed to me defenseless and reliant, I organized his life, laughed at his jokes, met his friends. There was certainly no conflict but I realized I really didn't fancy being a mother to such a grown-up child who was only looking for shelter."

"Well, he loved you a lot."

"Is that what he said? It may be true but I wasn't in need of a pretty lap-dog with a blue bow who demonstrated his loyalty, I needed a real husband."

"Crikey, Petra, you've thought a lot about your marriages!"

"Very typical of my generation, to try always to explain the past. You don't believe in psychology, do you?"

"I . . . I don't know, not to the extent of thinking it's always applicable."

"But then you were happy with your wife!"

I blew out the cigarette smoke in the direction of the ceiling. Garzón sipped his coffee thoughtfully.

"I suppose so."

"You suppose so?"

"The truth is I never stopped to think about it as much as you. Maybe because we had a son and, what with that and my work, I never had much time."

"You've a son, Garzón? And here I am drilling out the time with my nonsense! You may even have grandchildren."

"No, not grandchildren."

"Tell me all about it."

"There's not much to tell. I've a thirty-year-old son who's a doctor and lives in New York. He's the deputy director of an oncology hospital, so we don't see each other very often."

"Have you ever been to visit him?"

"I did once. I had a good time, though everyone thought I was South American and I had to keep on explaining I was Spanish."

"But that's great!"

"It seems he's very good at his profession and he'll go far."

I gave him a warm smile. Now we were friends in the presence of the Lord, we'd shared the things that really matter to people: marriage, children, mistakes, all of it vaporized by a succulent meal and outpourings of coffee. Garzón was human, a dad. It wasn't difficult to imagine him in America: a Chicano on

Fifth Avenue. He must feel happy with his life: a beloved wife, a talented son and the sensation of having done his duty at work, always the same. The sergeant had successfully sized up life, which involved obeying orders, not analyzing love or happiness and raising outstanding children to the greater glory of America—presumably the only way to reach the finish-line in one piece.

When we said goodbye, I was sure he'd head straight for the Ephemerides. Being submissive all his life had not saved him from the solitude of a boarding house. But he probably didn't care, he sought out company and conversation and found it there. He didn't succumb to self-pity and he hadn't set himself a worldly goal. To continue along his path, he didn't need to sublimate the ordinary and he didn't believe in the mirific properties of buying a house with a garden.

I couldn't sleep that night. One agitated dream followed another. My young companions from the gym miraculously managed to catch the rapist. They castrated him in the changing room, and all I could do was watch. They then asked me to dispose of his bloody organs. I placed them in a sports bag and wandered around the city, not knowing what to do with them. I finally had the brilliant idea of burying them in the garden and put them through the mincer. Once they were reduced to a foul, shameful hamburger, I went out into the backyard and spread them on the inanimate geraniums, which suddenly started to grow.

I had a hell of a job awaiting me at ten the next morning. Mr. Masderius had been left with no option but to allow his daughter to give evidence. They were both due at the station, where I would receive them on my own. Garzón was busy with the jewelers' workshops, of which he'd already visited forty-two to no avail. This business of the flower covered in rhodium seemed to be the devil's job, but perseverance was the only way. I could imagine perfectly what would happen: a tense and watchful

Masderius like a goalie keeping a constant eye on his daughter. And this is how it was. I was struck by the girl's appearance, she looked even worse than in hospital. Two black lines were drawn under her eyes, possibly as a result of the operation. But there was something in her look that went beyond any simple physical disorder, a runaway gleam, anxiety, perhaps fear. She was the rapist's archetypal victim: small, delicate features, the long, translucent hands of a Renaissance virgin. Why? Had he always been under the cosh of corpulent women? Was he just a coward who took on weak girls apparently unable to respond to aggression with aggression?

Cristina barely looked up, her feeling of shame was enormous, greater than that of the other girls. As she talked, she glanced, paralyzed, at her father. I'd willingly have shaken her to make her react, anything would have been preferable to seeing her in that state of intense dread. She referred to the series of events I knew by heart: no idea about the face, no idea about the voice, the wound on the arm . . . At this point, I interrupted her:

"What with?"

"I don't know."

"Something he was wearing on his wrist?"

"Maybe."

"Could you see what it was?"

She fell silent for a moment.

"No."

Infuriating. A phantom rapist or an extremely prudent and careful offender. The story was always the same. I was overcome by a fit of impotence. Why did that bastard never introduce any variations into his crimes? And what about circumstances? How could there possibly never be any witnesses, any trace? Why had he never felt the need to show himself? The individual we were dealing with really was methodical, cold, dispassionate, given to his obsessions with terrible strength.

Once Cristina had answered the final question, her father made as if to leave.

"One moment, Mr. Masderius, perhaps your daughter would like to add something or suddenly remembers something. It would be good to meet up again."

He didn't let me finish:

"Don't even think about it! Cristina's going to the States for a year to do an intensive course of English. So, unless there's a warrant, you won't be able to question her again. It's your turn now, do your duty, go after that pig and leave my daughter alone!"

"It's just that . . . "

He turned towards the girl:

"Have you anything to add, a new idea, details you've omitted?"

She shook her head, staring in front of her. I'd never seen anyone in such a state of stupor.

"Have a nice day."

They left through the door like an autumn wind. I slumped into my chair. Then I reacted, I went into the street and saw them get into their car. I took mine and followed them. Just as I imagined, he dropped his daughter at the door of their house, making sure she entered, and drove away. If there was still any chance of talking to Cristina, it was now. I parked and climbed up to the Masderiuses' apartment. I rang the doorbell, and, after a while, the mother appeared. She didn't recognize me. When I introduced myself, her face became contorted.

"My husband already talked to you, and my daughter was there."

"I know, Mrs. Masderius, but in front of your husband Cristina and I were barely able to communicate."

"She said everything she knows."

"Sure, but I have the impression she didn't answer freely. Please let me talk to her."

"Don't you understand? All this is like a bad dream, something alien to us."

"But I'm afraid it's not alien to you. Your daughter's been raped, nothing can change that."

"Please go."

"Mrs. Masderius, that guy's on the loose and we have to catch him, it's not a bad dream, it's the truth and you're involved. All of this really happened, open your eyes, you can heal the facts but never erase them. Let me in."

She moved back a little and I entered, closing the door behind me. She stared at the ground, staying quietly where she was, her hands hanging lankly on either side of her body. I decided not to waste any time and asked her where her daughter's room was. I was inside, but she could change her mind and I had no search warrant on me. We silently climbed the stairs of the large duplex. The mother abruptly opened a door and I could see Cristina's expectant face, her weary look. She was seated at a desk with two open suitcases lying on the bed, stuffed with clothes. The walls were covered in posters with Bruce Springsteen's unkempt image. I wondered what that moody teamster was doing in a room that was like a small, luxury apartment to scale.

"So it's true you're going."

"Yeah."

"What about your friends?"

She looked at me without understanding.

"I mean it'll be hard to leave them."

"It's only a year."

She'd clearly learned the lesson that justified taking a year out. On her return, no one would remember.

"All right, Cristina, I know we just talked at the station but I had the impression you couldn't really say what you were thinking."

"I was nervous."

"We were all nervous, your father as well, but now you and I are not nervous and whatever you say will be our secret. Is there anything that didn't come out?"

"No."

"Are you sure?"

"Yeah."

I sat at the foot of the bed.

"Cristina, listen to me, I know your father wants what's best for you. It's good for you not to get mixed up in such dark matters but you have to tell me what happened. The guy who raped you is a real asshole and we're definitely going to catch him. But he's not going to fall into the trap on his own, someone's going to have to give us a detail, the slightest indication, because, I tell you, we don't have a clue. That little detail will be like shoving him in our direction. Your mother understood that and she let me in."

She gazed at me through eyes blurred with tears.

"I was so happy at home and now I have to go to New York, where I don't know anybody."

I was wasting my time. This poor girl was lost at the end of a maze in which motives, a sense of reality, had all but disappeared. I had to leave at once because otherwise I'd succumb to the temptation of telling Cristina I thought her father was just as pernicious for her as the assailant himself.

"It's all right, Cristina, I'm going to leave. Don't worry about New York, I bet there'll be loads of other young guys. I wish you luck."

I patted her on the shoulder and, as I was going out, I heard behind me:

"I saw what he used to mark me."

I stood stock-still, without turning around, afraid that her words would vanish into thin air. Finally I looked at her:

"You saw it?"

"Yeah."

"And what was it?"

"A watch."

"A watch?"

"Yeah, I saw the reflective face shining in the dark, and I saw the luminous hands telling the time. Then he closed it."

"He closed it?"

"I heard like the click of a lid and then I couldn't see it."

"Was it one of those old pocket watches with a cover?"

"I don't know, I don't know what it was, there was no light, it could have been something else I heard."

"O.K., don't worry, that's already a lot. Now we're going to nail him."

"I hope so."

She didn't say anything else, but at least it was an openly expressed desire, she might even wriggle out of the plan of salvation her father had devised.

The sergeant was very pleased when I told him about my progress. So the first, absurd hypothesis was correct, we now knew what we were looking for: a watch. The fog began to take shape. He, meanwhile, had reached jeweler number fifty, which was a milestone in itself and gave us an excuse to celebrate. We went to the bar. The next step involved going backwards, we had to revisit our informer and ask him to narrow the search. Of all the workshops using rhodium, how many dealt more with watches than with jewelry in general? The answer would not rule out the others—any silversmith could mount barbs on a watch without it being his specialty—but by means of preferences we might manage to move certain names to the top of the list and save time.

"This is going swell," said Garzón.

"You have a lot of faith."

Even I, however, without having it, had changed my attitude. I'd immersed myself completely in the investigation, it was no longer something external and debatable, but our case, a case that, even if it cost us our lives, we were going to solve.

The cold abated. It was a clear night. I parked the car in the street and, as I was about to enter the house, someone appeared out of the shadows and called me. I was next to the wall and couldn't see a thing but immediately a woman stepped into the light from the streetlamp.

"Inspector Delicado, do you have a moment?"

"Who is it?"

"Ana Lozano, perhaps you remember me."

"No," I lied.

"I direct the show *It's a Complicated Life*. Can I come in?"

I should have realized the vulture would try again. The atavistic impulses of good manners made me invite her into the house. She took off her coat with ease and, without being asked, settled into one of the armchairs. She rummaged around in her large bag. It suddenly occurred to me I was a cop and in no way was it wise to show in a stranger. But it was a bit late for being cautious, I could only hope she would leave soon. She offered me a cigarette while eyeing the parcels of books.

"Have you recently moved?"

"That's right."

"You've a nice house here."

I suddenly felt in a bad mood.

"So how can I help you?"

She smiled peevishly, invested with a moral authority she was convinced of.

"You fulfill your obligation, don't you, Petra? Law enforcement is considered by society a sacred profession. But I'd like you to understand, so is journalism. Thanks to us, things happen for people. Till we open the doors to the public, facts don't exist for the vast majority. In our hands not only opinion but even reality is formed."

"You're like God."

"You could say so."

She stared at me as if I were a native of virgin lands who needed persuading of the existence of inventions as obvious as electric light.

"I wouldn't mind a drink."

That would have been the moment to give vent to indignation and turn that scene from a comedy into a Spanish drama. But, remaining in my state of civilized inertia, I served her a whisky with water.

"Listen, Petra, it's nothing to get upset about. You're not made of better stuff than the rest. The whole police force collaborates with us: inspectors, subordinates, even your own superiors. It's the sign of the times. What's more, if you like, we could suppress the source of information."

I smiled like an idiot, unclear where her propositions were leading.

"You see, Ana, it's not just a moral issue here, the thing is I don't like your program."

"Because we've been hard on you?"

"No, because it's a pile of garbage."

There was no way she was going to get offended.

"I understand, looked at from an aesthetic point of view it could give that impression. But you have to realize it's a kind of community service and the community is basically what it is. It's not for us to change it. Besides we're not asking you to reveal state secrets, just to keep us up to date with the investigation, confirm or deny the odd detail . . . For example, the house you visited today belonged to the latest victim, right?"

She touched a raw nerve:

"Have you been following me?"

She adopted a bored expression:

"Oh, come on, don't get all theatrical! You say it as if it were a crime, but it's not. We're following our own lines of inquiry and if you don't collaborate . . . "

"Are you sure that's legal?"

"Of course it's legal! And if we reach an agreement, we might even be able to compensate you financially."

"Is bribery legal?"

"For a journalist anything is legal."

"Please leave and don't expect any help from me."

She stood up in a rage.

"Fine! Thanks for the whisky. I said it as soon as I saw who'd been assigned the case: 'We'll have problems, you'll see.' It always happens when you're dealing not with real professionals but with amateurs and upstarts."

She rammed her cigarettes into her bag and left without saying goodbye. I had wasted her no doubt magnificently well paid time. I felt increasingly indignant while at the same time justifying my action. This was the limit. A cop could be expected to have to confront the underworld, crime, mental instability, the most marginalized areas. He might even have to deal with friction between operatives, clashes with his bosses or judicial authorities, but—my God!—journalists as well? Was this the new social conscience? It resembled an English fox hunt: trumpets, red riding coats and four hundred hounds howling all around.

My face was burning. Acting on a childish impulse, I brushed the dust off the chair where that predator had been sitting. I looked at my house. It was still foreign to me. Nothing to do with my life. This whole affair had exploded in my hands like a blasted firecracker and, if I wasn't careful, would wriggle loose, leaving a glittering trail in the air.

I filled the bathtub to the brim and flopped inside it. I sprinkled some bath salts on the water, which dyed it green. On the packet, it said: *These salts are made from the most exotic, natural herbs plucked from heavenly abodes where the vegetation follows its age-old course unimpeded by any external agents of civilized life. Simply irreplaceable when relaxation becomes a necessity.* I went under.

8

I had a chat with the chief inspector to bring him up to date. I probed his feelings towards us. Absolute calm. Once a case had been definitively allocated, any previous resentment vanished, so it seemed, together with any pressure or reproaches. Everything was in order. Once a train was installed on the track, it would have needed a serious collision to derail it. Something akin to apathy, in fact. But never question a system that is to your advantage—a golden rule for achieving success in life. The chief inspector treated me with greater respect than during the first part of the investigation. I attributed this to my feminist rant, not to any progress we might have made. Clearly, to take a step forward, you had to have a mouth that was trained to bite. I was thinking of mentioning this to Garzón, telling him that according to Darwin's theory women also had to develop large jaws and a deep-throated growl. I was sure he'd want to hear this, that it would get a reaction out of him. He was difficult to impress, after a life of boredom he was pretty much immune to life's novelties. When I told him about my awkward meeting with Ana Lozano, her attempt at bribery and my valiant effort at self-control, he barely raised an eyebrow, for him it was nothing unusual. Frustrating for me, since I needed cheering on in my first act of bravery along the path of duty.

As I was leaving the boss's office, a guard came up to me.

"Inspector Delicado, you have a *communiqué*."

"A what?"

"Sergeant Garzón has declared his urgent desire that you make yourself known as soon as possible at number 36 Avinyó Street. He didn't go into details."

I isolated the meaning of this text from its florid official delivery. It must have been important, Garzón was not in the habit of entrusting messages to others.

I took the subway to reach the center earlier. From a distance, I observed that the number belonged to a small workshop, one of those typical establishments in the old quarter that have resisted modernization. In the tiny shop window, various watches hung from a wire. I entered and, long before I could take in the scene, I was struck by the look of excitement on my colleague's face. I understood.

"Petra, this gentleman says some time ago he carried out the job we're interested in."

Next to him, there was an old man straight out of Dickens or Balzac. He looked at me in surprise:

"A woman!"

"That's right," I answered with a smile.

His pate was bald and translucent like a newborn's, he had on a gray, threadbare vest.

"There didn't use to be any women on the force. I suppose even if they'd been offered, they'd all have said no to such a job."

"Those were hard times."

Garzón looked at me ironically. I decided to concentrate on the matter in hand since the opening salvos were proving dangerous.

"Could you tell us what kind of job you did?"

"I set a crown of rhodium-coated silver barbs on a gentleman's watch."

"What kind of watch?"

"I don't know, the usual kind, a cheap watch you can buy anywhere, with a leather strap."

"Digital or with hands?"

"With hands."

"Did you put a lid on it, some kind of cover?"

"No, I just put the barbs and coated them in rhodium because he wanted them to shine and be strong."

I took out the box with the piece of evidence.

"Could this be one of the barbs you used?"

He changed glasses, putting on a broken, dirty pair.

"It could be."

"Do you recall who ordered the job?"

"Yeah, a young, tall guy in his twenties."

"Do you have his name and address?"

"No, I only ever take a contact number."

"Did you speak to him on that number?"

"I never got round to calling him, he turned up first."

"Didn't he tell you why he wanted the watch altered in this way?"

"No."

"Didn't it surprise you?"

"I get all kinds of weird guys asking me to engrave names or phrases on jewels, little hearts. I've made gold plaques for dog collars, what more can I say?"

"I see. Could you give us that telephone number?"

"I don't have it here. It's at home, which is where I keep all my old notebooks. Anyway, what is it you're after?"

"How about we visit your home?"

"What now? Impossible! There's no one to look after the shop. If a customer comes and finds it closed, who's going to make up my losses?"

It was hard to believe he'd lose a customer during a moment's absence, that is supposing a customer would ever dare set foot in such a dilapidated place.

"I close in an hour and a half, you can wait if you like. There's a bar next door."

A bull's head was affixed to the wall of that dingy dive, clad

in a Barcelona soccer cap. Depressing. I complained bitterly to
Garzón.

"Do you think it's normal? We've a hugely important lead
and that old scrooge makes us wait. I can't believe it!"

"Calm down, Petra, things are what they are, we can't force
him. Does he strike you as suspicious?"

"The old guy? No. But I bet the telephone number doesn't
belong to the rapist."

"Do you think he's that careful?"

"Sure he is, who'd give his own number in a situation like
this? You know, I'd like to catch the criminal right now and
bust his balls."

"Inspector! You're supposed to be a reserved professional."

"I smell blood, Garzón. Do you see what a nerve the guy
has, having a device made with total premeditation to mark his
victims? He has to be a monster, a real loony."

The sergeant shrugged his shoulders with the resignation of
a Franciscan prior.

"Your composure is beginning to get to me. Anyone would
say in Salamanca you came up against Jack the Ripper on a
nightly basis."

"I've seen a few things in my time."

I ordered another coffee. If I didn't manage to stay calm,
the investigation could run out of control at any moment. It
was better to brake, to keep the machine in hand. I was surprised to note that I hadn't felt this nervous in years.

"Stupid old man!"

I gestured with contempt. If it turned out he couldn't find
the telephone number in his notebooks, the solution to the
case, which was within reach, would sink perhaps forever in a
swampy marsh. I was sick with tension. The old guardian
finally appeared on the threshold of the bar. A pair of bow
legs completed his full-length portrait, wrapped in trousers
that were stained from overwear. He beckoned to us to follow

him. On the way to his house, every one of his weary steps made me wince with anxiety. We climbed the stairs of a ruinous building without an elevator. The old man stopped, caught his breath, climbed again. I'd willingly have pushed him. I couldn't understand my colleague's patience, he waited for him, helped him, listened to his complaints about the lack of light on some floors, the frailties of old age. We finally arrived, but the wait wasn't over. We had to stand there till he found the right key on a night watchman's crowded key ring and, having leafed through countless shabby notebooks, finally produced the right one from out of a bundle of archeological documents. The house stank of damp and cockroaches.

"I think it's this one." He read a telephone number aloud.

"Is there a date, a name, any pointer?"

"No. Just 'crown of rhodium-coated barbs for watch.'"

"Did he refuse to give you his personal details?"

"I didn't ask him for them."

I stared into his lifeless eyes.

"Now I'm going to ask you to describe him to us. It's very important you concentrate."

He stamped his feet:

"How do I know what the boy was like? I'm eighty years old, work ten hours a day without help, do you think I remember everyone who comes into my shop?"

This annoyed me:

"Listen, you're obliged to answer my question! This isn't a joke, we're after a rapist, so think about it before you say anything!"

He wasn't cowed.

"A rapist?"

"Answer me!"

Garzón intervened, bringing out the pot of cream:

"The inspector just wants you to make a little mental effort.

We understand the difficulties but the slightest detail will be of help."

"I don't know anything, I don't remember anything. I saw him for a minute the first time he came and another minute when he picked up the watch. You've no right to turn up in a poor old man's home and subject me to this kind of pressure."

I realized he was becoming hysterical and kept quiet. Garzón resumed control of the witness:

"It's all right, all right, calm down. We'll leave the station number and our names. If you remember anything, you can call us."

He pushed me towards the door. On the stairs, he gently remonstrated with me:

"You were too direct again. It's counter-productive."

"I have the impression he knows something. Besides, he's plain disagreeable."

"Don't be ridiculous."

"Don't give me that bullshit."

He looked at me in despair, made a compromising gesture.

"What do we do now, inspector?"

"Take the number to the station. They'll tell us who the subscriber is."

The telephone number belonged to a bar. It was too much to expect it to be the rapist's, but at least it wasn't made up. The Café del Picador was situated in the Clot district. In the car, on the way there, neither of us felt overly optimistic. The bar owner was unlikely to be involved. Loads of people go in and out of a bar, so it was pointless thinking about questioning. Besides what question would we ask? "Have you seen an individual with a watch like this?" However stupid the rapist might be, a hypothesis we'd already rejected, he'd never reveal his barbed watch in public. Imagining such a possibility could happen was like believing miracles always fall from the sky on the side of good.

The Café del Picador had a typical, filthy look. Grimy windows, a tiled counter and hellish game machines that from time to time played a fairground theme. Garzón wouldn't let me get out of the car.

"You should stay. If we have to go back undercover, it's better if they don't recognize one of us as a cop."

"You're right, the thought hadn't even occurred to me."

He was visibly pleased. I watched him make his approach in an unbuttoned raincoat with that incredibly ugly brown suit underneath. If a schoolchild were asked to paint a cop, this would have been my colleague's portrait. I lit a cigarette and sighed, wondering if my appearance were not equally obvious. He emerged after a while at a road roller's pace.

"The bar belongs to a couple without children. It's pretty normal, the local workers have breakfast and lunch there, it's closed in the evening."

"Anything untoward?"

"No. They haven't given out their number or been asked to take messages."

"Do they have any nephews, do they get any gangs of youths?"

"We'll have to put them under surveillance. What do you say we do it for a week?"

"Good," I bit my lips. "This is exasperating, we're close to something we cannot touch. Do you remember the torments of Tantalus?"

"You already know I'm not as cultured as you are."

"Oh, come on, Garzón, don't give me that again! Culture's no use in a job like this. The only really important things are facts, immediate, tangible, insignificant details: someone who went in, another who left, a third who saw them. I feel we're reliant on a string of spittle just to find something out. Don't give me culture!"

He stared at me quietly.

"You say interesting things, Petra, but it's strange, you despise your values, those you've been taught."

"I don't give a fuck about values, Fermín."

He laughed softly and shook his head. Discussing the meaning of life with a cop outside the Café del Picador in a car reeking of tobacco. Buñuel wouldn't have done it any differently, though perhaps in place of a cop he'd have chosen a cardinal.

We went to spy on that terrible bar for two successive days. What were we spying for? We didn't know for certain. There were no suspicious characters or movements. We turned up, parked the car nearby, listened to the radio. From time to time, Garzón stayed in the car and I went to the bar and drank a coffee. Within a few hours, I was the one acting suspiciously. What was I up to? The owners and customers eyed me with distrust. What did I want? I observed young, tall men, trying to work out if they were wearing a watch. Of course they were all wearing a watch. We were wasting our time wretchedly.

The second day, on returning home at night, I was surprised to find everything seemed distant and unimportant to me. I didn't attempt to put on any music or cook a hot dinner. I was absorbed in the investigation, it had become an obsession, and I couldn't care less about the house, my life, privacy. I didn't even care about the geraniums, they could carry on hibernating for centuries to come. I got into bed, feeling frozen, and wrapped myself up. Some bastard, a loony perhaps, was wandering around near us with a device for marking girls. I fell into a light sleep and glimpsed a field full of flowers, their corollas trimmed with bloody barbs. The wind swayed them to and fro with maddening regularity. They couldn't stop moving or dripping blood. They were fragile, exposed, but they were stuck firmly in the ground and couldn't escape. I took some time to come to and recognize the sound of the phone, which I could hear in the distance.

Having lifted the receiver, I then took some time to understand what Garzón was trying to tell me.

"Come again, sergeant, I'm fast asleep."

"The old guy just called me, he finally remembered."

"Does he have a name?"

"No, but he recalled a vital distinguishing mark."

"What is it?"

"A black tooth in the middle of his mouth, an upper incisor."

"Great! Now we've something to ask about."

"We'll give it a go. I'll pick you up at six in the morning. We need to speak to the bar owners before people start coming for breakfast."

"I'll be ready."

Of course I couldn't sleep. Our man's blank face now had a disturbing feature. The phantom opened his mouth. But were we sure the one who wore the watch and the rapist were the same man? Couldn't it be a friend, a go-between? It was at least a reliable lead.

I left the house at six on the dot. As a preventive measure against fatigue, I had consumed large amounts of coffee. I saw Garzón sitting in the car, waiting. Wearing sunglasses in the early morning mist, he was the quintessence of eccentricity. He acknowledged me with a wave. He looked happy.

"So he finally remembered something, eh. You see, inspector?"

"Don't you think he always knew and decided to keep quiet till he felt a prick of conscience?"

"I reckon so. He seemed a little scared when he called. He must have been weighing the consequences of furnishing that detail for quite some time."

"Does that make him suspicious?"

"Not really, you know what people are like with the police, the less they say, the better. They're brutally afraid of being implicated in something, of being called in by a judge to give evidence. For an old guy, it's even worse. What does he want to get into trouble for at his age? But, as you say, he then felt a prick of conscience."

"It was some time coming."

"I wouldn't be so sure, he could have taken a lot longer to call us."

He parked in front of the bar, which was still closed. We waited for the owners to arrive. Garzón started smoking and humming. I had wanted the night to pass quickly so we could cut to the chase, but I now felt intolerably sleepy and nodded off. After a while, Garzón gave me a nudge.

"Look, they're here."

The couple got out of a van and made to open the bar. We let them lift the metal shutter. They went in. Garzón smoothed out the tails of his raincoat.

"Let's go."

On seeing us together, the woman clearly thought, "Now I knew there was something . . . " The sergeant had accurately informed me about people's reaction to the police. Our mere presence terrified them. Their eyes told us to leave even before they discovered what we wanted from them.

"I'm Sergeant Garzón, I was here the other day, remember? And this is Inspector Delicado. We're looking for a customer of yours, or at least someone who may have come to the bar a couple of times."

"We already told you . . . "

"I know, but there's a detail I failed to mention, which you may perhaps have noticed. The man we're after, young and tall, has a black tooth right here in the middle of his mouth."

Garzón pointed to his upper teeth and frowned like a grotesque Chinese mask. They were silent. The woman started stammering:

"Well . . . I don't know . . . there's a boy comes round with a tooth like that." She turned to her husband. "Juan, I mean."

"But Juan's not a customer."

"He's a boy who works delivering beer. But he's not the sort to do anything wrong."

"We only want to have a chat with him. Is he tall and strong?"

"Yes. What's he done?"

"Nothing really. Can you tell us where he works?"

"Yes, a drinks warehouse a couple of blocks from here."

"Does he have the number of this bar?"

"Sure, he calls every week to take our order."

"Could you show me exactly where that warehouse is?"

The man proceeded to give Garzón directions. The latter turned to me.

"You stay here, I'll go and take a look."

I sat down at the bar. The man removed his apron and began bustling about in the kitchen. The woman wiped the counter and viewed me with curiosity.

"Would you like a coffee? I plugged the machine in when we arrived. It should be hot by now."

I nodded. While she served the coffee, she started chatting, directing her remarks to the topic that interested her.

"This boy, Juan, always brings the beer crates. He sometimes drops by for a drink, he only works around the corner. He doesn't come that much though."

"Does he come on his own?"

"Yes. The truth is he seems a good sort, though I haven't had much to do with him. But what can I say? Young people these days, what with drugs and I . . . "

"Does he take drugs?"

She ducked behind her outstretched arms, her eyes wide open, frankly alarmed.

"No! I was just saying. I know nothing about him, I don't even know his surname."

She stayed quiet after that, shot me fearful glances while slicing rolls in half. I asked her:

"Have you ever noticed if he wears a strange watch on his wrist, a watch with points and a lid that covers the face, or something like that?"

She shrugged her shoulders, shook her head. Then suddenly her eyes flashed wildly. Her jaw dropped and she said:

"I get it! You're after the flower rapist, the one who marks girls on the arm."

"Madam, don't be so ridiculous. Please calm down."

Public opinion. This is what those accursed journalists achieved by keeping the public informed: slowing down the work and making a mess of things. It'd been a mistake on my part to mention the watch. I got off the stool and went towards the glass door, this way I'd avoid having to listen to that woman, who probably swallowed every episode of *It's a Complicated Life* whole. Outside it was gradually getting busy, though the bar still had no customers. At that precise moment, a young man tried to cross the threshold I had occupied. He was rubbing his hands from the cold. I moved away from the door and he entered. I carried on looking outside. I then heard a suppressed cry behind me, the woman's frightened voice saying:

"It's him!"

I turned around. The young man came to a halt halfway between the entrance and the bar counter. He abruptly shifted and stared at me for a few seconds.

"Police!" I shouted.

He made a dash for the door. I caught him by one arm. I saw his gray, expressionless eyes in front of mine and then I felt it, I felt that great pain, I heard the bones of my nose crunch, the structure of my face crack section by section as if a huge cathedral had come crashing down. Lying on the ground, I tried to reconcile the noises inside my head with the screaming voice. It was the woman. I breathed in, swallowing blood. I didn't need to worry, it was the woman and I wasn't wounded or dead, I'd just received a punch in the face. A couple of chairs had been upended next to me. I got up gingerly. The bar owners came running over. The woman was crying:

"Oh, God! Please sit down. Are you hurt?"

She brought a clean towel, which was immediately soaked in blood. Neither of them knew quite what to do. The man went to serve me a glass of brandy. Garzón arrived as he was bringing it.

There were exclamations and hurried attempts to explain what had happened. The sergeant knelt down in front of my face, turning on me his kind owl-like eyes.

"Crikey, Petra, he got you there!"

"The guy escaped," I mumbled.

"Forget about that now, try and calm down."

In the clinic, they assured me I hadn't suffered a broken nose, only the bruising impact of an almighty blow. But when I looked at myself in the mirror, I was taken aback, a violet ring encircled my eyes. I had to spend three hours lying on a stretcher and they gave me an injection to stop the flow of blood. The doctor said, "A few anti-inflammatories and you'll be right as rain." In the meantime, Garzón took care of everything: contacts and informing the judge, arrest warrant, stationing guards around the suspect's house. He still managed to find time to come and fetch me from the clinic. I was grateful to him, though it wasn't really necessary, I could move by myself. I felt shaky and melancholy like a child who's just gotten over the measles and, most of all, stupid for having allowed the rapist to escape without putting up resistance. Garzón tried to appease me in the car:

"It wasn't your fault. The guy saw me enter the warehouse and, just in case, took off to the bar. There he could calmly drink a beer and come back later without arousing suspicion. He didn't know we were so hot on his heels. You came across him by chance, there wasn't a lot you could do, he caught you unawares."

"What did the warehouse manager tell you?"

"Nothing special. His name is Juan Jardiel and he does indeed have a blackened tooth. He's polite and hardworking. He was very surprised to learn we were after him for some crime. He said he'd bet his life Juan wasn't engaged in any shady dealings."

"Maybe he really isn't the rapist."

"Those who live alongside suspects always refuse to recognize a darker side. But it's difficult to believe the guy's not hiding something. The number of the bar, the black tooth, his aggression and escape . . . "

"Why did he give the jeweler the number of the bar?"

"It often happens, people can't even invent a phone number, he plucked one out of his head. In case of need, they knew his name there and could pass on a message that was meaningless to anyone but him."

"I suppose so. Do you really think he's the rapist?"

"Would you like to turn the other cheek?"

"I'm trying not to prejudge."

"Leave judging to the judge. What we have to do is catch the guy as if he'd been guilty from the day he was born."

I thought about the terrible implications of that statement. Garzón suddenly grew agitated:

"Did you get to see his face?"

"For a moment. What struck me were his dull, gray eyes."

"Could you recognize him?"

"If I had a good look, but if I saw him in a crowded subway car . . . "

"That should do it."

Even after offering my face in sacrifice, I hadn't been able to record the guy's features in my mind, taking advantage of the situation. What a disaster! Maybe now they would be justified in taking me off the case. I tried to smile at Garzón with a painful mouth. He, meanwhile, had acted skillfully and at great speed. Aside from seeing to judicial matters, he'd visited the home of the alleged rapist, who needless to say wasn't there. He gave me his impressions, which contained nothing unusual. Juan Jardiel's mother was a widow with no other sons, a fairly normal woman. A curious fact: the boy's girlfriend shared the apartment, having been adopted by the mother many years earlier. They were both incredulous about what had happened and then closed ranks. A search of the house produced no results. All the same, Garzón had arranged to question them more thoroughly. I could come if I wished, he didn't want to take the credit.

"If you're feeling all right tomorrow, we'll go back to the house, otherwise you should rest."

"Rest? No way! The only thing that bothers me is having to show myself with this face."

"It's not so bad. Listen, I have a suggestion, before going to sleep why don't we go and have one of your ex-husband's drinks. It'll make you feel better."

Pepe and Hamed spent a good while staring at me as one would stare at the slough of a snake, with curiosity and repulsion. The bruise by now must have been pretty conspicuous.

"What a brute!" said Hamed. "Among Muslims, striking a woman who's not your wife is considered a serious crime. Women are lofty, delicate creatures, like a flower."

I groaned:

"Oh no, another gardener!"

Pepe reacted sarcastically to my anger, but there was a kindness in his face. He abruptly asked me:

"Do you still like being a cop?"

"Of course I do. Do you think this is a game?"

He brushed his hair from his forehead.

"No, I don't think that, but you undertake novelties with real energy and then you veer off on a different tack."

He was referring to our marriage. I was surprised, he'd

never been at all ironic or critical. He'd accepted my arrival in and disappearance from his life like a biblical event and seemed to have borne them with Hebraic patience, invoking the name of Yahweh.

"I called you at home a couple of times but you're never in."

"What for?"

"To help you arrange your books."

"I don't have time right now."

"I thought you planned to lead an ordered, sedentary life in your new home."

"That's none of your business."

Garzón intervened:

"Did you hear that, Petra? Hamed says that journalist came back."

"She's a regular customer," added Hamed.

"I don't want you telling her anything, in particular that the guy punched me on the nose, is that clear?"

"But she already knew that! She asked Pepe when you were coming out of hospital."

"This is too much! I'm beginning to feel persecuted."

"Take no notice, Petra, it's the way things work nowadays."

I lit a cigarette. There was a pensive silence.

"Something's been bothering me, sergeant . . . " Garzón took his wet mustache out of his glass. "You see, when the suspect stopped in front of me, I shouted, 'Police!' Do you think that was right?"

He was a little bewildered.

"Well, I don't see what else you could have shouted."

"No, no, no, please understand me. I mean, was it formally correct? Or should I have said, 'Stop in the name of the law!'?"

For the first time, Garzón was caught on the wrong foot. He looked at me to see if I was joking. Pepe chimed in:

"It might also have been good to say, 'You're under arrest!' Right, Fermín?"

"Or the classic 'Hands up!'?" I added.

"That's more typical of a bank robber."

"I've always liked 'Police, surrender!'" said Hamed.

Garzón didn't open his mouth. He was amazed at our lack of common sense, above all mine.

"It doesn't matter what you say," he burbled uncomfortably.

I carried on unabashed:

"Yes, it does! Forms are always important, sergeant. Tell us which one you've been using all these years."

He took a long swig, reflected, spoke slowly, unable to get on our wavelength:

"Well . . . I suppose . . . I suppose the one my colleagues and I used was something like this: 'Stop, police, don't even think about moving, you bastard!'"

The three of us laughed wholeheartedly. Garzón, a little piqued, added:

"But anything else would have done just as well."

The following day, as was to be expected, the alleged rapist's escape was plastered all over the papers in great detail. I have to confess, since I hadn't read my colleague's statements, I found out about some things through those pernicious accident and crime reports. The suspect turned out to be a normal youngster. His family was modest but not in any financial difficulty. The long since widowed mother worked as a cleaner in a Social Security office. Juan Jardiel went to work every day, avoided marginalized places, didn't consume drugs or alcohol, didn't even smoke. In short, nothing seemed to indicate a criminal tendency. The journalists, however, pointed to his aggression and escape and questioned the motives that made him act in this way. He had to be hiding something if he ran from the police, but what could it be in such an impeccable character? I was of the opposite opinion. The suspect's details, the fact that his mother was a widow and his childhood sweetheart was in the family, were in my view tremendously significant. Too much feminine pressure, too much obligation. His immaculate, irreproachable attitude confirmed my negative opinion. What was that boy's life reduced to? Daily work, return home, a girlfriend-sister he's barely in love with . . . and the responsibility that the sons of widowed mothers seem to exude in front of the world. This didn't necessarily give rise to a rapist, but the neurotic family background I had been looking for was there and I was certain . . . Was I certain? Not anymore. I'd lost a large part of my initial strength. I felt extremely unnerved. It wasn't fear of the aggression I'd suffered, but seeing that young man's face had brought me back to an unexpected reality. Till now everything had been a sort of whodunit with clues, lines of inquiry, suppositions and conjectures. Not even the attacks on the victims had deprived me of an abstract, mental feeling. But suddenly the theories had taken shape. There was a man, he was alive, he had cold, vacant eyes which he had fixed on my face.

I tried to sleep. My bones ached and I couldn't find the right position. I'd always believed that reflection was harder for someone than action, but now I saw that action was not without its doubts. It pushed you forward, but didn't stop you falling in the ditch at the side of the road. Was this what I'd always wanted? Was I freer without being dedicated exclusively to philosophy? At least it wasn't boring. Was I going to ask to be transferred to Homicide permanently? My legs trembled slightly when I remembered that, the following morning, I had to interview those women, Juan Jardiel's tangible connection to the world.

Poor Garzón! He'd been outraged by our frivolous comments. There was no doubt he was the only real policeman in the Ephemerides that night.

The Jardiels' home measured sixty square meters. Three tiny bedrooms, a small lounge, a narrow kitchen and a single, communal bathroom. It was Mrs. Jardiel who opened the door. She and her adopted daughter had been told not to go to work that day so they could answer our questions. She was a tall, strapping, powerful woman, not at all the sort of widow to inspire compassion. She had on a grayish dress and her hair, to which a light perm gave a harmonious look, appeared to be dyed. Not a single muscle in her face changed expression when she saw us. She invited us in, serious and stony-faced. When she caught sight of my swollen nose, she imperceptibly grimaced. She showed an unwillingness to cooperate. When Garzón asked her to let us inspect the apartment again, she reluctantly agreed. Since my colleague had already made a search, he took me around the rooms. First, Juan's, seemingly unremarkable, but it attracted my attention. Nothing indicated that a young boy slept there. No poster, no cut-out of a football team pinned to the wall, no distinguishing feature. Only a few discreet pictures of landscapes and flowers, the same I then discovered were to be found in the rest of the house. A narrow bed, night table, and a small, fitted wardrobe. I opened a drawer, but it was almost empty: a shoehorn, some pencil stubs, paper handkerchiefs, a bus ticket . . . I mentioned this to Garzón and he remarked that nothing had changed since the day of the search.

"I don't think anything's been removed. I suppose it's always been like this."

We then went into the mother's bedroom. A large double bed filled almost all the space. An aseptic tidiness prevailed. Nothing out of place, no symptom of neglect. The same pictures on the walls as the only decoration. There were no symbols, religious or otherwise. When we re-emerged into the corridor, a girl was standing watching us, her hands hanging beside her body. It was Luisa, Juan's girlfriend. Tall, strong, athletic, black hair surrounding a face full of resolve and courage, just as I'd imagined her. She greeted us briefly. Her room was the last we examined. It was basically identical to the others, an old, furry dog lying on the bedspread was the only personal touch.

"We'd like to talk to you if we may."

We moved into the lounge and sat on a flowery sofa. Everything was clean and in perfect order. The television occupied a central place. On the sideboard were a few framed photographs which, from our position, I couldn't see.

"I suppose you've already been asked many times if you know where your son is at this moment."

"Yes, and I already told you I don't know. I'd like all those policemen to stop watching my house. Juan is innocent."

"Then why did he run away?"

"He must have gotten scared."

"But why?"

"Everyone gets scared if the police are chasing them."

"It doesn't seem very logical."

"It does to me."

The first exchange of fire made it clear resistance would be her attitude. She was determined, strong, unemotional, and she blamed us for her son's escape. I was still convinced this was going nowhere.

"Do you know if he was involved in anything strange or at least suspicious?"

"Juan never did anything illegal."

"Did he have any personal problems?"

"No."

"Had you noticed a change in his character recently?"

"No."

Garzón shifted uneasily in his seat. To speak, he adopted an ingratiating tone I knew very well:

"Mrs. Jardiel, do you realize that if your son really hasn't done anything wrong, you'd do well to help us?"

"How can I help you if there's nothing to say? My son got scared because you were chasing him for no good reason. He didn't have a problem before, but now he's hit a policewoman and might go up on charges, which is why he's hiding or he's gone far away."

I stood up and went over to the window.

"How about you, Luisa, did you notice anything strange about him recently?"

"No."

"Do you always live here?"

For the first time, the mother intervened spontaneously:

"Luisa's the daughter of my cousin, who was killed with her husband in a car accident. I took her in and brought her up. She's Juan's girlfriend and they are getting married in a month. As anyone can see, a boy who's going to get married doesn't tend to be a rapist."

"What do you do?"

The woman again responded for her:

"She works as a checkout girl."

I turned around. I glanced over the small, claustrophobic lounge. While that great protective caryatid was present, the daughter wouldn't speak.

"Does your son wear a watch?" I spat at her.

Her eyes bored into me:

"Of course he wears a watch!"

"What's it like?"

"It's an ordinary watch, I bought it for him."

"Do you always buy your son's things?"

"Yes."

"Clothes as well?"

"Yes."

"Did you know that it seems your son had a crown of silver barbs set around that watch?"

"That's ridiculous, he wore a normal watch, I bought it for him more than five years ago."

"And you've never seen another watch in the house?"

"No."

"Are you sure there's nowhere your son could have kept it?"

"Yes. I clean his room and I know what's in his drawers, there's no watch."

"Well, there's a watchmaker who's quite certain he set some barbs for Juan."

"People always make mistakes when they're forced into recognizing things."

I wandered over to the sideboard and asked for permission to look at the photographs. My attention was drawn to an old one, which showed a somber middle-aged man in a suit and tie.

"Is this your husband?"

"Yes."

I picked up another photograph.

"And this is Juan?"

"You should know, or didn't you see him? Maybe he wasn't even the one who hit you."

She was a snake ever ready to attack. I smiled. Actually I'd have found it difficult to recognize the features of the man who assaulted me. Curiously all the photographs were of Juan and her dead husband. None of them showed the woman or Luisa. The mother was watching me as if I might suddenly steal something. An undeniable strength flowed from her eyes.

"I'll have to take your son's photographs."

The girl moved forward:

"No, please don't."

The woman gripped her arm:

"Let her."

She came over to where I was and removed the photographs from their frames.

"I want them back."

"Of course, when we no longer need them."

The staircase landing smelled of food. They closed the door behind us with a precise click. There was no elevator. Back in the street, I took a deep breath.

"It's terrible to be hated so much."

Garzón came alongside me, took my elbow and directed me towards the car.

"Well, it's always like that, you'll have to get used to it. Would you like me to drive?"

"Please."

The old jeweler started cursing under his breath as soon as he saw us. Garzón waded straight in:

"Stop complaining, you won't like it if we take you to the station."

But the old man carried on cursing, inaudibly this time, as if he were reciting a prayer. We placed the photos in front of him.

"It's essential you concentrate and tell us if this is the boy who brought his watch for you to put barbs on."

He began banging his head as if lamenting his misfortune. At that point in time, he repented ever having recognized the job as his own. Only fear could check his unwillingness to collaborate, but he didn't seem to have any, he was too old to care. He looked at the photographs, screwing up his eyes.

"It could be."

Garzón made as if he had a frog in his throat.

"That's not good enough. Look at them more closely."

The old miser wrung his hands and bad-temperedly sifted through the photographs.

"What do I know? I already told you I get all sorts. My sight is failing. How am I supposed to remember someone who turned up months ago?"

"But it was a pretty special order."

"That's why I remember the job, but not him."

I intervened patiently:

"O.K. then. I can understand you don't recall the details of his face, so we'll take it step by step, which should be easier. Was he this tall?"

"More or less."

"Was he this well-built?"

"Well, he wasn't weak."

"With short hair and gray eyes?"

"I can't say. He was young and had a black tooth, do I have to repeat myself? Or maybe you'd like me to make it up."

The fact he was old and lonely did not arouse pity in me. He was like a character from Dostoyevsky, innocent perhaps, but contemptible and mean. I tried not to get carried away by the literary impression.

"If a judge summons you to give evidence, will you say you recognize him?"

His worn features twitched. Fat, swollen veins meandered beneath his transparent skin.

"Now that's quite enough! Some bastard decides to come to my shop. I render him a service as I would any normal customer and what I get in return is a bunch of cops and judges accosting me. I've no assistants or employees, who's going to pay for my lost time, who's going to make up for the inconvenience?"

"You will be summoned."

Garzón made a second attempt before leaving, though I had the impression he was doing it to wind him up:

"Are you quite sure you don't recognize him from the photos?"

Stubborn like a mule and close to a heart attack, the old man replied:

"I already told you everything I know."

I was glad to get out of that foul hole. We were dancing an absurd, tropical dance in which the arms and hips move but the feet stay in one place. It seemed impossible to make progress in that accursed case. I sighed.

"Do we have everything under control?"

The sergeant also sighed.

"Surveillance unit in front of the Jardiels' home, tapped phone, arrest warrant copied to all units . . . I don't think there's anything else."

"Is someone watching the bar and workplace?"

"Patrol cars are passing by."

"All right then. We'll have to question the victims again, show them the photos in case they notice something. You don't know how much I'd prefer not to see those girls again."

"I'll do it if you like."

"I'd be very grateful."

"What happened to that iron woman who puts suspects through their paces?"

"I'm a little bit tired. Besides I don't have to pretend in front of you anymore, do I?"

"You never know, you're still a woman."

We both chuckled.

"Do you think we'll catch that guy, Fermín?"

"I suppose so."

"Given that he's not a hardened criminal, sooner or later he'll make more mistakes. The telephone number was one and it won't be the last."

Garzón lit a cigarette and exhaled smoke with the verve of an old but well-oiled engine.

"I don't wish to alarm you but that's a common belief which usually proves groundless. A human being has a greater capacity for logic than you might think. In fact, just by remaining calm, a criminal is extremely unlikely to make mistakes."

"But this guy has nowhere to go, he has to feel surrounded."

"That's what would happen to a normal mind but you're convinced he doesn't have a normal mind."

"He behaves pathologically. Did you notice the mother?"

"What a woman! And the girlfriend?"

"She was punch-drunk. It has to be a real trauma for your boyfriend to be accused of rape."

"And yet she seemed indifferent, or distant at least."

He was right. Though such behavior was not unusual. The mind can digest or recycle bad things, but truly terrible things tend to stay outside, crouching down, too big to enter the fragile cave without warning.

"I have an idea, sergeant. This new ID the victims have to do, why don't we get Juan's mother and girlfriend to be present?"

"Crikey, Petra! Have you gone mad? Do you realize what you're saying?"

"I know it's pretty outrageous, there could be scenes, fights, unleashed emotions. But that girlfriend of Jardiel's might react, she might realize her future husband actually raped those girls. She could suffer a shock and go so far as to tell us where her boyfriend is hiding."

This suggestion affected Garzón deeply, it complicated his life and, more importantly, broke the orthodox scheme of an investigation. But, even after our tacit reconciliation and new explicit understanding, I was still his boss and he had no intention of questioning my methods. He simply remarked:

"You trust psychology too much, inspector. And I've always thought that's typical of the wealthy classes. The only psychology normal people have is their own interest, the most direct and material."

"Then only those who've nothing to eat suffer?"

"No, because they realize, even once they've solved the material, that life is still fairly disastrous."

"My word, Garzón! That doesn't tie in with your positive opinion of things. Would you like to explain yourself?"

"No way! You're the one who's making me philosophical. I'm talking nonsense. If you really want to take such a risk with the interviews, we'd better go home and sleep."

Sleep. Personally I didn't even try. I was too caught up by events to go to bed. I served myself a drink, put on some symphonic music and rested my feet on a pouffe. I gazed at the half-filled bookshelves, the walls. My distinguishing marks were there: Chagall lithographs, lawbooks and novels, the odd little statue, music by Beethoven and Chopin, jazz, old souvenirs, worthless handicraft items. . . Features which indicated that a person with their character, past, funny little ways, lived there. I recalled the Jardiels' home. There was something unnerving about it: the false gleam of the furniture, the regular, symmetrical arrangement of the pictures of flowers distributed throughout the apartment. A frightening air of unity, none of those who lived there had marked their territory, had grooved out their personality, they all moved in a limited space with the inoffensive taste more typical of a cheap hotel. The carefully folded cloths in the kitchen, the toilet-roll holder in the bathroom, the spotted toilet-seat cover. I imagined the kind of existence they would lead there. Breakfast at the small kitchen table, the mother probably in her dressing gown, presiding over the first meal of the day as she would preside over the others. Always under the influence of her austere expression. Order and cleanliness were the watchwords. Everyone disappeared off to work and then back home, dinner, evening in front of the telly. Sweep the corridor, put on a wash. Like in an anthill, duties conducted in a perfect organization. No strange fancies allowed. Yes, it was plausible, the constant feel-

ing of being on a microscope slide under the watchful eye of
Mother. A young man subjected to a depersonalizing iron dis-
cipline could burst, seek to be different or opposed, even take
revenge on such an absorbing feminine presence—and choose
weak girls to do it, fearful of the Cyclopean maternal figure.
The catalyst? His forthcoming marriage, which seemed to go
against nature. There were also the sticky mysteries, the dark
alleyways of a mother-son relationship of difficult extraction.

I was tired. I needed to get all that business out of my mind
before falling asleep. I went to warm a glass of milk and, on
passing through the hallway, I saw it, an envelope that had
been slipped under the door, a letter. It didn't even occur to
me that it could be related to anything but the case. I took it in
my hands as if it were a bird that could be scared off. I sat
down in the kitchen to open it. I had no doubt it was a confession, a denunciation, a certain clue. But it was a note from
Hugo. My God! Couldn't he use the telephone like other mortals, the postal service, messenger companies, a fax at least?
No, he had to give proof of his exceptional nature and distinguished methods.

Dear Petra,
I passed by, and you're obviously not here. I would ask that
tomorrow you find a gap in your investigative duties to have
luncheon with me. I should like very much to introduce you to
my new wife, who will be in attendance, at the same time as I
hand over your share of the profits from our final enterprise in
common. Please give your consent to my secretary by phone, and
she will arrange a time and place.

His style increasingly reminded me of that used by the station guards. I had to draw on all my Buddhist reserves to take
in the news. He clearly wasn't going to relinquish the last act
of the theatrical performance. He needed a drum roll, a

disheveled choir, the audience on their feet. His brand-new wife. How could his brand-new wife agree to something like this? And a luncheon! It could have been breakfast, an afternoon snack, an ordinary cup of tea. But no, it would be a long meal with a first course, a break in the middle and a final *digestif*. A torture. What did he hope to achieve? He wanted me to feel guilty about the outcome, to learn from his glorious *savoir faire*. This is how you do things, Petra, you can't just take off like that. You have to think, to try not to hurt someone who loves you: calm, knowledge, quiet. I considered not turning up. But there was the same problem as always, I couldn't. I was still afraid of him, afraid of seeing my disastrous image reflected in his eyes. Guilt. And me. The madness of someone who swaps everything for nothing. Whither goest thou, Petra? What will become of thee?

Fermín Garzón couldn't answer the phone because he wasn't in. "He's never back before one," his landlady told me, "but he's given me a number where he can be reached." I immediately recognized the number of the Ephemerides. There he was, of course, relaxed in the company of my second ex-husband's lot. God knows why! Maybe he was a lost soul, maybe Pepe reminded him of his son won over to the cause of science in America.

"Listen, sergeant, I'd be grateful if tomorrow you could conduct the interviews and early-afternoon business on your own. I have to have lunch with someone and I may be late."

"It's nice to know they're looking after you, inspector!"

He must have had one drink too many.

"Yes, but I assure you it's not for pleasure. I have to have lunch with a friend and his wife."

"Then why don't you invite me along?"

He must have had two drinks too many.

"Well . . . "

"Going unaccompanied to a lunch is an insult to a woman."

I should have realized he was joking. However, a glimmer of light had opened on my horizon.

"Listen, Garzón, you know that, with what you're saying, you'd be doing me a great favor?"

"I'm forever at your disposal," he said, suddenly getting serious.

"Really, why don't you come with me to that lunch?"

"Consider it done."

A madness, an absurdity. Of course Garzón didn't know what he was letting himself in for, he was completely unaware of the crux of the matter. Inviting him to sit down and eat with my first ex-husband and his current wife was a mess of vaudevillian proportions. Probably too much for him. He'd spent many hours wondering why I had gotten married and unmarried so often and now I was proposing to introduce him into another compartment of my privacy which might well raise a whole new load of questions. Too much for him. But he'd said yes, what else could he do after swearing eternal loyalty?

It was worth going to that lunch with Garzón, you bet it was, just to see Hugo's face when we arrived. And that was the least important reason. The restaurant where we had arranged to meet was luxurious, coldly and timelessly elegant. Thick, white tablecloths, china dinner service, waiters who came and went like the dear departed. I didn't want to stare at my successor in Hugo's heart, but straight away I got a first and reliable impression: short, straight hair, a little make-up, a round-necked dress, unobtrusive necklace . . . a woman who was discreet, discreet in the way she spoke and the way she dressed. Just the sort of woman I should have been. Hugo was proud alongside her, but he was embarrassed. So was she. We were all embarrassed with the exception of my colleague, the illustrious Fermín. He looked happy as if the situation were quite normal. He was a specialist in ex-husbands, I had to admit it once and for all.

We ordered and started eating amidst idle talk. Hugo was courteous but, when he looked in my direction, I could see irony dancing in his eyes like the flicker of a candle. His new wife seemed to have absolutely no curiosity about me or she was simply taking her degree of civilization so far that she appeared to be way above any interest. We talked about the inconveniences of urban life, the intricacies of underground parking lots, typical regional dishes, traveling by plane. Nothing intimate, no foray into private life or conjugal memories. Garzón was in his element, chatting, drinking, eating with his usual appetite and offering those present his most peculiar appearance: a dark suit, striped shirt and a horrific violet-spotted bow tie I hadn't seen. I thought he must have purchased that party piece for the discussion of banal topics during boarding-house meals. He probably sat down to dinner every evening with quasi-strangers with whom, like Hugo and his new wife, he had nothing in common. Hugo, however, was clearly fascinated by him. He paid him careful attention, observed his gestures, his way of speaking, and I suspect he kept wondering what on earth a guy like that was doing at a family occasion. I felt pleased, my ally's presence had dissolved any tension as if by magic. I was behaving like a child who, foreseeing a parental ticking-off, arrives at the awkward meeting with a friend. Anyway, Hugo had achieved his objective: to show me that he was married to a successful, beautiful and suitable professional. Everything was tickety-boo, he moved in sophisticated circles, his life was normal and prosperous. As for me, I had turned up in the company of a provincial cop in a bow tie, my days were spent in the squalor of my awful profession and I didn't even seem to have excelled at that. Ergo, I was the one in the wrong. And what was my mistake? To have abandoned our marriage, our promising life: the original sin.

During dessert, things inevitably turned acrimonious. Hugo became scathing because, however much he'd intended not to overact and to give moderate answers, a third and final act with the chance of showing off was too much temptation. He rummaged through his briefcase.

"Apologies all round but Petra and I have to talk business." He turned to face me. "Because everyone here knows we were married, don't they?"

His new wife, Elvira, chuckled softly. Garzón carried on following proceedings without any embarrassment, sipping coffee as if he were in the Ephemerides.

"Are you married, Fermín?"

"I'm a widower."

"And you haven't remarried?"

"No."

"Well, it's a mistake. A second marriage is the only sensible course of action open to a man. First time round, one learns, then one compares and is better able to appreciate. It's fabulous, believe me."

I sat with an artificial smile on my face, wondering how I would get out of there without being humiliated. Hugo, increasingly sure of himself, carried on his performance. His wife watched him with the slightly false alarm people have in front of an adored, spoiled child when they're not sure what the child is going to do next.

"One has the chance to see that one hasn't changed and yet it's not a disaster, everything's as it should be. A sign, one thinks, that one's initial error wasn't so bad. And having someone who truly loves one, one goes through a kind of flowering period, a renaissance. Seriously, Fermín, old chap, get remarried, it's a rare delicacy."

Garzón smiled with the air of a local policeman in the 1950s, surrounded by Christmas presents.

"But Petra won't marry me, Hugo, and I can't imagine I'd find a better woman. I don't have much luck."

We all smiled. Hugo's smile was so tight I was afraid blood

would start flowing from the corners of his mouth. *Chapeau*, my dear sergeant! Years and years of munching ham sandwiches in dimly lit offices and he'd come out with a Wildean quip. My heart would always be grateful to him for this occurrence. Hugo appeared not to mind, but I knew him well enough to see that he was vexed. Who brought this silly little man in here? How dare he ruin his dignified final scene? It could only be his frivolous ex-wife turning up in the royal court with jesters. He went on the attack again:

"Did you know that before joining the police, Petra was a prestigious lawyer with a brilliant career in front of her? She was conspicuous, intelligent, devoted. Far be it from me to belittle her qualities. My only surprise is that someone so sophisticated could change direction so easily, if that's what she's done. Because Petra was sophisticated, you see. I wouldn't wish to question her populist credentials but the fact is Petra always insisted on dressing for dinner, she couldn't retire at night without listening to Beethoven, she frequented the finest boutiques, wouldn't talk to those she considered vulgar or uninteresting intellectually, never set foot in the kitchen so as not to get her hands dirty, she knew how to dance, always spoke two semitones lower than other women, belonged to the odd club . . . "

Garzón swirled the anis he had ordered around his glass.

"Well, she's not bad as a policewoman. You should see her when she gets down to work. She mixes with thugs and whores as if it was nothing. What to tell you about the way she tackles rapists and brutes during questioning? The fact is from my point of view she sometimes overdoes it. The other day she stripped a poor pickpocket naked, stark bollock naked! Kept him there for over an hour, gazing at his balls, it's all she had to do, the guy almost died. He cracked, he finally cracked! And she can be pretty venomous towards suspects, cursing and swearing. I think it takes a strong stomach to watch her work."

Hugo stared at me with disgust written all over his face.

"Is it true?" he asked.

And I, whooping with savage delight, could only exclaim: "Yes!"

Elvira kept her eyes trained on the breadcrumbs on the table. Hugo blushed and pulled various documents out of his briefcase.

"I should like you to sign these papers, they certify you've received the money, it's all legal."

I signed them and took the check he handed to me, which I pocketed impassively. He paid the bill. There was total silence. Elvira looked extremely relieved when she saw her husband get to his feet.

"Under the circumstances, Petra, it's better if we never see each other again."

"My feelings precisely," I heard myself say.

There was the obligatory shaking of hands, though Hugo visibly avoided me and didn't make that simple, friendly gesture. His hatred would always come between us, as public and notorious as my abandonment had been.

The sergeant and I waited for them to leave before we stood up. We walked silently down the street. It was cooler. The impact of the last rays of sun was zero.

"Perhaps I shouldn't . . . " began Garzón.

I carried on without saying a word.

"I mean it's just . . . "

I stopped. I gave him a grave look. He was anxious and fearful like a child. I then exploded. A convulsive laugh rose from my chest and ran down my body. I couldn't help myself, I laughed. I went weak at the knees.

"Oh, Fermín!"

He smiled awkwardly but happily.

"Come on, Petra, stop, people are watching us!"

But I didn't want to stop, I felt a surge of liberation. I started walking very slowly. Garzón was grinning from ear to ear.

"You see, I just thought why do we always have to prove we're marvelous? What does it matter? Why does Petra have to be discreet, good, refined and all those positive things? Maybe it's not so necessary, why not also be a bit unpleasant? That's what I thought."

He was chuffed to have done something so daring. I managed to calm down.

"I'm sorry I got you involved in all of this. I was under the impression Hugo had arranged this meal just to show how perfect his new wife was, but I see he also wanted to throw a few stones in my direction."

"Does that bother you?"

"I suppose he ended up making me believe that his was the only way of looking at things."

"It's absurd, we always do our best to create a good impression."

"Yes but you see, after what you told Hugo, I don't think I have to worry about that."

"I repeat that I'm sorry, I went too far."

"No, you were fine, you may even have broken the spell. But moving onto more substantial things . . . Did you see that piece of paper?"

"Twenty thousand euros isn't bad."

"Do you need any money? I could lend you some if you like."

"I don't have great needs, I live well enough with what I earn."

"All right, then one of these nights we'll go and celebrate. What do you fancy?"

"A slap-up dinner."

"That goes without saying, but we'll do something special. Do you know what occurs to me? We could go to the Lyceum to see some opera or ballet. What do you reckon?"

"The tickets are pretty expensive."

"Remember the 20K."

"Would you do that for me?"

"I don't like opera but I would."

He looked at me gratefully. We carried on walking in silence. Suddenly a mischievous gleam crossed his face.

"Did you really use to dance?"

"Oh, come on, Garzón!"

"I'd love to have seen you in a tutu."

"Screw you!"

Back at the station, the whole case, momentarily forgotten, came piling into my mind. Garzón had convinced me not to question the victims in the presence of the Jardiel family, it was too much. But the suspicion that Luisa knew her boyfriend's whereabouts wouldn't leave me alone. I opted for a hybrid solution. While Garzón looked after the three girls and showed them the photos of Juan in hopes of an unlikely identification, I would interview Luisa on her own and show her some other photos, all the ones the pathologists had taken of Sonia, Patricia, Salomé and Cristina after they were raped. There was some pretty interesting material, images of the girls with marks on their arms, close-ups which focused on the pinpricks made with the flower. Bandages, trickles of blood. They'd do. Perhaps I was overly confident that Luisa's heart would soften. In the face of such a naked reality, she might even experience a feeling of hatred towards the victims, an outright rejection. It was equally possible she didn't know Jardiel's whereabouts, but the air of tranquility she gave off led me to believe she did know where he was, somehow they may even have managed to meet. I'd do everything in my power to lean on her emotions. Something told me she had a fragile, humane, surmountable side in direct opposition to the steel wall that surrounded her adoptive mother. In any case, getting her to speak on her own, away from the other woman's paralyzing influence, was essential. I used a complicated official citation to summon her to make a statement, specifying it was only her evidence we were interested in.

At seven in the evening, I was informed the girl had arrived. She was frightened and suspicious. She sat down. Without a word passing between us, I started handing her the photos, which I'd arranged on what I thought was a suitable psychological scale, the most shocking first. I watched her face very carefully to see if I could detect any variation. Her hands trembled so that the photos quivered in the air. She went through them, stopping at times. She showed horror, disgust, fear of the truth, and began slowly shaking her head. She swallowed hard, hypnotized by the images, mortally serious.

"He didn't do any of this," she managed to say.

"Everything seems to indicate he did."

"It wasn't him."

"How can you be so sure?"

"Because I am."

"Did he tell you?"

She fell silent. I pulled up a chair.

"Maybe it's just that you want to believe he's innocent."

"Juan couldn't do anything like this. He could have slept with me if he'd wanted, living together we had plenty of opportunities, but he never touched me. He preferred to wait till we were married. He was brought up very strictly and has a sense of morality."

I sighed.

"That doesn't prove anything, quite the opposite in fact. Forced always to behave impeccably, he vented his frustration in this terrible manner."

"No."

"Is your mother hard on you?"

"We were well brought up. She can't stand people who do what they feel like, youngsters who act like animals, who drink alcohol and take drugs."

"But wasn't your education too rigid?"

"No, she's a good, hardworking woman who taught us a sense of morality and dignity, to be well thought of."

"And what's Juan's opinion?"

"He doesn't mind. Juan and I try to avoid dissolute people, we're disgusted by those who don't know how to meet their obligations."

"Were you taught that as well?"

She stayed quiet, looked at all four corners of the office, wrung her hands. She opened her mouth as if to say something and then closed it. She wore a heavy, stubborn frown.

"You're totally mistaken . . . " she said abruptly. "Didn't my mother tell you anything about our family?"

"I only know your parents died in an accident and she took care of you."

"Well, it's not true."

My pulse quickened.

"It's not true?"

"No. Juan's father didn't die, nor did my mother. They ran away together and haven't been heard of since. Juan's mother took me in and raised us both."

"What about your father?"

"He didn't want to know, he said a man couldn't live with a girl on his own. He handed me over to Juan's mother. She told him, 'You won't see her again, don't even think about coming back, claiming you're her father.' But he never came back, wasn't even interested in how I was. Now you can judge whether she's a good woman or not and how well she's treated us. And you can also guess what Juan and I think of immoral people."

I had to shut my mouth for it not to drop open completely. What a story, a rare mix of Eugène Sue and Sigmund Freud. The poor girl had no idea that the more she argued his innocence, the more she drew a circle of suspicion around her boyfriend-brother.

"Why does Juan's mother keep all this a secret and say she's a widow? Why did she invent that business about your parents and the accident?"

"What do you want, everyone to know who our parents are? Who cares! I've heard her say a thousand times that though we're modest people, we've as much right to our honor as the next."

"Did your mother or Juan's father ever get in touch?"

"I already told you no one ever got in touch and if they'd entered our lives, my new mother would have thrown them both out."

"I understand."

"Now you know why Juan couldn't have done those horrible things to the girls."

"Why did he run away?"

"I don't know."

I remained silent. She contorted her face in a sneer.

"I've one last question to ask you but I want you to think carefully before you answer, I want you to think about what is going to help Juan in such circumstances, especially if he's really innocent. Luisa, do you know where he is now?"

She didn't even hesitate:

"No."

"Are you sure?"

"It's the truth."

"All right, you can go but if you hear from him, tell him for his own good to give himself up."

She didn't reply.

Before going home, I wanted to see Garzón. I was desperate to fill him in on the details. He was tired when he arrived, having just questioned the victims. He threw his coat on the stand and slumped into a chair.

"Did they recognize anything about Jardiel?"

"Not a thing."

"Not even his stature or complexion?"

"They only know how to say no. All evening working away for nothing. One of them even burst into tears."

"Salomé?"

"Yeah. She avoided me as if I were a monster."

"That girl's going to find it difficult to get over the trauma."

"And of course we're missing the statement of the one who's gone to the States."

"I wonder if her father had a legal right to send her away."

"Don't talk to me about legal rights, I've just about had enough."

He let his shoulders droop. To cheer him up, I told him what Luisa had confided to me. I thought he'd be excited about this awful melodrama, but he was unmoved like a parcel left in a bus terminal.

"Don't you find it important?"

"If you say so."

"Do you realize what it means to be subjected for part of your childhood and all your youth to a constant climate of moral dogmatism?"

"Sounds like what I was subjected to."

"It's not the same! These kids have grown up in a stale, hermetic universe full of hatred and feelings of shame, guilt, revenge. They've been taught to conceal the truth and despise those who brought them into the world. It's terrible, it's . . . the ideal breeding ground for any kind of mental pathology. It could easily give rise to a rapist."

"Which would prove something I've always thought: problems with one cunt lead to problems with the rest."

I started.

"What was that, Garzón?"

He gave me a look of innocent surprise.

"You said you didn't mind swearing."

"But that was an impertinence, a vulgarity unworthy of you."

He turned very serious and ill-tempered like a child. He muttered:

"It's far from simple to know what's pertinent and what is not."

I stood up and took my bag.

"It appears you've had a bad evening. I'll see you to-morrow."

I was more angry about Garzón's indifference to my dis-coveries than about the impropriety itself. It was difficult to make him understand that, if the psychic profile of a rapist fit, then the case could be considered solved. But psychological motives held little weight with him. He'd have understood it better if a guy raped out of spite or for sex. Anyway, this defor-mation of the family that clarified things for me like a ray of light, for the sergeant was no more than problems with cunts. Praised be primitive mentalities! And all this a few hours after he'd behaved like a real gentleman in front of Hugo. There's nothing worse than continuing to live with a hero after the act of heroism.

I returned home in a foul temper and looked in the fridge for something to eat. Provisions were thin on the ground and I thought I should do something about it, but not tonight. Tonight I needed to sleep. At twelve, however, I was woken by the phone. I recognized a voice destroyed by life.

"Fermín Garzón speaking."

"What is it, has he been arrested?"

"It's not that, I just wanted to say how sorry I am."

"For what?"

"For what I said earlier about problems with one . . . In short, it was a stupid thing to say and I should have realized it would offend you. But you know what? I find it increasingly difficult to appreciate I'm with a woman."

"Thank you, that's very flattering, though I'm not sure how to take it."

"Take it in a good sense. Were you asleep?"

"Yes."

"Then now I've two reasons to be sorry."

"Forget about it, I'll go straight back to sleep."

"Good night, inspector, see you tomorrow."

I curled up with the pillow and switched off the light. I suddenly felt an irrepressible desire to laugh. And I laughed, rhythmically shaking the mattress. It was the first time I'd laughed in this way, in bed, alone, in the pitch-darkness.

The search for Juan Jardiel continued the following week. Although we had so many active units at our disposal, there was still no sign of the alleged rapist. The journalists remained on the alert, closely monitoring the situation. I took a roundabout way to work and back home again, but always with the impression I was being followed. With the torch of social unrest still burning, I couldn't afford to send any reporters to hell. In the meantime, Pepe kept me up to date with the TV journalist's visits to the Ephemerides, which he didn't seem to mind too much. I began to suspect it amused him and he encouraged her intermittent presence by pretending to know things. I laid low, continually going over the facts. I thought, as if thinking by itself would carry the investigation forward. Garzón didn't follow my example, he moved, accompanied patrols which were out looking, met with the judge. He had contact with his informers in that mysterious case of smuggling he didn't inform even me about in order to maintain the veil of secrecy. I admired his capacity for action.

One morning, I went to the bank to deposit my twenty thousand. This was the final windfall I could expect, so I planned to make it last, the dying embers of the past would cast their beneficent shadow for some time to come. But my savings would start after I'd fulfilled my promise to Garzón. I went to the Lyceum and bought tickets for *Aida*. When I told my colleague over the phone, he became emotional. We arranged to meet the following day.

It was a freezing evening in February. We were to wait for each other on the Ramblas. When Garzón arrived, I did a double take, he looked so different. He was dressed in a suit as compact as the armor of a medieval knight, dark gray with milky white stripes, a yellow shirt, a blue tie held by a pearl pin and, in his buttonhole, a tiny police insignia. He was impressive, like a mafia boss on the day of a wedding. His hair was slicked back and his mustache meticulously brushed like a glistening seal rescued by Greenpeace. I had put on my black party frock and gold necklace but, next to him, I was a little anonymous, victim of a certain pale discretion.

He was jumpy like a kid, crazy to see some opera, go inside the Lyceum, walk around what seemed to be for him a sanctuary almost. I wondered how it was the bright image of opera became a decisive myth in such a Cartesian mind. He made me take the tickets out of my bag and show him. He begged me at the end of the evening to let him keep them as a souvenir.

"They'll have set you back a bit," he said.

I remarked he could have gone to the Lyceum whenever he'd wanted, it wasn't so much money that he couldn't have spent it given the circumstances.

"I'd never have come on my own. I'm too in awe of this place that isn't mine, I'd have been afraid the whole time of acting the fool, committing a faux pas. I could never have taken the decision to spend money on something so unnecessary."

"You don't have to justify yourself to anyone."

"True, but so many years obeying orders make it no longer possible to do what one feels like."

I burst out laughing. The sergeant was weighty and sententious as Tacitus. There was something magical about him, a kind of positive energy that could quash any uncertainty. That night, he was especially brilliant and profound.

On entering the theatre, we bought programs and walked through the majestic hall. Garzón was in some unfathomable seventh heaven which gave off rays and beams of light. He literally shone and, if he'd been hung from the ceiling, he'd have looked like another lamp. He was absorbed, greedy and grateful for each moment, he didn't even notice other people, his transport was private, a happy ecstasy. He murmured disconnected phrases: "years and years of luxury . . . harmonies and reservations . . . Mariona Rebull . . . " I found it difficult to believe the ancestral gloss of the Catalan bourgeoisie was responsible for his enchantment, but I didn't ask him anything and let him get on with it. He was in a state of grace also during the performance, but no more than on the stairs, in the salons and foyer. He didn't talk to me in the intervals, he didn't even dare smoke. I admit that opera was never my passion, but I had to watch with so few distractions I eventually became engrossed.

Outside, Garzón floated on the damp sea air, his eyes a little fogged. He still didn't speak, lost in his mystical experience, nor did he notice the biting cold.

"Did you like it, Fermín?"

"It was unforgettable."

The elegant theatergoers merged with the people in the street. We walked aimlessly.

"Are you going to stay silent all night?"

He awoke from his dream.

"Excuse me. I've been a bore, bad company, but I was so taken up with the spectacle. I am grateful to you, Petra, thanks to you . . . "

"Don't get all solemn and tell me where you'd like to have dinner."

"You decide, I'm not sure the emotion will let me eat."

"You'll get over it."

He did get over it and ate ravenously: avocados stuffed with prawns, baby lamb cutlets. I asked for a bottle of cava, which we finished before dessert. I ordered another without Garzón protesting. It went down well, allowed the thoughts to dance on a bubbly cushion.

"Do you see, Petra? Happiness must be something like this."

"Champagne and opera?"

"Not exactly. I mean it must be magnificent to have inherited from your ancestors so much cash and refinement you no longer have to wonder if it's allowed to indulge in pleasure."

"No one's forbidden to have a good time."

"I must belong to the eighth or ninth generation of slaves, I've always been taught the value of things, duty first, working to pay for what I have. It's better when things come from before."

"You could always have changed your luck."

"Maybe, but what would have been the use of slogging away if my mother doesn't speak French? There's nothing I can do about that. I saw it once in a movie, the height of class is for your mother to speak French."

"Garzón, you're unbelievable!"

"You know, you may be right."

We both laughed wholeheartedly. He quickly filled our glasses, emptied his in one gulp.

"Let's go, ours is the only table still occupied, that makes me feel guilty. You see I feel guilty for everything, when I overstep the mark having fun as well. What do you say we have a drink somewhere else? This time on me."

We crossed the restaurant to the surprised looks of the waiters. We clearly didn't make an ideal couple. Back in the street, the sergeant gave free rein to a whole series of humorous fantasies. We were both decidedly tipsy.

"Can you imagine, Petra, if we suddenly bumped into the rapist? I'd throw myself on top of him, get him in a judo grip and force him to bite the ground. 'Get back, you bastard!' I'd shout at him, 'don't you dare touch this lady again!' At which point you'd jump on top of me and, offended, reply, 'Garzón, have you still not realized it's humiliating to try and save a woman?'"

He was in his element, and a little drunk.

"Then the chief inspector would congratulate us: 'Well done, boys, a copper should always be prepared, even after seeing *Aida* at the Lyceum.'"

He laughed good-naturedly. We entered a bar where some soft jazz was playing. Garzón ordered a double brandy and relaxed.

"I've never understood jazz, it's intellectual music."

We let the languid drip-drip of a classical quartet flow in silence, the plucking of a piano, a low murmur . . .

"Talk to me about guilt, Garzón."

"About guilt?"

"Yes, the guilt you feel when you overstep the mark."

His smile vanished, he drank some brandy.

"It's an old story, Petra."

He rubbed his eyes, which were red from cigarette smoke, and sighed.

"My mother was extremely religious. She taught me I should never feel too much pleasure. 'When you get stuck into a good piece of meat, think about those who've nothing to eat,' she would say. 'When you're nice and warm in bed, remember those who've nowhere to sleep.' On and on with things like that and if I ever answered, 'But, mother, I don't know anyone in need,' she'd react as if she'd been stung and say, 'Well, there are people, even if they're far away, in Peru. At the moment a square of chocolate is melting in your mouth, at that very moment a poor child is dying of hunger, breathing his last, commending his soul to God.'"

He took his weary eyes off the memory and fixed them on me.

"Good heavens!" I exclaimed in order to say something.

"There you have it. The worst thing was that I couldn't do anything for those starving hordes that stretched all the way to Peru. But it didn't matter, my tea still stuck in my throat. Sometimes I'd chuck my chocolate in the gutter so that when the next kid expired, he'd catch me only eating bread. I think that's why I joined the police, to help the vulnerable. And then, the way things are, I've spent the whole of my life screwing them and landing them in the clink. Because it's almost always the vulnerable or the poor who commit crimes, isn't it?"

"I suppose you're right."

"And it wasn't only my tea or the warmth of my bed she cast in my teeth, it was all the rest: amusements, friends. I even married the woman who was best for me spiritually, not one I really liked."

"But you were very happy with your wife."

He remained silent for a moment. He drained his brandy and asked the waiter for another. When it came, he took a savage swig that was almost a bite.

"That's what I've always liked to think so as not to go mad. But my wife was like my mother, or worse, since I didn't have to share my bed with my mother and I did with her. She was obsessed with cleanliness, prudish, sanctimonious and stupid. I wonder quite why I was faithful to her. She couldn't make love on a Friday or during Lent or at Christmas because it was unseemly to be 'doing it' while our Savior was being born. And when she had a hysterectomy and couldn't have any more children, then she argued, 'What for, Fermín, why be together if God doesn't love us as husband and wife?' You don't know what it is for a young, hearty man to go to bed clean-shaven, wearing fresh pajamas and cologne, and always to get the same response."

He looked through me. I realized I shouldn't say anything, just let him speak.

"Then I'd arrive at the station and find myself in an atmosphere of mental misery. My colleagues winding up whores we'd arrested. Farewell dinners when someone retired, everyone drunk at the table, doubled up with laughter, operating a sausage for phimosis. That's been my life, Petra, not much. So now, which should be the time to feel happy with my memories, just the thought of them drives me crazy."

"You have your son."

"My son? When I went to see him in New York, he didn't know what to do with me. He introduced me to people who only spoke English. After a fortnight, he was clearly desperate for me to leave and vacate the sofa in his tiny apartment. All his friends were weird, people I couldn't be with for five minutes. Now he barely writes. Maybe he's also traumatized by the education he received from his mother, like me, as you say the rapist is we're after."

He was bloated and pale, with twisted features and purplish rings. He had drunk and talked too much and was showing all the tiredness of the night, the week, a life perhaps.

"Don't think you're the only one on your own, Fermín. Me too, so many mistakes . . . abrupt changes, sudden projects, failed marriages . . . Everyone's alone but that's the way it is, if you're alive you have to keep on going. Besides, it doesn't matter whether you decide to join the Trappists or go to a deserted island, there's still no rest, in the end you get fed up with the abbot or annoyed by the caws of the parrots in the coconut palm under which you've chosen to sleep. The important thing is inner peace, and that's something no one knows how to achieve."

He was KO'd like an old boxer.

"You talk well," he said. "It's obvious you've studied."

We were both empty, silent and exhausted.

"Shall we go, Fermín?"

"Do you think the Ephemerides will be open?"

"At this time? I don't know. Is it a good idea to drink any more?"

"No, it's late, you're right, we should go to bed."

He staggered to his feet. I wasn't in a much better state, but I tried to ride the crest of the alcoholic wave bearing down on top of me. We emerged into the icy night. The jazz music fell quiet. It would have been sensible to take a taxi, but there was none in sight. I got behind the wheel and Garzón slumped beside me. I took him to his boarding house. He stared through the windscreen. When we arrived, he seemed not to recognize the place. I shook his arm gently.

"Are you all right, sergeant, do you fancy a breath of fresh air before going inside?"

He awoke from his sleepless torpor.

"No, I'm fine. Thanks again for a wonderful evening."

"Good night, Fermín."

I watched him go up to the front door, thickset beneath his armored suit, impossible quadrature of a circle. I drove away, not entirely sure I would arrive home in one piece. But I did. When I went inside, the silence of the rooms struck me as a haven of peace. I lay down on the bed in my clothes, in my coat even, and thought the easiest thing would be to sleep like this. A second after making this courageous decision, the phone rang.

"At last we've found you, inspector."

I was so confused, took so long to understand, that all I remember of that moment is staying very quiet, nodding like a child who doesn't know how to speak into the receiver. When I hung up, funnily enough the only thing that worried me was how to inform Garzón without his landlady kicking up a fuss. She was inevitably going to get livid, and she did.

"It's a serious police matter," I mumbled in excuse.

"Hold the line."

Two minutes later, I heard my colleague's voice.

"Sergeant? It's Petra Delicado. I'm sorry to disturb you at this hour but I had no choice. Juan Jardiel's turned up dead in a side-street. It seems he was murdered."

I expected to face a string of strong words, a murmur of surprise, a hung-over groan, a curse, a pun, but all I heard was a laconic and dispassionate "My God!"

10

He'd been found around eleven o'clock at night, lying in an alleyway near his home, with various stab wounds in the left part of his neck and chest. It was the first murder victim I'd seen, it was actually the first corpse in general. I observed it coldly, trying to appear professional, but I'd have liked to get away from there.

The murder scene was crawling with cops, including the chief inspector.

"A nasty business, eh, Petra?"

"What happened?"

"He was attacked from in front. There's no sign of a struggle."

"Caught by surprise."

"From in front and by surprise. Strange, isn't it? Must have been someone who knew him, don't you think?"

"Someone must have arranged to meet him here. It's a good place for him not to be heard shouting out if he shouted at all."

"How do you relate it to the case?"

"I don't know. It's a bit soon for conjectures. Let's see what evidence they find on the corpse, we'll draw up a list of suspects and . . . who identified him?"

"One of the cops, with the photos you gave out."

"Good work."

"The police generally function well. Is it the same man who attacked you?"

"Yes, I'm sure of it."

No one had closed his eyes. I looked at them again and recognized that great emptiness, they had been almost as inexpressive in life as they were in death.

"Where's your colleague, Garzón?"

"With the judge."

The chief inspector then glimpsed my festive outfit under my coat and smiled ironically.

"You're looking very elegant, I don't suppose it's to meet with the journalists? There's a horde of them behind the cordon. I expect they're waiting for you."

"Please, sir, I'd be grateful if you could have a word with the judge and ask him to place a ban on reporting the case."

He laughed out loud.

"Don't be naive, Petra! We're always trying to have a ban put on reporting, but judges do what they feel like. We'll have to get used to living among journalists, I'm afraid."

He moved off with a somewhat studied spring in his step.

"Keep me informed! And let me know if you need any help. I'm sure I can scrape together a few extra officers."

I squatted down next to the corpse. Now I could look at him closely. He was pathetic, his large eyes staring at the dark sky. The coagulated blood on his wounds resembled a shapeless pile of coffee grounds. Legs sprawled, arms open in a cross. I held out a trembling hand and, barely touching him, lifted his upper lip. The blackened tooth appeared. I dropped it with disgust and it formed a slight sneer. A horrifying smile. I turned about, overcame the instinct to leave and went back to the corpse. Taking care not to touch anything, I examined his wrist. He was wearing a watch, a seemingly ordinary watch. When they removed the body, I could study it, trawl for significant details. It obviously wasn't fitted with the device for marking girls. The fact he didn't have it ruled out the possibility that someone had killed him repelling an attack. But could anything really be ruled out? He could have attempted to rape a girl without meaning to mark her this time. Though it was hard to believe! How could a guy on the run, alone, unbalanced, ever have committed another crime? Unless he wanted to throw the police off the scent. Maybe the coldness we'd attributed to him from the beginning was even greater than we imagined, maybe he'd deliberately stopped wearing the fateful barbed watch to rape another girl, she'd resisted, been carrying a knife, stabbed him and then gotten frightened and left without informing the police.

"Too complicated," said Garzón.

"Who knows, my friend, who knows," I replied unconvincingly.

Two days later, we received the forensic report. In effect, there was no sign of violence prior to death. The murderer, whoever it was, had not punched or scratched him. The victim had not defended himself. Whoever it was, they'd appeared in front of Juan or been talking to him and attacked him without warning. No counter-attack. Incredibly, he was surprised and gave up. Five medium stab wounds revealed the attacker had been determined.

"It smacks of revenge," I asserted.

"Or else someone who'd been in on his secret for some time and suddenly, for some unknown reason, decided to murder him."

We pored over the dead man's watch. It was new and vulgar, one of those watches you can buy anywhere for five or ten euros. Garzón quickly deduced he'd bought it with the intention of erasing all memory of the barbs.

"That way if he'd been caught, he wouldn't have been wearing any incriminating evidence."

I reflected.

"Something doesn't fit. First of all, it's not logical for someone who's guilty to foresee extenuating circumstances in case of arrest. Besides, even supposing he'd ditched the barbed watch, why was he wearing such a new one?"

"Because he bought it as a replacement!"

"That would mean he usually wore the barbed one, something I do not believe. So where's the watch he wore every day? His mother said she bought him one years ago, so it can't have been this one, which is brand-new. In which case, where's the other watch, his old one? Why wasn't he wearing it when he was murdered?"

"He didn't want to be identified wearing any of his watches."

"That's daft, Garzón."

"The mind in a panic doesn't always work at full capacity. He must have thought wearing a new watch would get him out of trouble."

I shook my head distractedly, sighed.

"Has his family identified him?"

"Yes."

"And?"

"A drama, you can imagine."

"Yes, I can."

"But not as tragic as I'd expected. The truth is Juan's mother and girlfriend were more aggressive than sad."

"Aggressive?"

"They were crying but they didn't stop blaming you for Juan's death."

"I'm not surprised, they were bound to reach that conclusion. I marked him out as guilty without having definitive proof and now somebody's done him in for being the rapist. I was sure they'd see it that way, it's easier for them. What about the watchmaker, has he been to identify the body?"

"Not yet. He said he won't come till his shop closes."

"Unbelievable!"

"He also said he was a worker and the police couldn't just tell him what to do."

"What a crank!"

We had to wait in the morgue for almost two hours before

the jeweler decided to put in an appearance. I was furious. He arrived, as always, sullen and grumpy. He was wearing a large checked cap, which he didn't even remove out of respect for the deceased. We summoned the person in charge, who opened the refrigerated drawer. He peered inside with a marked expression of disgust.

"Is this the young man you saw?"

He examined him as if he were just another pile of garbage. "Maybe."

"Take a closer look."

He turned around, his countenance warped almost to distortion:

"Listen, I told you with the photos and I'll say it another twenty times. I'm old, I see a lot of people and I can't remember everyone. I think it's pretty clear."

I approached him, seized by a fit of nerves.

"Now you listen to me. Since the first time we met, you've done nothing but create difficulties. We're dealing with a murder now, you understand. If you refuse to collaborate, I shall personally see to it you get done over, I'm serious, I don't care how old you are."

He was frightened and retracted his body like a slug. He looked to Garzón for mercy.

"Look at me!" I screamed. "And then look at the deceased and tell me if that's who you did the job for."

He still hesitated. I took him by the arm and pushed him to within inches of Jardiel's corpse. He was trembling.

"Yes, he does look similar, yes. The boy who came had the same color hair, and the face, yes, I think it's him."

I lifted the dead man's lip and showed him the blackened tooth.

"Yes, that's him, I'm sure of it."

"All right, you can go."

He took to his heels. Garzón gave me an ironic look.

"You let out the beast you carry inside, didn't you, inspector?"

"The bad thing is that this time it was for real and not to impress you. I shall have to start worrying."

"Why does that honest tradesman annoy you so much?"

"To hell with honest tradesmen!"

"If I'm not mistaken, you're pretty angry."

"And what do you expect? What else can happen? We have the culprit practically in our grasp and he slips through our fingers. A week later, he gets killed and we don't have a fucking clue who did it and why. Do you think it's a laughing matter?"

"Let's go and have a coffee."

We left the depressing morgue. I was grateful for the dense and ordinary aroma of coffee, the chatter of people.

"Let me tell you something, Fermín. If we were taken off the case now, I think we'd deserve it."

"Afraid of making a fool of yourself?"

I took a bitter sip from my cup.

"You're right, a man's just been killed and all I care about is my professional reputation."

"What else can you do?"

"I don't know, feel pain, sympathy, or be pleased because there won't be any more rapes, anything except worry about my boss. The life of a cop is cruel."

"They all are, cruelty's in our souls."

"My word, sergeant, that was poetic! Now let's go, we've no time to waste sitting in bars."

"Where to?"

"The Jardiels' house. I want them to identify the watch Juan was wearing when he was murdered."

"If you prefer, I'll go on my own."

"No, I'll come with you. Are you afraid they'll assault me?"

"It'd be strange but even if they don't, it could be disagreeable."

"And you'd like to protect me from harsh reality. I don't know whether to thank you or be offended."

He left behind me, emitting a characteristic clucking sound, laughing, cursing maybe, I didn't want to find out.

The claustrophobia surrounding the Jardiels' apartment affected me long before we entered, on the dark green flights of stairs, hearing voices and noises coming from inside people's homes. It was augmented when Juan's mother opened the door and showed us in. I was once more confronted with that icy, tidy order, the impersonal banality of the pictures and furniture. This must be the pride and joy of modest people, to be able to live and not to live in chaos, to be clean, organized, not to let a speck of dust escape from their tight control. This must be the source of their sense of dignity.

Unexpectedly, the mother looked at me without a hint of hatred, with no sign of having cried, with no expression.

"When are you going to give me my son back so I can bury him?"

"Once the autopsy and studies are complete, they'll inform you."

"And what do you want?"

I produced the watch found on the corpse, showed it to her:

"Madam, is this the watch you bought for your son?"

She took it with her fingertips as if she couldn't bear to touch it. Her short, worn eyelashes fluttered in a gesture of surprise.

"No, it isn't, I've never seen this watch before. The one I gave him was old by now."

"Are you sure?"

"Yes."

"Is your daughter at home?"

She frowned.

"I don't want you to disturb her, she's crying all the time."

Garzón intervened:

"It's just a moment."

The mother tensed, came up to me:

"Are you never satisfied? I've spent my life working. From one day to the next, I lost my husband and gained a daughter. No one's ever had cause to think badly of us. My children went to school, wore clean clothes, ate hot meals, always had what they needed. We never gave rise to gossip. And now people stare at us at work, in the street. Because of you, my son is dead and everyone thinks he was a criminal, a rapist. Leave the girl alone, go away."

The sergeant came between us. He probably feared my reaction would be violent.

"We understand, madam, but that's not the way things are, you can't explain them away like that. Please call your daughter so we can talk to her."

She clenched her jaws and left the room. She came back a moment later with her daughter. Her eyes were red from crying, her face blurred, her nose swollen. Without saying a word, I held the watch in front of her.

"Is this Juan's watch?" I asked.

She looked at it for a split second and nodded. Her mother confronted her.

"What do you mean it's Juan's watch?"

"I bought it for him a month or two ago."

The woman couldn't take her eyes off the girl.

"Why?"

"No reason, I wanted to. The one you gave him was pretty old, mother. And then he bought me this."

She felt under her jersey and pulled out a tiny gold heart hanging on a chain. The woman looked at her as if she didn't understand.

"Why didn't you say anything?"

"We were afraid you'd be offended, mother, since the other one was from you . . . But it's usual for couples to give each other presents, everyone does it. And since it's almost Christmas, we were going to tell you then. It was just a whim."

The mother gritted her teeth and gave her a cold stare. We witnessed the scene in silence. I devoured the expressions on both their faces. The woman abruptly turned to us and cut in:

"Is there anything else?"

I shook my head. We made for the exit down the narrow corridor. As we were about to open the door, we again heard that strong, flat voice:

"I've been invited onto a program, I'm going to appear on television. I shall explain to the whole world that you're to blame for my son's murder, that he was innocent. I'll tell them I want other policemen leading the investigation, not you, I'll ask for you to be dismissed. So now you know."

I turned around.

"Will you be paid to appear on that program, Mrs. Jardiel?"

"That's none of your business."

"Of course not, I just wanted to know if you were going to make a profit from your son's death."

"Get out!"

Garzón was alarmed, he must have thought I was warming up for another fight, he pushed me gently outside. Back in the street, I looked at him.

"What a woman, did you see? She had them perfectly controlled, a form of slavery. And then you're able to deny the influence of psychology. If my mother had been like that, even I could have turned out a rapist."

He pulled out the car keys with a sigh.

"For God's sake, stop talking nonsense!"

While he was driving, I burst out laughing. Poor Garzón! Hard and insensitive as a stone, but terrified of strife, verbal controversy, in favor of peaceful coexistence and indifference.

"What are you laughing for, are you in a better mood now?"

"No, but if I let myself be ruled by my mood, I could do something serious, like attack you."

He looked at me like an incomprehensible, pampered child.

"Do you know what we're going to do, Fermín? For once we're going to conduct the investigation the way they do in American movies . . . "

His face showed patience and a little irony.

" . . . We'll go home, prepare something to eat and put a blackboard on the wall."

"And then?" he asked.

"And then we'll think, we'll think till we're half dead."

I wasn't joking. We went home. I switched on the heating. The first thing Garzón did was inspect the geraniums. He didn't comment on their lack of biological activity. My own home was as strange to me as a nuclear shelter or an oil platform. I took two pizza bases out of the freezer and lit the oven. Garzón shyly edged towards the kitchen table. I rebuked him.

"Come on, Garzón, don't just stand there! You'll have to help me a bit if you want to eat. Behave as if you were in your own kitchen."

"You know I don't have a kitchen. I have lunch in a bar and dinner in the boarding house. Ever since my wife died . . . Besides, I've never been any good at cooking. Some colleagues know how to make paella or a barbecue, but as for me . . . "

"Open that cupboard and take what's in it, then look in the fridge. Put whatever you fancy on your pizza and I'll do the same with mine."

"All mixed up?"

"It'll be fine. Do you want an apron not to stain your suit or would that be humiliating?"

He grinned. I pointed to the drawer where he'd find one and went to the lounge because the phone was ringing. I returned a moment later.

"That was Pepe, he wanted to pop round. I told him not even to think about coming now."

Garzón had his hands full trying to open a can of anchovies.

"You're a hard woman."

"Why?"

"Perhaps he'd like to maintain a relationship."

"Oh, no! He'd turn up whenever he was depressed or had a toothache or was hungry. He has a tendency to let older women take care of him. No way! You have to look to the future, never to the past. Pass me the salami."

"Although you women have been liberated, you're still as hard as you were before."

"You think so? Strange interpretation!"

We carried on covering our pizzas with ingredients. The sergeant's had quite a pile. He'd mixed a whole range of things: anchovies, Gorgonzola cheese, slices of ham, capers, tuna. He stood contemplating his work.

"Would a little chorizo go amiss?"

"No, throw it on!"

We ate in the kitchen, washing the food down with two cold beers. Garzón seemed content, hungry as always.

"I never realized cooking was so easy."

"You should leave that boarding house, find yourself an apartment. You'd have more freedom in your own home."

"It's all so complicated! Cooking, shopping, clothes . . . "

"There are laundries, supermarkets, freezers, ready-to-serve meals . . . "

He swallowed a string of mozzarella with docility. It was as if I were listing the labors of Hercules and the plagues of Egypt at one and the same time. He was incapable of the first and unwilling to accept the second falling on his head, destroying his tranquility.

I made a liter of coffee and we got down to work. I put the blackboard on the bookshelf and at the top wrote *Jardiel Case* and underneath *First Possibility*. We agreed our first hypothesis, if only to reject it, should be that the murder was in self-defense in the face of an attack. The sergeant scribbled down the drawbacks:

No sign of a struggle
Barbed watch missing
Girl unlikely to be armed
Couldn't have snatched the rapist's knife without signs of a struggle
Strange that the alleged girl hadn't gone to the police
Victim of usual physical stature wouldn't have had the strength to stab him so deeply

I pointed at Garzón with the chalk like a schoolteacher.

"If Juan Jardiel was caught defenseless, we have to think his assailant was someone he knew and didn't feel he had to be on his guard against."

"Even if it wasn't someone he knew, at least someone he'd arranged to meet," said Garzón.

"O.K., so the next hypothesis is that of revenge, though I warn you it has its weak points. For example, how did the avenger know the whereabouts of a fugitive from justice? How did he or she make contact?"

"It could have been someone from his world. A settling of scores."

A settling of scores? I couldn't see the reason. Jardiel didn't move in the underworld or in circles of drug addiction. It was absurd to surmise that he had a second life in this sense, we had no grounds to suspect it.

"No, sergeant, Jardiel's death has something to do with the rapes, there's no other motive."

"In that case, we need a list of suspects."

The list would be short. Who could have wanted Juan

dead? We raised two suspects to the top of the list: Salomé and Mr. Masderius. Salomé was the most evasive, the most mysterious of the victims and probably the one who had suffered most. Masderius, with his belligerent, indignant attitude, made himself a favorite. But in both cases the question remained the same: how had they managed to locate the rapist?

"Salomé could have found him by means of youngsters, friends of friends, people who, not mistrusting her as they do the police, could have given her details."

"Despite not being from the same neighborhood? I'd be surprised, Fermín, but all right, let's admit it as a working hypothesis. However, do you really think Salomé wanted him out of the way?"

"We both agreed on her as a favorite when looking for suspects. She's a strange girl, reserved, reacted badly during questioning. Who knows if there isn't violence lurking beneath her cool exterior? Think of it like this: she decides the police investigation isn't going well. She knows someone from Juan's neighborhood and asks questions or gets a friend, maybe even a boyfriend, to ask questions. The police is a slow, institutional, weighty organization, young people know shortcuts and ways. So this boyfriend, friend or she herself locates Juan and tricks him into meeting them in a side-street, where . . ."

"Does Salomé have a boyfriend?"

"I don't know, that's something we'll have to find out. We should jot it down on the list of things to do."

A big picture was taking shape on the blackboard. In the meantime, we were drinking inordinate amounts of coffee. And Mr. Masderius, how the hell had Mr. Masderius located Juan? The difficulties Garzón pointed out were clearly logical. There didn't seem to be any common ground between them, any possible link. We stared into thin air or, rather, into thick smoke.

"He could have hired a private detective," I suggested.

"Crikey, I hadn't thought of that! Though that would mean a private detective was able to find what we couldn't."

I had rubbed his professional pride up the wrong way.

"You yourself just said the police force is a complicated organization, sometimes guerrilla warfare is more effective."

He poured himself some more coffee without appearing convinced.

"I'll look into the possibility of a detective."

He noted it down on the blackboard, which was almost full. This system of ongoing reflection was illuminating, but it hadn't produced a substantive hypothesis. Even the one about Masderius was weak. A member of the establishment, a successful architect with money and a reputation . . . I found it hard to imagine him stabbing rapists in the dark. And yet he'd been so worked up, so determined to remove all trace of his daughter's rape . . . maybe he'd decided to go that little bit further in his clean-up of the past. He could even not only have hired a detective, but have included a paid assassin in his plans, who agreed to take out Jardiel. Killing a guy without getting your hands dirty is frighteningly easy.

I started noticing the first symptoms of a coffee overdose. My heart took off at a light gallop from time to time, my hands tingled and my mouth was bitter. It was two in the morning. I slumped back on the sofa. We remained silent. I looked at my feet, which were a little swollen.

"Unless . . . " began Garzón.

I was too tired to prompt him. He fell quiet. Then he took up his sentence with renewed vigor.

"Unless, Petra, we're completely wrong. Listen carefully."

He stood up and began pacing about the room. He then came back to where he'd started and turned to face me. His eyes gave off an intense, somewhat demented look. Then, between pauses, reflections, stutters and excited outbursts, he began to elaborate a complex new theory. He thought Juan

Jardiel wasn't the rapist. Serious considerations led him to believe he was really just covering for someone else, even helping him to carry out his plans. He had in mind a friend, an alter ego, someone depraved like Jardiel but much braver, bolder, cleverer. He was the real rapist. Using Jardiel, he had him visit a jeweler and put barbs around the watch so that he couldn't be identified. Each time this man committed a rape, he'd then meet up with Juan and relate his misdeed to him. In this way Juan, a timid, weak-willed individual castrated by his mother, derived morbid pleasure and became an accomplice, so that the real rapist was assured of his silence. Till the net of evidence tightened around Juan and made him nervous. It all coincided according to the sergeant. The day we went after him and he slipped out of work, he headed straight for the bar to use the phone, to contact the phantom man and, frightened, to receive instructions and let him know the police were searching for him. But he bumped into me and I spoiled the maneuver. All the same, having escaped, he went to the phantom's home, where he was in hiding all the time he was a fugitive. Till the phantom realized, even wielding such influence over Juan, he couldn't get rid of him and Juan was turning into a liability. He then put the second part of his perfect plan into practice. He set him a trap, arranged to meet him in a side street for whatever reason, perhaps promising to help him leave the country, and—bam!—he stabbed him to death. Which is why the deceased failed to defend himself. Free of risk and suspicion, he'd given the police the rapist they were searching for and could carry on with his normal life, whatever that was.

He looked at me, still dazed by his own capacity for deduction. My upper eyelashes hadn't dared unite with the lower ones for a moment during his reasonings.

"Crikey, Garzón, why aren't you chief inspector yet?"

"Lack of studies."

"You don't need them."

"Tell me what you think of my theory."

"Well . . . it's one hell of a theory. But let's see, it has a weak point. If what you say is true and the phantom wanted to shirk responsibility, then why didn't Juan's body turn up with the watch for marking girls? Why didn't the real rapist put it on his wrist so he'd be found with it? That would have been a clear statement: 'Here's the rapist and here's his weapon.' He could then have ambled home, it would have been a perfect crime, leaving no room for doubt."

"You're obsessed with watches."

"Answer me, Garzón, how does that fit into your theory?"

"In short, Petra, no plan is perfect. Maybe the phantom forgot to bring the watch the day they met, maybe he didn't think . . . "

"Someone who's that perceptive?"

"Maybe he'll need the device again."

"To commit another rape?"

"It's possible."

"Oh, come on, Garzón, that's ridiculous! First he searches for an accomplice to take the burden of suspicion, even at the risk that the latter might make a mistake and spill the beans. He kills him to prevent his name from coming out and then brazenly commits another rape. There's something there that's not quite right."

"But you were the one who always believed in the idea of a madman committing these crimes. The fact he's intelligent doesn't mean he's any less around the bend. Imagine, he's not just a degenerate but he likes to play, to show his mind is one step ahead of the police, he might even come up with more strategies like that of Juan Jardiel."

"I don't know, Garzón, a clever psychopath's gambit, it sounds like a movie."

"But tell me, since we know nothing about him, if he decided to commit further rapes, where would we start to look for him? All the preparations for the crime were carried out by another, who's now dead. It's a catch-22, it'd be like starting again. He may even feel tempted."

"You want to drive me crazy, Garzón, we've no proof for any of this."

"How can we have proof against someone we haven't been looking for?"

"You're like a Hollywood scriptwriter."

"Could you reject this path at a single stroke?"

He was euphoric. Giving voice to the theory had not, as often happens, made it less credible in his eyes, on the contrary, having honed it up, he believed in it more passionately. It must have been the coffee. I tried to appear convinced to keep him happy.

"I wouldn't reject it outright, of course not, it is in effect another possibility. I just think we should be basing ourselves on something more tangible."

Garzón's occurrence had amazed me. You can't start with prototypes, it's a fallacy. The stubborn, experienced cop who can't get away from the most Cartesian evidence starts building castles in the air. But, expounded like this, it was another possibility. Why not give the phantom who'd appeared out of nowhere a place in reserve?

We wiped the board clean of deliberations because we had to start summing up. Our conclusions were nothing new. We had to conduct interviews we'd already undertaken. We had to talk to the girls again, Salomé especially, find out about her friends, apply pressure. Then there was Masderius, whom we had to investigate in connection with the possible hiring of a detective. Maybe Garzón was right, maybe the epicenter of the case had always been somewhere else.

"Fermín, I think you're more qualified to locate Masderius's supposed detective. Do you want to take charge of that?"

"And what about my theory? Aren't we going to investigate the phantom?"

"I'll make inquiries about Juan's friends if you like."

"Good. Though we already know he never had many friends."

"There'll be one who'll put us onto the mysterious man, if he exists."

"I'm increasingly sure he does."

I looked sympathetically at his fleshy nose, which was alert; he was holding his breath, ready to go bounding down a trail.

"Is there any more coffee?" he asked nonchalantly, as if he'd just arrived.

In the morning, before I left home, Pepe called. He wanted to know if I'd seen the television. What he said when I told him no didn't surprise me in the slightest. All the signs had been there. Juan's mother had appeared on the program following the case and apparently expressed herself with harsh clarity. The sergeant and I had not come out of it well. Luisa had been relegated to second place.

"She hardly opened her mouth and, when she did, it was always to say her boyfriend wasn't the rapist. She was obsessed by it: he wasn't the rapist. The mother was more explicit, she accused you both of having caused Juan's death. It sounded plausible, she did well. Everyone must hate you and Garzón by now."

"I suppose she carried out what's known as an impartial analysis. Did you record it?"

"Yep."

"Then we'll have to pop by and see it."

At that moment, I should have felt harassed, constricted by the media, but some internal defense mechanism prevented me from feeling like part of that circus. The champions of good turned instigators of murder? Too crude! On the other hand, it annoyed me to think of that waspish journalist sniffing around in the Ephemerides, following us in the dark, giving rise to some mawkish conspiracy. Though what did a little more hatred matter? The role of witch was actually quite fun. The alleged defenders of the people were now their enemies. It had never occurred to me that, to be marginalized with all the honors, you only had to stand on the side of the law.

Of all our declared detractors, the one who detested us most was Mr. Masderius. The muffled drill of his contempt pierced the skin long before you were in his presence. I endeavored never to look him straight in the eye because I was instantly overwhelmed by the terrible sensation of wanting to be erased from the world. On learning that I wished to question him, he directed me to his lawyer, "his official spokesperson," and, when I informed him the police didn't accept proxy evidence, he lost his temper. He had no choice but to receive me, however, and we arranged to meet in his office. I suppose he meant to intimidate me by appearing installed in his kingdom. I was calm, but my mood changed as soon as we started speaking. He behaved with such superiority! He made me wait more than ten minutes sitting opposite him before he deigned to take his eyes off the documents lying on his desk. He finally looked at me with a sneer halfway between irritation and disgust.

"What is it?"

I asked him if he'd heard about Juan's death. He answered that he had. I asked him where he was that day when the crime was committed. He opened a bulging diary and searched.

"I had a meeting with the office staff."

"All of them?"

"A routine, quarterly meeting."

"I understand."

"Do you suspect me?"

"We have to consider all possibilities."

He smiled, monstrously stretching his facial muscles.

"Do you really think I killed him?"

"Anyone with motives could be the murderer."

He slammed a drawer shut.

"How dare you turn up here attempting to intimidate me? Don't you realize where you are? This isn't a slum where you're carrying out a raid on some whores, I'm a prestigious architect, I don't belong to your world, I don't just go about stabbing people, I've something to lose, you have to be blind not to see that."

I heard the sound of breaking glass in my mind, arched my body over his desk.

"Mr. Masderius, when it comes to murder there's no social class. You could have been in a meeting with a hundred others, that doesn't prove your innocence. I've seen more solid alibis fall to pieces."

"Get out of here!"

He'd lost control, his forefinger furiously pointing to the door. He's kicking me out, I thought and realized that till then, in all the days of my life, I'd never been thrown out of anywhere.

"I assure you, Mr. Masderius, if you killed Juan Jardiel, I shall personally see to it you pay. You might meet a worse destiny than that of those raided whores."

"Get out of here!"

He was white, stiff with rage, pop-eyed with indignation and disbelief. I stood up and left as proudly and deliberately as possible. My dignity had taken a severe blow. As I walked through that impressive building of offices in between glass and wooden partitions, I was overwhelmed by a savage desire to wreak revenge, to kill. Yes, anyone could do it, could kill, and not in a fit of temper, but with the sure conviction that nothing will change in the world if another pest disappears from it. Masderius the rapist . . . it wasn't a bad idea to let them exterminate each other outside what is ridiculously termed "the rule of law."

My hands were still shaking when I reached the Ephemerides. Garzón was there. They were watching the offending video that tore us apart. I asked Hamed for a beer and swigged it down. Juan's mother was talking on the screen, with a perm she'd just had done.

"It's amazing, isn't it? They're raped, their sons get killed, but they all have time to go to the hairdresser's before appearing on TV."

Garzón didn't react, he was absorbed by the program and smoking.

"Would someone please switch that off?"

They looked at me in astonishment. Pepe walked over to the set and turned the volume right down.

"Are you in a bad mood?" he asked.

"This is all a fucking mess."

Pepe whistled slowly.

"I sense something's not right."

Garzón came over to me without letting go of a tankard of beer in which he wet his mustache.

"You should hear what she has to say. She basically has a go at you. She thinks a woman shouldn't be in charge of investigating a rape."

"Oh no? Why not?"

"She gets too emotional, is influenced by the victims' feelings, has to find a culprit somehow, even if it's the wrong one. She's not stupid, this woman."

"Perhaps you even agree with her."

"I didn't say that, I only mean she's good at putting forward an argument. What's up, why are you so upset?"

"I just had a run-in with Masderius."

"Was that a good idea? He's an influential man. This time they might take us off the case."

"What do I care? Or have you acquired a taste for rummaging through the garbage? I hope they do take us off it!"

"But I thought that your . . . "

"That my professionalism was tied up in this, my sense of the absurd, my feminine conscience? No, Garzón, I've had it up to here with all this soup, in which victims behave like assholes. The rapist can go fuck the eleven thousand virgins as far as I'm concerned."

Hamed frowned, suffering as he always did when I used a vulgar manner of speaking. Pepe looked at me, playing with the remote control.

"Petra, Ana Lozano, the director of the show, was here. She wants to give you the opportunity to defend yourself and explain your reasons on TV. Why don't you accept? I think you need to, that way you could cut short all the gossip and slander."

"Do me a favor, Pepe, darling. Next time that vixen shows her face, tell her if she gets in my way again, she'll be sorry."

"Petra, be reasonable."

"I am being reasonable."

Garzón opened wide his eyes.

"Are you going to resign?"

I downed the rest of the beer.

"No, I am not going to resign!"

I made for the door, leaving a gawping threesome behind me.

"Oh, good God!" I heard Hamed exclaim.

"Quiet, let's not wind her up any more!" Garzón snarled. Clearly the three of them had reached the conclusion I was unbearable. This amused me, flattered me, encouraged me to persevere.

I preferred to question Salomé on my own. Garzón carried on trying to find out if she'd had some way of knowing where Juan Jardiel was. I hoped when I saw her to detect a particular expression on her face, but it was still a closed book. What could I really ask her?

"You heard that boy Juan was killed."

"Yes."

"We were wondering if you could tell us something about that."

"No."

The hypothesis that she was the murderer immediately came tumbling down. A girl who's been raped, who adopts a position somewhere between resentment and fatalism, does not come across as guilty. I was the one who felt guilty. Perhaps Ana Lozano was right and I was letting myself be influenced by my feminine subjectivity. I needed to be more rigorous.

"Where were you when Jardiel was killed, around eight or nine?"

"I don't know, going for a walk."

"Alone?"

"Yes."

"Do you walk alone at night?"

"Sometimes after work. If I go straight home, my mother wants me to help her. So I rest a bit."

"And don't you have any friends who go with you?"

"Not at night. Everyone's doing their own thing."

Simple, understandable, fitting a plausible whole like another piece.

"Did someone see you when you were out?"

"I don't know."

"How about you? Did you see someone, anyone you know, who could identify you now?"

"I don't think so."

"You didn't pass by a local shop, bar, amusement arcade, or greet a friend?"

"No."

And yet the alibi was so unstable, so fragile, unpaired and inconsistent like an old shoe on a waste tip. Her fringe was ruffled, her eyes tired, she was wearing a black blouse buttoned up to the neck. She despised me.

"Are you going to say I killed him?"

"Someone had to."

"Was the corpse marked in any way?"

"No, why do you ask?"

"Because if the corpse wasn't marked, then I couldn't have done it, I'd have marked him as he marked me but on the face."

She pulled up her sleeve and showed me her skin. The mark with the flower was still there, dry, wrinkled around the edges, the color of parchment. A shudder went down my spine. I prayed to God that Masderius had taken out the rapist, not that girl. My own thought horrified me.

"Did someone tell you where Juan was hiding?"

"No."

"Did a friend of yours kill him for you?"

"No."

"Had you known where he was, would you have gone after him?"

She reflected deeply, spoke with a sneer:

"I don't know."

If she didn't feel the need to defend herself vigorously, it was a good sign. Besides, she was right, a victim's attack should have been more vicious, more vengeful, and no cruelty had been inflicted on Juan's body, only the stab wounds needed to end his life.

I asked her what her job was. She worked in a factory, sewing cups on bras, eight hours a day. That's all she did, she just assembled the pieces that in her hands acquired the shape of semi-globes. Pretty hard. After the factory, presumably her mother had her peel potatoes for supper. Of course washing hair couldn't be much more fun, or doing the dishes for a coarse, despotic mother who's tired after work. None, not one of the victims could have killed the rapist, some time ago they'd lost the necessary pride, the impulse of individualism needed to do it. And the fourth victim was also out because she was in

New York, possibly as restricted by her daily life as the others. And yet Salomé's unemotional account retained a tiny amount of inner rebellion that could finish her off. Her passive revolt lay in that laconic "What do I care?" she always used as a farewell.

"If you can't prove you were out walking when the murder was committed, I can't promise you there won't be any more questioning. We'll probably have to turn you over to the judge."

"What do I care?" she replied.

Garzón had reached the same conclusion I had after questioning Sonia and Patricia, neither of them could have been the culprit. In his case, the decision was made easier by the fact they both had verifiable alibis and it was crazy to think they might have hired a paid assassin. A friend who did the job for them? It was too big a favor to ask for out of friendship. The sergeant listened to my comments about Salomé and, despite the weakness of her statement, agreed with me that she wasn't the killer. I was surprised to note that he didn't reproach me for my subjectivity, perhaps because deep down he was guided by instinct. But his subjectivity and mine had little in common. For me, the centuries-old repression of feminine dignity made a violent reaction impossible; he again wielded the pedestal and the flower as arguments. How could a woman, an ethereal being above this world's dark substratum, be capable of murdering someone in revenge? He was still determined to search for his man, the phantom rapist in whose hands Jardiel had been putty and finally a broken toy.

"I found out he was seen recently with an unidentified friend, a guy more or less of his age, perhaps a little bit younger."

"It could have been anyone."

"He didn't have many friends, or indeed any."

"But talking to someone doesn't mean much."

"I'm questioning all the guys he had the slightest relation with."

"What about Masderius?"

"Don't worry, I haven't forgotten about him. It's just that when you're dealing with private detectives, the investigation gets much more complicated. They're like eels that slip out of a net. But if he hired one, we'll know. Trust me. Remember I have experience in this kind of street search."

"Are you still helping the Civil Guard?"

"The case is almost solved, the smuggled goods will turn up soon."

"Where do you find time for everything?"

"It's not very pleasant being at the boarding house. And you want me to move to an apartment! If I settled down, well, my work would suffer."

Garzón, suddenly so content, who could understand him? Proud of his disordered life, majestic like Henry VIII in front of a chicken, with greasy hands consigning the smugglers of Chesterfield to the Tower. I didn't want to disappoint him, but I had spoken to the chief inspector. He advised prudence in every step we took. We still enjoyed his confidence but, if his superiors suggested changing the guard, there wouldn't be much he could do about it. Did I understand? I told him I did, we were no longer in a bargaining position. If things carried on in the same way, our heads would soon be worth more than Jack the Ripper's. We were about to reach a fairly absolute limit: the entire world's deep and total enmity. In this story where victims and executioners were confused, we couldn't count on a single comforting support. I remembered only the friendly gesture of the bar owner who brought me brandy after I'd received a punch from Juan Jardiel. Perhaps I had to turn the other cheek or finally appear on TV, swearing cops also know how to cry and say they're sorry. At that point in my melancholy thoughts, the filterless cigarette in my mouth disintegrated a little, which gave me the perfect excuse to spit.

11

The events left me no choice but to order Salomé's arrest. Her alibi was too weak given the magnitude of the pointing finger. The reports of the psychologist and social worker also went against her. Salomé had been accused of having an evasive personality, an uncooperative attitude and a fatalistic indifference out of keeping with her age. According to the report, a violent act could not be ruled out of her possible reactions. The self-sufficient isolation she was so proud of was considered a cynical feature, a generic mistrust of society. What I found cynical were all those circumlocutions abounding in abstract concepts that sounded like chats over a coffee. Of course she mistrusted society! It was the only healthy, logical thing to do. Everything from her birth had formed part of a tenacious machine. She was limited in her freedom, in her opportunities, she washed floors, sewed bras, put up with a family who saw in her only two working hands. In the bloom of youth, she had been raped and shamelessly exhibited on television. She was the only one who seemed reluctant and didn't willingly take part in that horrible circus. In fact, hers was the only possible elegant attitude, she kept her sorrow hidden and felt contempt for everyone, aggression, which has yet to be outlawed. But one thing was my personal explanation of what had happened, quite another the general imperative of the investigation.

All the same, it would be difficult to turn a technical suspicion into a real accusation, however much police theory appeared to be in command. How did we plan to prove that Salomé had been able to locate Juan Jardiel? We kept returning to the theory of an intermediary friend or boyfriend who moved in juvenile circles more easily and could find a clue that led to the rapist. And then there was Garzón, still on about his phantom and extending what till then had been the borders of the case. I, however, remained convinced all the pieces of the puzzle were before our eyes and we were looking like a dumb child at a whole we simply didn't know how to put together. A piece or two may have been missing, but there was sufficient material for the drawing to begin to take shape. An inkblot in the Rorschach test awaiting a wise interpretation we couldn't give.

Salomé's bail was fixed at three thousand euros, which her family refused to pay. I took a more or less rigorous approach; I thought about it, thought again and finally decided to pay, creating a disturbing dichotomy between my intimate and my professional self. Garzón was furious when he found out. It struck him as an excessive act, an attack of sensibility. He warned me I'd be sorry before long.

"Are you going to get involved like this in all your cases?"

"Once we're out of this mess, I don't plan to take on any more cases."

"You did that because she's a girl, right? Feminine solidarity and all that."

"I did it because deep down I don't think she's guilty, even though I feel obliged to treat her as a suspect."

"All right, but paying her bail . . . "

"I don't see why she should take more shit after all she's suffered. Anyway, I thought we'd agreed that for you women are like a flower."

"Each flower has its gardener."

"There are flowers, Garzón, that sprout by the side of the road without any attention. No one waters them, no one takes care of them. All they receive is the blessing of sun and rain . . . "

He remained silent and absentmindedly took out his cigarettes.

"That was poetic. Seriously, I mean it, I continue to think you speak very well."

"I'm a lawyer, remember?"

"But standing bail . . . "

That evening, Garzón and I had dinner together in a bar. He was obviously melancholy and eventually confessed it was his birthday. I tried to be effusive when congratulating him, but this didn't help pull him out of the pit he was in. He wasn't in the mood for talking, he bolted a plate of tortellini with the same concentration Einstein must have used to sketch out his theories. I respectfully gave attention to my pasta and left him alone till my mind regurgitated the case with all its obsessive details.

"Sergeant, we have to go through the pieces again. I propose another session with the blackboard. I'm convinced there's something we haven't seen that's escaping our attention, even though it's right in front of us like a transparency."

To my amazement, Garzón replied:

"Do you know what my wife always gave me for my birthday?"

His hippopotamus-with-a-cold eyes were fixed on me.

"Underwear," he said as if this were the greatest tragedy for a man. "Socks, shorts, undershirts . . . just enough to spend the year appropriately dressed underneath. Can you imagine? No aftershave, no surprises, nothing . . . socks that inevitably ranged somewhere between black and brown. One birthday after another, always the same."

My food stuck in my throat. I realized my colleague was going to get emotional.

"A sensitive man like me. When you were talking about flowers by the side of the road, I thought of myself."

I found it difficult to imagine such a rotund gentleman as

anything but a blooming carnation, but his feeling of loneliness clearly wasn't funny.

"I see that life has slipped out of my hands in the most stupid way. And I've understood that since meeting you."

I sensed the pasta wouldn't go down well.

"But, Fermín, I . . . "

"You've moved, Petra, chased after true love, got married twice, got divorced, changed profession, studied, thought about your conflicts and problems . . . maybe you've even been to see a psychiatrist."

This caught me off guard.

"A psychiatrist? . . . No, but do you think I should?"

"Of course you should! If I'd had a psychiatrist who'd listened to me, my life now would exist in another place: in their records, in a file, in the guy's mind, at least it wouldn't have evaporated like a puddle!"

"Psychiatrist as witness? Now, that is a policeman's vision!"

"Don't poke fun, I'm being serious."

"Sorry, Garzón. It's just I'm not used to your unusual way of seeing things."

"Well, that's some consolation."

We ordered coffee. If only the sergeant had known that what I liked about him was his monolithic character, his sense of duty, his unanimity! But the props on which I hoped to support myself always came tumbling down like the walls of Jericho. I couldn't allow him to get all existential on me, it wasn't his role, for all kinds of depressions and abrupt changes I had myself to turn to. Why the hell did my attitude have to be so contagious? Since I didn't want to spend the whole night moaning, I upbraided him in my most colloquial style:

"Don't give me that, Fermín! The only life that really matters is what hasn't happened yet, what's to come."

Dumbfounded by the sound of my own vulgarity, I continued in my attempt to get him back to detective orthodoxy.

"Think about the complicated case we're on. Without your experience we'll never be able to solve it and that shows your past is valuable, it's there, it left a trace, it never evaporated."

He gave me a lackluster look. He was weary. He reminded me of a gladiator sentenced by the emperor.

"Let's have a glass of grappa, and tell me what's planned for tomorrow."

"Planned for tonight, but you don't have to come, I'll go on my own."

He'd arranged to meet a few boys that knew Juan in an amusement arcade. We were on the phantom's trail.

The glass of grappa was all that gave me a little warmth as we emerged into the rain-stained night. My colleague was still as withered as yesterday's lettuce. We reached the vile, neon-lit arcade in silence. Four boys were waiting for us there. They had the coarse, spotty look that comes not from crime, but from a lack of education. They laughed and nudged one another. Garzón addressed them with little style:

"When did Jardiel use to come here?"

"When his mummy let him."

"And when was that?"

"On occasion, he'd sometimes escape after work, but he immediately had to go home and clock in."

"His mother's pretty harsh. One day we were playing table football when she turned up."

"Did she kick up a fuss?"

"No, she gave him one look and that was enough."

"Did he mind? Did he talk against his mother?" I intervened for the first time.

They looked at me as though I were a dumb fly.

"Who's this then?" the youngest asked Garzón.

"My boss, Inspector Delicado."

They turned their now ironic attention to me. I repeated my question.

"No, that's none of our business. We weren't his friends, savvy? Nor did we hold his prick while he went for a pee."

The three of them laughed. Fortunately the level of melancholy in the sergeant's blood prevented him from responding to the provocation meant for me and I could carry on impassively.

"Had he been seeing any particular man lately?"

"Do you mean was he gay? But I thought we'd agreed he was a rapist."

They again burst out laughing. I looked to the end of their long, gangly legs. There were their feet, big, almost deformed, clad in frightful sportswear. I think it was due more to the disagreeable aesthetic impression I suffered than to anything else, but the fact is I reacted.

"I haven't come here to fuck around. If you've agreed to talk, then talk, why don't you?"

"We're not criminals," one of them protested to Garzón.

"Causing the police to waste investigative time is a crime. So if I feel like it, I can take you down to the station, where you might immediately get out but not before you've had a good beating."

They became serious, looked at Garzón, who shrugged his shoulders and smiled. The youngest talked again:

"Recently Juan started turning up with a new guy. I think he was into selling some of those weird porno magazines."

"Where does he live?"

"I don't know. As I said, he's a new guy."

"Is there a bar where we might find him?"

"You could try the Diamond Pub."

"It's been a pleasure."

We left without looking at them. Garzón whispered to me:

"You've gotten much better at the level of violence needed."

"It's all a question of learning."

Continuing with our nocturnal round, we reached the

Diamond Pub. My colleague was utterly at ease in such dives. He talked to the owner, an aging man who looked as if he'd been through all the stages of a descent into hell. He acted friendly, put a couple of complimentary whiskies on the counter. A guy selling porno magazines? *Connais pas*. As was to be expected. But he had a lot of useless things to say about some of his customers. Nothing interesting. It seemed he was keen to help. We told him we were after a rapist. He appeared unmoved, the world was like that, youngsters, too. Nothing surprised him anymore. We downed our whiskies and took our leave.

Outside, a boy came up to us. He wanted to talk, but not in front of the pub. We arranged to see him two blocks away. He followed us at a distance.

"Let him explain, don't ask him anything," said Garzón.

"I know the guy you're after, I heard you in the pub. I also know where he lives. But I'm not going to tell you my name."

"Fine, no problem."

He dictated an address, which my colleague immediately wrote down.

"I don't like rapists."

I nodded as he made off, looking in all directions.

"That's it, let's go."

We took the car. I understood Garzón was preparing to go into action.

"It's three in the morning," I reminded him.

"Even better, he might be at home."

He had cheered up since his disappointment with the underwear. I was slightly scared, all this was new to me. Questioning suspects at the station wasn't the same as trapping a pornographer in his lair under cover of darkness. Garzón murmured to himself:

"Earlier, we should have gone there earlier."

I realized from his nervous state that he was convinced the

end was in sight. It seemed to me that everything was coming
together too well. In a single, perfect move, both murderer and
rapist fell into our hands. Too much of a carom to be true.

We ended up in an outlying suburb where I'd never been.
Garzón parked the car and took me by the arm into a tall,
ruinous building without an elevator. We rang at a bare door
on the fifth floor, but no one answered. We rang again and this
time heard some weary slippers sliding towards us and at last
the bolt was removed. We were faced by a very young, tall, athletic man. Garzón showed some ID and the boy immediately
piped up:

"I'm not doing anything illegal."

"You have pornography in here," said my colleague.

"That's allowed."

"That depends what kind it is. Have you any videos of children, murders, tortures?"

"Absolutely not. It's all artistic material, you can check it
out if you like."

"Let us in."

He moved aside. We entered a small lounge full of bookshelves containing rolls of paper.

"They're posters," said the guy.

Pictures covered the walls, depicting mind-boggling scenes:
a serpent twined around the body of a woman, incandescent
rubies in the eyes of both; a hairy dwarf with his back to us,
performing fellatio on the classical statue of an ephebe.
Garzón stared in amazement at the images.

"Is this what you have in here?"

"I already told you, it's pop art."

Garzón sat down on a sofa covered in filthy cushions.

"How do you know Juan Jardiel?"

"Who?"

"You're perfectly aware who I mean."

"No, I'm not."

I took my cigarettes out of my bag and offered one to Garzón. He gestured to me to take over the questioning, but I declined. I wanted him to continue.

"You've been seen several times with him recently, so it's pointless trying to deny it."

"Loads of guys come round here to buy material, I might then meet up with them in a bar, but that's not to say I know them."

"The one I'm talking about is a bit special. He was accused of rape and has just been killed."

"I've no idea who you mean."

"O.K. Where were you on the twenty-fifth between one and three in the morning?"

"I don't know. Here, I suppose. I'm always here at that time."

"Can you prove it?"

"Right now if you like. My girlfriend lives with me."

He entered a dark passageway and after a while returned leading a sleepy girl by the hand. She can't have been more than fifteen. She was dressed in panties and an undershirt, her flesh was white like wax and she had beautiful, Renaissance-style hair.

"Tell them where you spend all your time," the boy ordered her.

"Here," she replied, giving us a timid look.

"Always, all the time?" Garzón became frustrated.

"Yeah, with him."

She moved closer to her partner, who put his arm around her shoulders to protect her.

"You see."

"We see all right." Garzón turned to me, "Inspector, if you agree, I suggest you notify a patrol and go in search of an arrest warrant. I'll stay here with these guys till it arrives."

I felt a huge sense of relief on leaving that building. I did everything my subordinate commanded and then went home. I desperately needed to cleanse my skin of foul air and my mind of images. I filled the bathtub to the brim, added musk salts and quietly slipped inside. Had we reached an outcome? Garzón thought he had the rapist, an astute, enigmatic individual, a degenerate who hatches a plan alongside his misdeeds to pass on the guilt. Someone capable of controlling another's will, gradually drawing him into his pernicious game and then doing away with him. I found it extremely hard to recognize such a monster in the young man we'd just arrested. And the girl in the undershirt . . . was this the companion of a depraved rapist? Difficult to say since it may not be necessary for monsters to have two heads or a forked tongue and we may happily give up our seat to them on a bus.

But there was a lot that needed explaining. Why had the owner of the pub denied knowing Juan Jardiel? Of course it's normal to refuse to collaborate with the police on principle, as Garzón said. He hoped he could keep that boy in the station long enough to make him talk. Otherwise, we barely had any evidence against him. No, no one who sleeps next to a girl in an undershirt can be a rapist. Garzón's inquiries were leading us astray, but I couldn't find anything solid enough to make him change direction.

The following morning, I arrived at the station early but of course Garzón was already there.

"Questioning the suspect?" I asked a guard.

"No, I think he's talking on the phone."

I sat down in the meeting room, lit a cigarette and exhaled but, before I could put my brain into gear, Garzón burst in as if pursued by the Furies and slammed the door shut behind him. He was in a state, his cheeks flushed and his tie loosened.

"Petra, you may have been right," he began.

"What do you mean?"

He started wheezing.

"Calm down, sergeant."

He sat down, took a cigarette out of his shirt pocket and lit it.

"For fuck's sake, Garzón, calm down but say something!"

"I've located the private detective Masderius hired."

"No!"

He nodded gravely. The detective was a lesser light working for a small agency in Barceloneta. Nothing special, one of those insignificant set-ups that look into marital infidelity and outstanding debts. It was obvious Masderius had gone for discretion, otherwise it was hard to imagine someone choosing a place like that. But Garzón was a bloodhound of invaluable instinct, able to obtain the specimen even before the shot did.

"Good work, sergeant, you've hit the nail on the head."

It seemed the guy had not wanted to admit the truth, had started going on about protecting a client's anonymity, and my colleague had had to threaten to charge him with covering up a murder to make him see sense. He did finally, there were no two ways about it: Mr. Masderius had hired him to locate Juan Jardiel. He claimed unfortunately not to have done so. "And what would have happened had you found him?" asked Fermín. "Well, of course I'd have handed him over to the police," the jerk answered. Needless to say, the director of the agency did his best to distance himself. Mr. Masderius? A case his employee had taken on without prior authorization. He left him stranded, as often happens.

Garzón had rushed straight to the station and called Masderius in for immediate questioning, but his haste was in vain, the owner of the agency had clearly forewarned him and he turned up in the company of his lawyer.

I noticed a patina of fear on the architect's face that hadn't been there before. As soon as the lawyer opened his mouth, I understood he wasn't going to let him say a word.

"At the time the murder was committed, my client was at his club, playing a game of tennis with his colleague Pedro Pifarré. This is something you can check out immediately."

"I don't suppose it's necessary," I replied.

"Well then?"

"Just as, Mr. Masderius, you hired someone to find Jardiel, you could easily have paid an assassin."

His lawyer carried on answering for him.

"That has yet to be proved, just as we'll need to find out if the private detective was coerced into making a statement."

"Are you going to try to buy off the witness?"

The lawyer unfurled his sumptuous peacock feathers.

"Do you have any idea who Mr. Masderius is?"

"I know he's someone who hired a detective on the margins of a police investigation."

Masderius intervened at this point, much to the alarm of his lawyer.

"Police investigation? Don't make me laugh! You haven't been able to clear up anything. Total ineptitude if you ask me. This is how everything works in this country: health, commerce, mail . . . "

"Am I to understand that to make up for official inefficiency you felt obliged to turn to private enterprise?"

The lawyer chimed in:

"My client didn't say that."

He laid a hand on Masderius's arm. I continued:

"Thinking like that, you must find it very painful to pay your taxes, Mr. Masderius."

The lawyer gave me a conspicuous look.

"I'm afraid I don't understand."

"That's how they caught Al Capone. He didn't pay his taxes and went to prison for it."

Masderius reared up like a cornered cat.

"I will not permit such slander!"

"It's logical, Mr. Masderius, you shouldn't be offended. Once you start breaking the law . . . "

The lawyer's hand moved to Masderius's other arm, he'd have muzzled him if he could.

"Inspector Delicado, you're well aware my client has many obligations, I'm afraid we don't have time for your tom-foolery."

"Of course not. I'm also a lawyer and can instantly tell the kind of business someone's involved in. And yet I must warn you your client's gotten himself into a mess. I shall hand the results of our investigation over to the judge and he will decide."

They left almost without saying goodbye. As Masderius passed next to me, I saw he was shaken, nervous, close to an attack.

Garzón looked at me.

"Great, inspector, great. It's obvious I'm good at questioning in the lower reaches but when it comes to higher things . . . "

"Don't underestimate yourself, Garzón. Who found the detective and got him to talk? And just how did you do it?"

"In the time-honored way, I put the jeepers on him."

I smiled.

"I suppose you could say we make a good team."

"I liked that bit about Al Capone. What made you think of that? Masderius almost died!"

"A simple desire to piss them off. Besides, I've recently found out it helps to add a small surrealist touch when questioning."

"A fantastic team, you're right!"

"Don't count your eggs, Garzón, this case just keeps on getting more complicated."

"Have no fear, in the end we'll see the light."

"You find a beam in the eye illuminating?"

"You're a pessimist."

"Why don't you apply your marvelous powers of deduction to the case, that'd solve it!"

He chuckled at my jokes.

"Al Capone, that's a good one!"

His gelatinous belly shook like a Yorkshire pudding. I felt an enormous wave of sympathy for him and then suddenly I froze. Was this man my brother, my friend, my accomplice? Had his professional life not had a dark, sinister side? Brutal nights of questioning at the station, repression, beating and humiliating detainees, abuse of power. Was he some kind of benign soul levitating down corridors without coming into contact with corruption? I had to erase that image if I wished to continue with the investigation.

"Shall we have a drink?" I cut in.

We went to the Ephemerides, where Hamed regaled us with two cocktails called "Sweet Oasis." It was their day off, but we enjoyed special dispensation. That said, the impression of leafy palm trees didn't last long because Pepe insisted on switching on the TV.

"It's Ana Lozano's show."

"Oh, please, turn it off!"

"But you're the main attraction! For weeks now, you've been the only theme."

I laughed, after all what did it matter? Unfortunately my laughter took as long to go out as a fire in a frying pan. Salomé was the first image that reached our eyes. It was an exclusive interview, they'd pulled out all the stops. Fair enough, why shouldn't she make a bit of money like the others? She answered as if she were being forced to swallow live toads, but she answered. Again and again, bestowing oodles of dignity on Ana Lozano.

"This must have been very difficult for you."

She stared at her quiet, empty hands.

"I've often regretted having reported him to the police."

This was the worst thing she could have said, the final link in the chain around my neck called depression. I felt like a poor Delacroix castaway raising his arms to the sky. It was too much for me, I couldn't wait till the end.

"Switch it off, Pepe."

Garzón gave me a bitter look.

"You see, Petra? She didn't even mention the fact you stood bail."

"She regrets having gone to the police. If that's what she really thinks, then why's she going to feel grateful to me?"

I left the bar, walking slowly. It was a calm, iridescent evening. When could I go for walks again, slowly mingle with other people, allow my mind to wander over innocuous images, get away from all these obsessive details? I stopped, not wanting to go too far. I was in Muntaner. My feet had taken me there almost without wanting. I looked up. The light was still on in Masderius's office. When I pressed the button in the lift for the fifth floor, I had only one aspiration: for his secretary to have left. It was late enough for this to be possible. Perhaps for the first time since I'd been born, God was on my side and Masderius himself opened. He was amazed, horrified to see me, but he didn't shut the door in my face.

"You're well aware I won't talk unless my lawyer's here."

"A mistake."

Facing each other off in silence. He was tired.

"Mr. Masderius, I'm quite sure you didn't murder Jardiel. Let me in, I shan't stay."

Unexpectedly, he stood aside. I followed him into his office. He sat down, gestured to me to do the same.

"Think about it carefully. If you carry on denying you hired that detective, the evidence will pile up against you and breed suspicions. It'll then be difficult to rectify without falling into contradictions. It'll get more and more complicated, believe me."

He lowered his head, took off his gold-framed glasses and

started rubbing his eyes in defeat. He kept his fingers pressed against his eyes and began to speak.

"Yes, I hired him. I hoped he'd find Jardiel before the police, but he didn't."

"What made you do it?"

"I wanted to beat him up, castrate him even, I don't know . . . then dump him in front of a police station."

"But you're a civilized man, Masderius, I don't understand . . . "

He looked up violently.

"What do you know? Since my daughter was raped, I haven't been able to sleep, I can't concentrate, I can't eat, it's an obsession. I thought when Cristina was away I'd feel better but it hasn't worked. It's useless, my life's changed and will never be the same. Do you think it helps that the guy's dead? I promise you it doesn't, I still wake up in the middle of the night and I know it happened, it really happened."

"But life . . . "

"Oh, please, don't talk to me about life."

We remained silent. I'd never seen anyone looking so deeply depressed, so exhausted.

"Had we found the guy, I might not even have touched him. But at least by paying the detective I was doing something, right, I wasn't just sitting there, getting desperate."

A man of action. But now, if a psychiatrist didn't attend to him soon, he'd have a nervous breakdown before long.

"Mr. Masderius, if the judge ever summons you, tell him exactly what you've just told me."

"I didn't kill him."

"I know."

I stood up and he made a weak attempt to accompany me.

"It's O.K., I'll find my own way out."

He sank back into his cherry-colored, leather armchair. When I reached the door, I heard him say:

"Now no one will be able to prove he was the real rapist and he won't pay for his crime publicly."

I didn't reply, he may have been right. Anyway, there was no point in promising a broken man I'd fulfill my duty.

Back home I had serious problems finding something edible. When this was all over, I'd buy in supplies, vast supplies, enough to keep me alive during a new ice-age: fresh vegetables, cereals, cheeses from twenty different countries, a leg of pork, dozens of quails' eggs and bread, heaps of bread: brown bread, white bread, sliced bread . . . Like a ship's storeroom before a crossing. But for now I'd make do with a pack of biscuits and a cup of tea. Night had already fallen, I went out into the garden. I turned on the light to water the cadaverous geraniums and suddenly I noticed them: I had to kneel down to make sure my eyes weren't deluding me, but no, there, on one of the tall stems, were some small, green bulges, buds struggling to open. I ran into the house and called Garzón.

"What is it, Petra?"

"It's the geraniums, sergeant, they weren't dead, they're starting to go green, you managed to revive them!"

"My God, you gave me a fright! I thought something terrible had happened."

"Excuse me, you're right, I shouldn't have bothered you with something so trivial. What were you doing?"

"Having dinner."

"I'm very sorry, forgive me, it was a childish impulse."

"Oh, don't worry too much, my landlady hasn't gone to town today, a few watery French beans and a minuscule omelet."

"Get yourself an apartment, break free! You'll soon find a way to prepare delicious meals."

"Perhaps, inspector, perhaps."

Stunned by the caliber of my lie and envying Garzón's

French beans, I got into bed, feeling exhausted. I couldn't have stayed awake a moment longer, I slept like a log.

A ring woke me at five in the morning. I was so fast asleep that, when I picked up the receiver, my voice refused to come out of my throat.

"Inspector Delicado? I'm calling from the station. I'm sorry to wake you but the chief inspector would have you present yourself immediately at the following address. Do you have something to write with?"

"What's happened?"

"I don't know. The orders are to inform you and Sergeant Garzón. I'll dictate the address to you."

As I drove, a series of mournful possibilities went through my mind. I was disoriented. And yet I had a strange feeling that overrode any other thoughts: Masderius had committed suicide. Despite my earlier conviction, he had been guilty of doing away with Jardiel. Unable publicly to face up to the crime he had committed, cornered by the evidence and racked with guilt, he had decided to take himself out of the equation. In this way, the double case would be solved by means of its own destructive force and all Garzón and I would have done is run like hunters after specimens that were always dead by the time we arrived.

I saw the patrol cars from a distance, mobile barriers, cops moving in the dawn. As I came closer, I could make out the chief inspector and Garzón's rotund figure. I parked the car and got out. It was then I saw the shape lying on the ground, covered in a blanket. It was clearly the outline of a body. Masderius?

"Morning, gentleman. What have we here?"

Garzón's eyes were blurred from astonishment or a lack of sleep. The chief inspector gave me a stern look.

"As you see, Petra, we can't get away from it, another murder."

"Whose?"

"Salomé, the first girl to be raped."

I felt the blood in my veins slow down, without the strength to carry on circulating.

"She received a heavy blow to the head and then they slit her throat. Terrible, isn't it?"

"I don't understand . . . "

"Wait, I haven't finished yet. They'd lifted her skirt and removed her panties."

"Rape?"

"Rape by the same rapist."

"How do you mean?"

"What you heard, you can see for yourself."

He bent down and pulled the blanket off the lifeless body. There was Salomé, white and fragile like a broken doll, her neck twisted, a large, black stain stretching over all her clothes. I swallowed with difficulty. The chief inspector took her arm and with his flashlight focused on a specific point. There, next to an old, dry mark, was a new flower, swollen, bloody, identical to the one made months earlier. I looked at Garzón, who remained speechless. He returned my look, phlegmatic and serious.

The chief inspector told us we didn't have to wait till the body was removed, but he wanted to talk to us. We went for a coffee in a bar that had just opened. He found a corner table.

"Well, you see how things stand. This case gets more and more complicated. Of course I wouldn't even think of taking you off it at this stage; on the contrary, you have my full support, I think you're doing pretty well. Circumstances, however, oblige me to take a decision I wouldn't normally take. I've decided to apply to another station for help."

"Do you think that's necessary?" I asked.

"Listen, Petra, events have taken a turn that society is going to interpret in the following way: the police tracks a rapist till it seems they find him. They point him out to the whole wide world, saying, 'Here he is.' This gives someone a target on whom to vent all their vengeful anger, so they go and murder him. All right so far, but it turns out the real rapist wasn't Jardiel but another guy who's on the loose, joyfully watching this confused ceremony unfold. Of course this guy's completely crazy and decides to confront the police he's already made fun of. He loops the loop and starts raping the same victims a second time, not only that but he also murders them. Sounds logical, don't you think? It's as if we ourselves have tied the strings and enabled the crimes."

"That's just an appearance."

"One we can't allow. We have to do something even if it's just to placate public opinion."

"But before going to another station for help . . . " Garzón started. The chief inspector interrupted him in a determined voice.

"I'm sorry, Garzón, but I've already asked for it. Tomorrow an inspector will be dispatched from Girona headquarters. I believe I know who it is, a very able young man, a top-rate matador who'll come in handy."

"What about the command?"

"The command will be joint with Inspector Delicado, as is only natural."

In truth I should have asked that question myself, but I didn't have the energy to worry about my stripes. The chief inspector had actually been very understanding towards us and I was grateful that, instead of sending us a top-rate matador, he hadn't thrown us straight into the arms of a picador.

I ordered surveillance and protection for the two other raped girls. If this strange game continued, they'd be next on the list. Garzón looked like a man who'd been defeated.

"Do we have time for a coffee?" he asked.

"Not now, sergeant. They're going to conduct an autopsy

on Salomé's body immediately. I'd like to be there as soon as they have details."

Half an hour later, we were in the corridor of the Forensic Anatomical Institute. We sat down on a bench to wait. The noise of traffic could be heard in the distance. Inside, there was a thick silence. A wave of sadness swept over me. Salomé, another mouse who'd disappeared from the city. A short, absurd, wretched life.

"It reminds me of the day we were waiting in the hospital," said Garzón.

"Horrible, isn't it? It's as if we were always at the start."

"No, now it's much worse."

"Well, at least we managed to have three people charged at the same time. By the way, has the phantom rapist been released yet?"

"He's still in jail as a suspect."

"Hasn't anyone been to see him or inquire after him?"

"I've no idea. The truth is I'd forgotten all about him. We'll have to let him go, he can't have done this while being locked up."

A metallic sound came from somewhere, possibly the sound of one surgical instrument knocking against another. It was tragic. Entrails, blood, and yet I couldn't permit myself the luxury of thinking about that girl or death. My mind continued debating the rational arrangement of the pieces, like in an intellectual game. How and who? And if Jardiel wasn't the rapist, why the evidence about his blackened tooth and why escape? I looked at Garzón, who had fallen asleep. I couldn't remember the last night I'd slept well, without dreaming or getting a fright, without the sensation the phone could ring at any moment, breaking the silence. The sergeant's head flopped forward from time to time. He'd half-opened his mouth and the air whistled in between his teeth. I'd never seen him looking so tired, at the mercy of his fat, ugly body. How long before he retired? Perhaps he'd end up in an old people's home, telling other pensioners how he'd spent his life taking part in high-risk, top-secret missions. And what about me? I might have a similar destiny, after all I was as alone as he was. Well, if that's the way it was, it'd be better to start facing up to it with humility. I stretched my legs, leaned my head against the wall and proceeded to nod off, wrapped in my overcoat.

The pathologist found us shamelessly dozing. By the time I managed to come to, the poor man was coughing so much the health of his throat was at risk.

"I understand there's not much to do round here," he said, diplomatically offering us an easy way out.

"It's peaceful," I agreed while at the same time nudging my colleague.

"If you don't mind, I'll have them type up the autopsy report. It shouldn't take long."

"Did you find something?"

He brushed back his hair. The smell of disinfectant mingled with his aftershave.

"Well, it's strange . . . she was raped by the penetration of a smooth object. There are no tears, no signs of aggression, just the simple introduction of this object. I think I'm in a position to state the object was inserted into her vagina after she died. The tissues were completely relaxed, which means there was hardly any friction."

"Well, that is interesting! And what about the mark, doctor, was it the same as before?"

"I'm sure of it, exactly the same, just like the photographs I got from the station. In short, if it wasn't done with the same object—and we cannot know that for certain—then the new object was an exact copy of the one the rapist always used."

"I see. And were there no signs of a fight?"

"I'm surprised but no, absolutely none."

"Why should that surprise you?"

"Sometimes the death of a girl who's been attacked with the idea of rape is the result of the attempt failing. If the rapist is impotent or makes a mess of it, he'll often take it out on the victim and may even kill her. We're talking about highly unbalanced individuals, of course, such as the one you're looking for."

"If it's the same guy, he's shown himself on other occasions not to be impotent."

"But he could have been feeling guilty, afraid."

"Do you think a man who's afraid would dare rape a recent victim? I find it hard to believe."

"When dealing with deranged individuals, anything is possible."

"Yes, I suppose so."

He bounced off down the corridor. Garzón kept scratching his eyes.

"Now we can have a coffee," I told him.

We dipped our donuts in our cups and listened to the pleasant murmur of conversations that contrasted with the deathly silence of the place we'd just left. But I couldn't stop thinking. Dead, then raped with an object. Why? Had she seen his face this time, so he had to kill her? But even so, why rape her like that? I couldn't find a satisfactory answer.

"What do you plan to do?" asked Garzón when he finally managed to clear his mouth of donuts.

"I don't know, I really don't know. This thing with the object . . . "

"I mean about the inspector from Girona."

"What do you expect me to do?"

"Are you going to stand for it?"

"Garzón, I don't understand you."

"I thought at least you'd protest. Truth is we've put up with the worst of it and now this guy arrives to see what he can find. And you're the same rank, so he'll try to out-command you."

"Well, it doesn't really matter."

He looked at me as if he didn't understand a word.

"But . . . you're a woman!"

I burst out laughing.

"Yes, I know that."

"And aren't you going to do anything, lodge a complaint, show that you can manage on your own?"

"No, I'm not going to do anything."

He took a steady sip of his coffee. It was funny, Garzón thought he could count on my usual feminine demands to solve his problem with competitiveness. But no, he couldn't, after all I wasn't proving to be such a great cop, even if I was a woman.

12

G arzón dropped me in front of the station. I opened the car door and got out. He was going to release his "phantom," he couldn't keep him any longer even for illegal possession of pornography. I took a few steps down the sidewalk and it was then this human bulk crashed into me. I couldn't see the face while I was being shaken by the lapels, but from the high-pitched voice and the wavy hair I could tell it was a woman. "It wasn't him! It wasn't him!" she screamed. I tried to push her back to find out who it was, but barely managed. "It wasn't him! It wasn't him!" Luisa, Jardiel's girl-friend, vented her anger while continuing to shake me vigor-ously. The two guards who were at the entrance to the station came towards us, but there was someone else on the scene, a camera recording at a safe distance. "You accused him, but he'd never have raped anyone, now we know it wasn't him!" The guards took her off me, but she carried on shouting, "Murderer! You killed him, he wasn't guilty!" A small crowd of onlookers had gathered around us. Someone took me by the arm, it was Garzón.

"Let's go inside, inspector, this way."

I let him take me, I was too disconcerted to do anything for myself. One of the guards came over:

"Shall we arrest the girl, inspector?"

"No, let her go."

Inside the station, Garzón went to the machine to get me a coffee.

"I saw it all from the car, she was waiting for you, but I didn't have time to get to you. Are you O.K.?"

"Yes, yes, don't worry. What about the camera, where did that come from?"

"I've no idea, I only noticed the girl, I left the car and by the time I arrived they were already there, two journalists. I can't understand where they popped up from so quickly. It must have been set up and they were waiting with her."

"Yes but they're always following me, so it could have been a coincidence."

"Are you sure you're O.K.?"

"Yes, I promise, go and do what you have to."

"Don't leave the station before I get back, we need to stay together if they're going to try this stunt again."

"I doubt they're going to."

He left a little reluctantly. I had to keep on smiling and show I wasn't in the least affected, which of course was absolutely not true. I could feel my heart beating, a glow in my cheeks, my hands were quivering. But I had to carry on pretending because one of the guards took over from Garzón.

"Would you like a little water, inspector? What a performance, eh?"

"What to do? Do you have anything for me?"

"The chief inspector gave me this note for you."

I put it on the desk to stop it trembling in time with my pulse.

The inspector from Girona arrives tomorrow. I've sent him the file on the case so that he's fully informed when he joins up

The guard remained standing in front of me.

"Is there something else?"

"Yes, inspector, a young girl would like a word. She didn't look suspicious to me, to tell the truth, but if you like I'll stay here with you."

"No, please, that won't be necessary. Wait five minutes and then you can show her in."

I cleared my throat, cupped my hands in front of my face and began deeply inhaling my own breath as a way of calming down. Right, I had to think for a moment. Masderius was out on bail. The judge didn't believe him and the recent rape didn't count in his favor. Of course they were two different things. Even if Jardiel wasn't guilty, whoever took him out didn't realize this and killed thinking he was the rapist. That's why Luisa had attacked me at the entrance to the station, though she could have done so when her boyfriend turned up murdered . . . but then she also was convinced of his guilt. Terrible, even when you're dead, the judgment that makes you innocent or guilty continues hanging over you, even outside this world its concepts hound you down to hell.

There was a knock at the door of the office. I had managed to calm my breathing. My voice sounded firm:

"Come in!"

A very young girl appeared in front of me, a girl I didn't know, who for the moment didn't seem to want to assault me.

"How are you?" she asked.

"Fine, thanks. Who are you?"

"Don't you remember me?"

I raised my eyebrows, studied her carefully.

"No, I'm afraid not."

"I'm Esther Sánchez, we met the other night when you arrested my boyfriend."

The image of the slender girl in an undershirt now came to me clearly.

"Yes, of course, I know who you are."

"He's been in prison for several days but he didn't do anything, really, I can prove it."

I could have told her that at that very moment Garzón was freeing her boyfriend not far from there, but something stopped me, I wanted to hear her speak, to know what made her so sure.

"Take a seat."

Sitting down, she looked even more childlike.

"No one's been to see him or to seek his release. His father hasn't shown any interest and has kept his mouth shut. He's an asshole. Emilio, my boyfriend, prefers me to stay silent, he'll take anything, perhaps even being charged with murder, but I won't. I didn't talk to begin with but he's been in jail long enough."

She clenched her harmless fists on my desk.

"What did you want to tell me?"

"Emilio is Juan Jardiel's half-brother."

The breathing I had so solicitously attended to raced off again.

"What?"

"It's true, they have the same father. I don't know if you're in on the secret but Juan's father took off with someone else and left his wife, Juan's mother. A few years later they had a child, Emilio. Do you follow?"

"I think so."

"Juan continued to see his father on the sly, without his mother's knowledge. He loved him a lot, they were pretty close. He also saw Emilio. But the father's an asshole and hasn't looked after either of them. He almost kicked Emilio out, Emilio had to earn a living with porno posters. I don't wish to sound arrogant but thankfully he found me and the two of us get by."

"What about Emilio's mother?"

"She died."

"Why doesn't Emilio have the same surname as Juan?"

"He wasn't legalized, his father never even recognized him, he has his mother's surname."

"Right."

My mind was churning, locating and contrasting details, trying to store them like a disciplined computer.

"Talk to his father, he knows everything about Juan, I bet he'll have some interesting things to say. I'm tired of protecting him. Emilio never had anything in common with his brother, they didn't even get on. He said it wasn't fair that his father preferred him, gave him his surname, whiled away the time with him."

"Where can I find him?"

"He has a bar, the Diamond Pub, it's—"

"Yeah, I know where it is."

When I told her to go back home because I'd personally see to Emilio's release, she didn't believe me. She had suffered too much to think that something in her life could be easy. And she was right. Even if she hadn't told me any of this, her boyfriend would have been freed the same. All she had to do was wait. Now, having acted in this way, she'd have to listen to his recriminations for having betrayed the mysterious father figure. Some people really have no luck.

I asked two guards to go with me and headed in the direction of the Diamond Pub. Wasting a minute in such circumstances could have proved fatal for me, I needed to know. I remembered perfectly the prickly guy who put us off the scent, his impenetrable features, his apparent friendliness. I shouldn't blame myself, it would have been an act of superhuman heroism to have recognized that man from the photographic image Juan's mother kept; they had little in common, the heavy build, the determination in the eyes perhaps.

He was behind the bar. I only had to look at him for a moment to see that he remembered me.

"How's it going, Jardiel?"

"What's that?"

"Oh, save me the effort! You are Ricardo Jardiel."

He started nonchalantly washing dishes, adopted a jaunty expression.

"So what?"

"You hid your son Juan when he ran away, didn't you?"

"My son is dead."

"And maybe you know who killed him."

"Are you crazy?" he raised his voice. Some boys playing pool turned to stare at us.

"Come with me to the station, you'll have to make a statement. Don't make me call the guards."

He entered the kitchen and came out with a much younger woman.

"Stay in charge, I'll be back soon."

Before we went into the office, I asked for Garzón, left a message for him to join the interview on his return.

Ricardo Jardiel wasn't nervous, he asked if he could smoke. He looked proud and weather-beaten. I sat down opposite and offered him a cigarette.

"To tell you the truth, Jardiel, you're in a mess. Think carefully about what you're going to say and try to be honest. If you contradict yourself, you could be charged with anything: rape, murder, whatever."

"You're well aware I haven't done anything. What's more, I can prove it. Don't you think I have enough witnesses with all the customers of my bar? I'm always there."

"All right, that means you've nothing to hide. Tell me about your son Juan."

"Juan? I hadn't seen him since I left his mother. A couple of years ago, someone must have told him where to find me and he turned up in the pub. We got chatting. It was nice suddenly finding you had a son."

"But you had another son with your second wife."

"Emilio? Did he tell you I was Juan's father?"

"No. Tell me about Juan."

"What's there to say? I don't know much. He was a good lad, lived in the shadow of his shrewish mother. He'd come round, drink a beer . . . All his life hearing I was a bastard, he could have despised me but he didn't."

"Did you give him advice?"

"What?"

"I mean, did you tell him to get away from his mother?"

"I might have said something of the sort."

"Don't get all defensive, Jardiel. I repeat you'd do better to be honest."

"O.K., so I told him, I told him not to put up with her all his life, not to marry the girl she'd found him. What else was I going to tell him?"

"I can understand you trying to save your son, even hiding him at home when he was on the run. No judge would condemn you for it."

"I didn't know he was a rapist."

"So you did hide him."

"I didn't say that. Listen, it's pure chance I was that boy's father, ask his mother what you like, she's the one who raised him. I don't know anything, so I'm not going to say anything. He may or may not have been the rapist. He's taken that secret with him to the grave."

"Perhaps not. Why didn't you say who you were when we visited your pub last time?"

"Who wants to get involved?"

"All right, you can go then."

He was amazed.

"I can go already?"

"If you don't know anything . . . "

He stood up, seemingly unconvinced the outcome could be so easy. What else could I do? This guy was a hard nut to crack and wouldn't talk if he thought all the evidence had vanished with his son. Garzón was waiting at the door. He gave me a quizzical look. I went to fetch my coat.

"Has the boy been released?"

"Yep."

"When?"

"An hour ago."

"I imagine he'll be at home, let's go and see him."

In the car, I brought the sergeant up to date. He was subdued.

"We're very close now, Petra, I feel it."

"Don't count your eggs, we've a load of unanswered questions, a load of crimes waiting for a culprit."

"But at least a path has opened up."

Emilio was at home. When he answered the door, his face expressed tiredness, curiosity, exasperation.

"Now what the hell do you want?"

"Your father's confessed the truth."

The girl in the undershirt came out and stood beside him. She'd been crying.

"Fair enough, why are you telling me?"

"Don't play the fool with us. Let's go. This time you're not going to get out so easily."

His girlfriend clutched the sleeves of his shirt.

"What have I done?"

"Hide your brother Juan Jardiel when he was on the run. You knew perfectly well he was the rapist, he told you."

"That's not true! My father didn't say that."

"Listen, that's enough, you can say what you want to say to the judge."

The girl came forward.

"No, don't take him, he hasn't done anything wrong."

He held her back.

"Shut up!"

"No, I won't shut up, if you've already gotten angry with me for speaking once, it doesn't matter if I do it again."

"If only you'd kept quiet!"

"You'd still be in prison. Do you think your father's going to do anything to get you out? He's just a pig."

Garzón and I witnessed the scene in silence. There was

nothing we could do to tighten the trap. Either it worked or we had to go back.

"You know what I'm saying is true, he's an asshole. He risked hiding your brother but he wouldn't even visit you in prison or stand bail."

Emilio lowered his eyes. The girl turned to me.

"His father was perfectly aware what Juan had done, he knew what he was accused of. He hid him in the cellar and if he hadn't been killed, he'd have given him enough money to go abroad. He had a guilty conscience and wanted to help him."

There was a tense silence.

"You know it's true, Emilio, he even seemed to like the fact Juan had been capable of rape, of causing such a commotion."

"You don't know what you're talking about, shut up," he murmured.

"It'd be better if you told the judge that, Emilio, better for you, for your father, for everyone."

I tried to make my voice sound sweet. The girl looked at me:

"And after that will you let him come home?"

"I think so."

I sighed deeply, it had worked. I took them both to the court and Garzón went off in search of an arrest warrant for Ricardo Jardiel.

We met up for lunch. Garzón was nervous.

"When are we going to reel him in?"

"Let him stew for a bit, I want him to think about it, to see the mess he's in. Besides, we're not going to beat about the bush. We'll put a copy of Emilio's statement under his nose. If we want him to talk, he has to feel he's cornered."

"Can't we just tell him? That way, we'd gain time."

"Why the hurry?"

"What do you mean, why?"

"Well, you're not a man to rush into things. What's gotten into you?"

"Crikey, Petra, all this investigating is bad for your health! The trouble is that the inspector from Girona's arrived. We have a meeting with him this afternoon. He's spent the whole morning reading our reports."

"I see, and you want us to solve the case in a couple of hours so that when we meet him, we can say, 'Sorry, matador, you're late!'"

He fidgeted as if I were talking nonsense.

"Are you going to tell him, Petra?"

"Tell him what?"

"Our recent discoveries about Jardiel's father?"

"Are you joking? Of course I am!"

A black cloud settled over him.

"Just to be clear, I don't plan to obey direct orders from him. You've been the boss here all along. So if he decides to start telling me what to do . . . "

"Calm down, Fermín! At least he's a man. Imagine if we'd been sent another woman!"

He scowled at me.

"That was out of order, admit it."

Well, I thought, even if we didn't manage to solve this blasted case, the experience would have been positive for the two of us. We'd both learned things, our relationship was genuine and lacking in affectation. He had understood that he could be under a woman's orders without necessarily falling into discredit, and I . . . I had been much more mistaken than he and so my change was greater. I had acquired humility. Immersion in the wretched world of crime, the lack of glamour in my profession . . . I certainly no longer felt like ticking off social workers, stripping suspects or making demands of superiors. I realized the difficulties of being a cop go far beyond mere sexual discrimination. But now it seemed Garzón wasn't in the least amused by this change.

"So you're not going to oppose the involvement of another boss," he insisted.

"Forget it, Fermín, everything seems to indicate that instead of solving the case in a reasonable time, we've made it more complicated."

"But the cat's almost in the bag."

"Oh, yes? Explain it to me."

"Juan Jardiel was the rapist and Masderius killed him."

"All right, and who then raped and murdered Salomé?"

"How the hell do I know?"

"Give time a little more time. This inspector may help us. By the way, what's his name?"

"Ramón García del Mazo. A ridiculous name."

I burst out laughing.

"Come and have a coffee in the Ephemerides. We won't have Emilio's statement till four. What do you say?"

He didn't want to, but he accepted. What was making him so anti-authority at this stage? A late stand in favor of individualistic principles?

In the Ephemerides, there was a moment of calm. Pepe and Hamed were eating side by side, so we went in and sat down with them at the table, waiting till it was time for coffee. They were tucking into an exotic lamb dish with mint, which the sergeant couldn't resist.

"Only a taste, we just had lunch."

I admired his ability to recover when it came to gastronomy, the extent to which he enjoyed his food. Lucky him! He always had a last resort in life to hold onto.

"How's the case going?" asked Hamed.

"Well, you'll have seen the television."

"Yeah, you were on the other day, you didn't come across at all well in the images."

"It's true, I didn't know they were following me with a camera. Since then I've been much more careful about which dress I put on before leaving home."

"They weren't following you," said Pepe very seriously.

"How did you find that out?"

"Ana told me. That girl, Luisa, Juan Jardiel's girlfriend, called her to say she was going to pull a stunt, asked her to be there and film it."

"She asked her?"

"Yeah, she was very keen to prove her boyfriend's innocence."

"She may have been wrong about that."

"Then why was another girl raped with the mark and everything exactly the same? Jardiel couldn't have done it."

"I don't know, Pepe, and even if I did, I suppose you realize I couldn't talk about it, especially knowing Ana Lozano is still a regular of this bar. Is she still spying on us in the dark?"

Pepe lifted his pretty brown eyes from his plate and fixed them on me.

"Don't you think you're developing a persecution complex? Ana Lozano is a regular but that doesn't mean she's after you, you may not be so important."

Pepe assaulting me? This was something new, a milestone, an exception, it almost called for a celebration.

"You may be right, I feel like a fox being hunted."

Hamed stood up.

"I'll make some scented tea."

"That girl seems to care an awful lot about showing the world that Jardiel wasn't a rapist, more than about seeing him dead like a dog."

"At least that way she protects his honor," said Hamed from the kitchen.

"What was that?" I asked.

He came out, carrying a steaming copper teapot.

"All a dead man has left is his honor."

"Oriental mentality," said the sergeant while preparing a cup.

"Possibly," I added.

We concentrated on the tea. Small pine nuts swirled up and down in the liquid.

"Delicious Arabic tea," commented Garzón.

"Maybe East and West are not so far apart," I said thoughtfully.

"Are you philosophizing?" asked Pepe ironically.

"What makes you think that?"

"Your natural tendency to philosophize for no reason."

I was amazed, another right hook, what was going on? Garzón gave me a sidelong glance and smiled.

"Aren't we running a bit late, inspector?"

In the car, I couldn't stop thinking about what had happened. My colleague immediately cottoned on:

"Is there something bothering you?"

"Did you notice how aggressive Pepe was towards me?"

He nodded matter-of-factly.

"It's probably healthy."

"What do you mean, healthy?"

"You came to terms with the new situation some time ago, maybe it's his turn now."

I lit a cigarette.

"Oh, come on, Garzón, if what you're trying to tell me is that he's going out with Ana Lozano, it seems pretty obvious. But that relationship won't help him resolve anything."

"Are you sure?"

"That journalist is the same age as I am!"

"Not everyone's like you, there are those who like to repeat past experiences."

"All the same, there's no need to react in that way."

"It's just an initial phase, he'll get over it."

I watched him while he drove. He was like a closed coffer, but a gleam of gold escaped from the corners of his mouth.

"You told him, didn't you? You told him to learn to be hard with me."

"I didn't tell him to do anything but we're friends, remember? So we've talked about loads of things."

I stared at him in surprise, as if I'd just discovered this sardine meat was actually pure salmon.

"Unbelievable, Garzón, you're unbelievable, really."

He laughed with delight.

"You've achieved something impossible for me, you've rid me of all my husbands."

"Are you annoyed?"

"No, I'm not. I'm grateful!"

My surprise took years off Garzón, he had stopped feeling like a provincial hick and was fluffing up his brand-new peacock feathers as an expert in urban sentiments.

"Here we are," he got out, reached my door, increasingly listing to one side. "Ladies first," he said, full of pride.

"Unbelievable, Fermín, I'm not joking."

Emilio's statement was waiting for us, signed and sealed: his father had sheltered Juan Jardiel while the latter was a fugitive from justice. I clutched it with satisfaction. This piece of paper was the only weapon we could use to make the man speak.

"Has Ricardo Jardiel been brought in?"

"He's in room twenty, inspector."

"Shall I wait outside?" asked Garzón.

I shook my head, Jardiel didn't seem the kind of person to be influenced positively or negatively by the presence of anyone. I wasn't mistaken, he didn't even glance at my colleague. His air of contempt hadn't changed despite his preventive detention. Psychological games wouldn't work with him, he'd only admit what he couldn't deny on the grounds of evidence. It seemed essential to me to go straight to the point. I placed the statement under his nose. He read it. Only by paying careful attention to the movements of his face could I detect the contraction of his jaw. He dropped the piece of paper and looked at me equanimously.

"So what?"

"I suppose you won't now deny you hid your son."

"What else could I do? He was my son, I won't deny it. You can accuse me of that."

"We can accuse you of a few more things. You knew your son was the rapist we were after."

"No."

"That's what Emilio's told us."

"Of course he'd think that, but what does he know? He didn't even see him. Besides, if that's what he said, why isn't it here, in his statement?"

"Let's not be childish. Why did you think your son was on the run, for jumping a red light?"

His answers were well prepared, at no point did he appear to be nervous.

"I'm the owner of a pub, I get a lot of young people. I talk to them, I know them well. Young people today have lots of problems, scrapes with the police, drugs, whatever. My son turned up and said he had a problem, I didn't ask him what it was."

I stood up and began to pace around the room.

"Listen, Jardiel, I can understand you not wanting to be charged with being an accessory after the fact but what I find hard to stomach is you don't do anything to find out who killed Juan."

"Juan is dead."

"That is very true, about as true as the fact you're the rapist and murdered your own son."

Out of the corner of my eye, I saw Garzón make an almost imperceptible gesture of surprise.

Jardiel raised his hands to his head in mock disbelief.

"That's right. And I also killed John F. Kennedy."

I needed to draw on all my theatrical powers. I smiled sarcastically:

"Go ahead, laugh as much as you like. To make your joy

complete, I'm going to give you a rundown of the case the judge is preparing against you. Are you ready?"

He arched his eyebrows as a way of canceling out any expression on his face.

"Ricardo Jardiel, you were the rapist from the start. No one doubts you have a stronger character than your son. You probably wielded huge influence over him recently. Your son Juan knew you were raping and marking those young girls, you told him so and used him for your own purposes. You had him prepare a special barbed watch so that if things came out into the open, the watchmaker would only recognize him. But your son started getting nervous when he saw the net of suspicion tightening around him. He sought your protection and you hid him in the cellar. Of course this wasn't a plan that could last, so you promised your son a substantial sum of money to smuggle him out of the country. A sum you don't have and never will have, so you did the only thing you could do to take him out of the equation: you killed him. Then you raped again because needless to say you're sick, Jardiel, you're a madman, who would only deserve pity were you not so dangerous."

Garzón stared at me, amazed by the sudden reappearance of his theory concerning the murder victim. Jardiel's face had lost its color but, despite suffering this first setback, he said in a voice of apparent calm:

"You can invent all the stories you like but when Juan was killed, I was serving beer. Let's see how you're going to prove your fantasy."

"Your son Emilio has declared you felt proud talking about Juan's rapes. The judge was interested to hear that. He also declared you were going to pay for him to go abroad. It's as if you did your best to ply him with false evidence. The judge was also interested in this. The pieces all fit together perfectly. Especially since your son Emilio has just declared you didn't seem surprised to hear about Juan's murder. And that's not the end of it, the last thing he said is that the watch used to mark the girls is now in your possession."

"I didn't read any of that in his statement."

"There's a second statement. Nor does the one you've read say you encouraged your son in his alleged offenses, you hid him in the cellar and planned to abet his escape, and yet you see how I know all of this."

Now he was affected. My arrow had reached its target, we had yet to find out how deep the wound would be.

"Think carefully, Jardiel, things are serious. You'll be brought back into the station again tomorrow for our last interview, the next will be with the judge, on formal charges. Think carefully about what you need to declare before it's too late."

I stood up and left the room. Garzón followed me. Out in the corridor, after taking a few steps, my colleague could no longer suppress his curiosity.

"I don't understand, inspector. Did Emilio really confess his father had the watch?"

"No, he didn't but I think Jardiel has swallowed it. I gave Emilio an incomplete statement to sign, lots of details were missing, I thought in our hands those details could be more elastic and useful, include the odd lie that also passed as the truth."

"Brilliant, inspector, brilliant."

"Don't flatter me, please, the theory of the phantom rapist was yours, I just used it for other means."

"I take my hat off."

"Well, put it back on. If that guy recovers the composure he lost for a moment and pauses to think, he'll ask us to show him the second statement tomorrow and then . . . "

"God is with us, Petra, he won't."

"God isn't interested in these things, Fermín. If he wanted

to manifest himself, he'd choose something more glamorous, he'd appear to Ana Lozano, showing her the way, and she'd give him a televised interview."

At five o'clock sharp, we were in the chief inspector's office. García del Mazo had already arrived. He was more or less my age, not very tall, with a finely clipped mustache that ran along his thin upper lip. He was serious and stony and, if his face emitted any data signals, I have to admit my radars were not well enough equipped to receive them. Coronas introduced us, trying to lend a cordial air to proceedings. He then dotted the i's and crossed the t's.

"I don't wish to add to the burden you're carrying but you know this case is receiving an unusual amount of publicity, so I'd urge you to try and solve it quickly. Needless to say, this will be a joint command. Are there any questions?"

The three of us remained quiet. After he left, García del Mazo attempted a smile.

"All bosses sound the same, they must attend courses in oratory."

I also had a go at a smile.

"You've read the reports?"

"You can address me as *tu*. The name's Ramón."

I nodded.

"And mine's Petra."

Garzón kept his mouth shut and our new colleague didn't say a word to him.

"I've read them. If you'll allow me one comment, I think they're fine, only that they're a little clichéd, they lack a certain vision. Correct me if I'm wrong but you haven't been very methodical, now have you?"

"I'm afraid you're right, we've somewhat staggered along in the wake of recent events."

"That often happens, I shouldn't worry about it."

Garzón stirred uneasily.

"Well, I suppose we can still make use of the computer, you've barely touched the police data banks."

"There are some recent developments you don't yet know about, I'll tell you about them if you like."

I related the whole story of the interview with Ricardo Jardiel. He nodded from time to time without changing his expression at all. He didn't seem impressed, nor did he consider my revelations crucial.

"Well, maintain that course but . . . the most we can expect from that interview is for the father to state that Juan was the rapist, which may or may not be true. The question is who killed him, because it's obvious the boy's murderer is the subsequent, possibly the initial, rapist and of course Salomé's murderer too."

He spoke with confidence, so slowly the listener felt obliged to accept his conclusions or at least to follow his reasonings as if they contained something new.

"There's one thread you've left dangerously loose in my opinion."

The sergeant and I glanced at each other with a guilty air, as if we'd been caught.

"It has to do with Salomé's death. No one's bothered to follow her final movements while alive, the people she may have met, changes she may have introduced into her routine."

Garzón intervened:

"I went round to her house, where they told me she'd done the same things as always at the same times."

"That's not enough, sergeant," he didn't include Garzón in the more intimate form of address. "What does a family know about a young girl's doings? Doesn't it strike you as too much of a coincidence that the same victim was picked twice? What's the meaning of that? Is it just a challenge to the police? But this isn't a soap opera!"

His professorial tone began to grate on me, but he was

right, by all the demons of the wilderness that stubby little technocrat was right!

"Not to worry, Petra, I'll follow that line of investigation, you carry on with Jardiel and you, sergeant, have a look on the computer at the list of reoffenders."

"The first thing we did was check the list of suspects, to little effect," the sergeant gave himself the enormous pleasure of saying.

"But I'm talking about hardened offenders, noticeably hardened offenders, I might say. The IT Department has such data, in fact Barcelona's data bank is pretty complete."

Garzón turned serious:

"As you wish, inspector, will do."

I knew his icy style of official obedience. This fellow was rubbing him the wrong way.

García del Mazo consulted some notes he had with him.

"Let's see . . . what else was there? Ah, yes!" he adopted a casual air. "There's a question of procedure I also disagree with. It has to do with media relations. We're not living in the Middle Ages, now are we? Why refuse so steadfastly to make statements? This can't carry on, the force has special departments for external relations. It's been clearly proved that obstructing the work of journalists only makes our own life more difficult. There's an easy solution: pick an official spokesperson and give the odd press conference. That's all. Is it necessary to say something substantial? No, just a few general conclusions to placate the public's curiosity. This ensures the integrity of our image and avoids excessive speculation."

He gave me an understanding look.

"I know you don't approve of this," he added.

"Right, but now there are two of us in charge. If you're so sure, why don't you take care of it?"

"I will if you don't mind, that is unless you prefer to."

"Go ahead, I think your knowledge of police departments is better than mine."

He made a unifying gesture with his hands.

"As for methods, I suggest two meetings a day, one in the morning and one in the evening."

Garzón reacted:

"Two meetings? What for?"

"A meeting is an end in itself, a tool of the trade, a basis for the exchange of ideas, hypotheses."

"What if we've nothing to exchange?"

"Let me tell you, sergeant, that in the States there was an experiment over one year to put all the managers of a company in the same room for two hours a day. There was no set agenda, no order of the day, no specific topics up for discussion and, strangest of all, no one was appointed to head the meeting. Do you know what happened? At the end of this period, the company's sales had increased by forty percent, its internal structure had been optimized and all those employees with potential had acquired greater responsibility. What do you say to that? Of course it seems there were days these gentlemen remained silent for minutes on end, on the brink of despair, not knowing what to do, but eventually someone always found a thread to pull on that led to the skein."

"They probably played spoof," said Garzón.

García del Mazo chuckled indulgently:

"Who knows?"

He took his leave with just the right amount of cordiality for the occasion and bounded out of the door. He was wearing a dark blue tailored suit and a tie decorated with tiny stirrups.

"What a guy!" exclaimed Garzón. "Modern and efficient, I know his sort like the back of my hand."

"He wants to make a name for himself. Do you fancy a beer, Fermín?"

We crossed the street in silence. My colleague was fitting up

the chariot of demons that would spirit him off. I waited philo-
sophically for him to turn into a charioteer and race past me at
the speed of Ben-Hur. I didn't have to wait long.

"You were caught with your pants down, weren't you,
Petra?"

"Do you think?"

"You bet. All that business about command and authority
and feminist bullshit, and you turn around and say yes to
everything."

"He was right about some things."

"About the press as well?"

"I don't know what your problem is, you've always thought
the same as he does."

"What does my opinion matter? You're the boss."

"That's what really gets to you, isn't it? Command and
authority. Only a man could think like that."

"Listen, I don't think, I'm not paid to think, but it's obvious a guy can't just walk in here and take over a case others
have been slogging away at for months."

"Why don't you leave your armor at home for once?"

He drained his beer in one gulp. He was annoyed, clearly
disappointed at the turn of events.

"I'll be off then, Petra. See you at a meeting some time soon
to exchange ideas."

"Give my regards to Pepe, and some good advice while
you're at it . . . "

Now he was irate. He walked, sinking his feet in the ground.
I ordered a second beer. Not investigating Salomé after her
murder had been a real blunder, and probably not the last we'd
made. Refusing to give up the case when we'd had the chance
was another act of irresponsibility. I felt the weight of the
atmosphere increasing over my head. Stubbornly resisting all
contact with journalists was further proof of a childish mentality
that—García del Mazo was right—had seriously hampered the

course of the investigation. And as for our improvisations . . . I began to hurry the second beer in preparation for a third. Of course the guy was smug, unpleasant, a theorizer and a social climber, but he was a true professional, one of the new batch who'd come out and said some sensible things. And yet I shuddered at the possibility of having two meetings a day with Garzón and him, silent accusations stifling the air, the angel of death waiting for us at the door with his flaming sword.

A guard from the station suddenly entered the Jarra de Oro and came towards me.

"Inspector Delicado, there's a message for you from the police cells."

I took a deep breath, the effect of the alcohol dissipated.

"Is Sergeant Garzón at the station?"

"No, he left with you and hasn't come back."

"Try to find him and tell him he's needed."

I had been convinced and in the end it had happened: I was told that Ricardo Jardiel wished to make another statement.

"O.K., bring him straight up."

He arrived in under an hour. As soon as I saw him, I knew he'd suffered a moral collapse and uncertainty had prevailed over his cold, contemptuous cynicism.

"Right, Jardiel, let's start again. One fine day Juan turned up and told you the police were on his tail. You took him in and hid him in your cellar, thinking that no one would connect you and you'd be safe. We'd gotten that far. Now here comes the first question: did you know your son was the rapist?"

"Yes."

"How long had you known?"

He shielded himself behind his hands, opened wide his eyes.

"Whoa, hang on a minute! He told me the same day."

"I don't believe you."

"I swear to God."

"Oh, come on, don't give me that! You heard each time he got up to one of his tricks, you had a good laugh and probably egged him on as well."

"Do you think I'm crazy? Juan was found dead but he could have been caught alive, why would I risk being charged as an accomplice?"

"Because you took pleasure in your son's misdeeds."

"I'm not a dirty old man, I have other ways of enjoying myself."

"But you don't care what happens to women. You abandoned Juan's mother, Emilio's mother, and you'll abandon the one you have now when you get tired."

"Emilio's mother died."

"But you'd made her life impossible and left her long before."

"Did Emilio tell you that as well?"

"No, I worked it out for myself."

He rubbed his nose, his hands were trembling. By exploiting his sense of guilt, we might get somewhere. Good, well spotted, even vermin have that blasted sentiment tucked away somewhere. I sighed, offered him a cigarette.

"Did Juan give you the watch he used for marking girls?"

"No!"

"But he showed it to you."

He hesitated for a moment.

"Yeah, he showed it to me."

"And you let him?"

"I don't know what you mean. He stood in front of me and said, 'Look, I've worn this twenty times under your nose.' Then he opened it and showed me what was inside."

A shiver ran down my spine.

"Describe the watch."

"I thought you already knew what it was like."

"Describe it to me."

"It was an ordinary watch, fairly old, nothing obvious, but the face was mounted on another face set with barbs. I imagine when he attacked a girl, he took the upper face off, then put it on again so that it appeared he was wearing an ordinary watch."

"Very clever, your son, I can understand why you were proud of him."

"I wasn't proud of him! I owed him the favor of taking him in. But I told him he couldn't stay there forever."

"You offered to get him out of Spain."

"He already had someone to help him."

"Who?"

"I swear I don't know but whoever it was turned out to be the same person who killed him."

"Explain that to me."

"Juan made a phone call, arranged to meet someone, went out to that meeting and never came back. I found out he'd been murdered the following day on the radio."

"He didn't tell you who he called?"

"No, that's the truth, I promise you."

"Was he wearing the barbed watch when he left?"

"Yes."

"Are you sure?"

"Yeah, I noticed. I told him not to go about parading that thing but he ignored me. He was crazy, his mother made him like that. I'm not a monster, you see. I had my reasons for abandoning her. And the next one as well, she was a weak, unbearable woman. When we split up, she begged her daughter to see her and even she didn't want to. Why should I be a saint if no one else is?"

"I'm not here to judge your life, Jardiel, you know what you've done. I hope for your sake you haven't lied to me."

"I'm not a rapist or a rapist's accomplice. I simply wanted to lend my son a helping hand."

"You picked the wrong moment. Perhaps if you'd offered earlier, you'd have been of some use."

I was so excited when I left the room I didn't even know what I should do. I started heading down the corridor, retraced my steps to where the guard was:

"Did you find Sergeant Garzón?"

"I haven't been able, inspector. He's not at the boarding house or at the bar where I sometimes call him . . . "

"All right. What about Inspector García del Mazo, do you know where he is?"

"I have the impression he went in . . . "

I put a hand on his arm.

"Not to worry, it's not important. I'll see you tomorrow."

Any attempt to locate Garzón before dinner would have been useless and del Mazo could go and get stuffed, so I returned home. I needed a drink and a rest to extinguish the fire that was beginning to devour my brain.

I drove by instinct, without noticing, and I was almost surprised to find myself back home. I never even thought of preparing something to eat.

I flopped down on the sofa as soon as I'd served myself a margarita that was heavy on the tequila. So things had taken a new, perhaps illuminating, turn. Slowly, I said to myself, go slowly this time, no sudden movements or hasty conclusions. Where the hell had that dimwit Garzón gotten to?

13

I woke up with a sharp pain in my neck and pins and needles in my legs—my muscles were tense from shock. I looked at my watch. Great! This was just the way to embark on a new direction in the case. I picked up the phone.

"Sánchez? Put me through to Sergeant Garzón."

"He's in a meeting with Inspector García del Mazo."

"It doesn't matter, tell him it's urgent."

After a short while, I heard my colleague's woolly voice:

"Where were you, Petra? We've been waiting for you to start the meeting."

"I want you to come straight to my place for a study session."

"What about García del Mazo?"

"Make some excuse and get out of there."

"What about the chain of command?"

"The chain of command can go and get stuffed."

"I was sure you'd end up reacting. I'll tell him there's been an emergency in the smuggling case. It won't be such a lie, I was on it till late last night."

"That's why I couldn't find you."

"What about you? Why aren't you here?"

"I overslept, Garzón, I overslept, do you have to know everything?"

He took less than an hour to appear. He wasn't particularly curious about the reasons for my calling a meeting at such short notice.

"Will we make a pizza today?" he asked.

"Not today."

"Will we use the blackboard?"

"No, Garzón, we have to keep all the possibilities in our head, embody them there, purify them by fire and if we reject one, root it out and lay it underground."

He gave me a perturbed look. He obviously didn't feel like taking reality quite so seriously that morning. He must have been hungry, and my bloody dialectics no doubt seemed to him disproportionate. Though, needless to say, when I told him about the interview with Ricardo Jardiel, he was open-mouthed at the ace up my sleeve.

"Farewell phantom, Fermín. Juan Jardiel really was the rapist."

"Then how do you explain his death and the latest rape and Salomé's murder?"

"Let's take it in stages. Why don't you sit down?"

He asked if he could remove his jacket and loosen his tie. He scratched his mustache with his forefinger and then twirled it in the air as he spoke:

"So it turns out the person he arranged to meet must have murdered him and taken his watch."

"Right."

"Someone with a desire for revenge."

"Let's suppose so."

"And if they took his watch, it must have been with the intention of attacking further victims and marking them with the selfsame instrument."

"Probably."

"But who the hell could it have been? Masderius?"

"I can imagine Masderius hiring a detective, I could even conceive of him killing Juan Jardiel, but there's no way I'd consider him capable of raping and murdering a young girl."

"You're right, it doesn't make sense."

Garzón stood up, went to have a look at the geraniums, and paced back and forth nervously.

"Perhaps we shouldn't reject the hypothesis that there are two people involved: Jardiel's murderer and the girl's murderer. As for the watch . . . "

"No hypotheses, Garzón, this time no hypotheses. Let's go over the facts from the beginning. Do you want to make a pizza?"

"Not now, Petra."

We stood facing each other. I spread open my hands:

"Four girls are raped. They're marked on the arm with a strange flower. By means of a witness, we locate the alleged rapist and he escapes. Days later, he turns up dead. Shortly after that, we find the first victim, who's been raped like the first time and now murdered."

"Not exactly like the first time, the second rape was carried out using an object."

"Correct. Finally we have a new, reliable witness who assures us Juan really was the rapist. Absolute surprise. Why? The chain of events had led us to believe Juan was innocent."

"There was another rape after his death and he wasn't found with the barbed watch. Good enough reasons to think he wasn't guilty."

"True, he wasn't found with the barbed watch but not only that, his wrist wasn't bare either. If his wrist had been bare, we could have supposed the device had been stolen. But no, he was wearing a watch."

"An ordinary watch his girlfriend had given him."

I remained silent.

"A watch his obsessive, super-vigilant mother knew nothing about."

"It escaped her attention."

"Other things escaped her attention such as the fact Juan had been seeing his father secretly for some time. But if his father told us the boy had been wearing the barbed watch when he left the pub, why the hell was he found with the other one?"

"Maybe he'd been wearing them both."

"Not likely if he wanted to avoid embarrassing questions. I'm convinced it was the murderer who removed the barbed watch and put the other in its place."

"But where could the murderer have found a watch Juan's own girlfriend identified?"

"Good question."

"Do you think the girl lied to cover up for her boyfriend?"

"Listen, Garzón, I only think the person who killed him wanted Juan Jardiel to appear innocent. So they removed the incriminating watch, put another one on and lest anyone should be in any doubt, raped and marked again."

Garzón scratched the tufts of hair on his forehead.

"Who could have wanted both to kill him and to exonerate him? Besides, it wasn't just any old watch but one his girlfriend had given him."

"One his girlfriend *said* she had given him."

We stayed silent. Garzón shook his head as if he'd sucked a lemon.

"I think I know what our next step is going to be."

"Do you?"

"To question Luisa."

"Wrong! Our next step is going to be to make that blasted pizza! There's no need to hurry this time, we have to work out whether we should ask Luisa to come in or . . . "

The phone rang. I picked up the receiver, agreed, agreed . . . Garzón's round eyes following my every gesture were making me nervous. I hung up.

"That was García del Mazo, he wants us to have lunch together in the Jarra de Oro."

"Why didn't you tell him to go to hell?"

"Calm down, Fermín."

"Are you going to tell him anything?"

"Only Ricardo Jardiel's evidence, nothing about our own deductions."

"Ah, no! No way! Don't tell him anything!"

"What about the chain of command?"

"I also don't give a damn about the chain of command. The guy can't just turn up and award himself a medal."

"I assure you even if he takes ours, the case will be solved by us."

"You'll never get a promotion like that."

"Who said I want a promotion?"

We emerged into the street, putting on our raincoats.

"Don't be too upset about the change of plan, Garzón, a pizza would have been difficult, I only have olives . . . "

"A pizza crust with olives wouldn't have been bad."

"You see! I bet you've a flair for cooking you didn't even know about."

Garzón grunted and tetchily put the car in first.

The lunch went on for ages. García del Mazo discoursed on the importance of the human factor allied to technology in police praxis. I thought that deep down he was a good guy, he hadn't even gotten angry about our absence from the first meeting. He was even nice, it was just that he'd arrived at a bad time and was interrupting, slowing down the investigative process. I was sure we'd almost reached the end of our case and it bothered me to have to give explanations to wear him around like a broach as we pursued the remaining lines of inquiry. Garzón gave his new boss a look that was criminal while I found it difficult to understand what he was saying. I couldn't stop turning it over in my mind: only one person could have wanted Jardiel's public rehabilitation, and that rehabilitation necessarily involved death. When I finally managed to pay attention, García del Mazo was spouting forth:

"The father, lads, he's very important. I'm going to question him myself to see if I can catch him out, who knows if he isn't selling us a dummy, the guy's highly suspicious. Meanwhile, I shall ask for a computer-generated image of the double watch. They look great, they're used to make photofits as well. In the course of an investigation, it's absolutely essential you ask for things, request data from all the different departments, inconvenience, make demands, otherwise they take you for an idiot."

Garzón glanced at me. I smiled:

"You clearly have a lot of experience in internal affairs, Ramón."

He looked at me with pride oozing out of every pore:

"I assure you no one ever catches me out!"

"The guy's a prick," observed Sergeant Garzón as we left the bar.

"Stop being hostile and concentrate on the job in hand. What time is it?"

"A quarter to five."

"Then we'll have to wait till the shops close."

We arrived at the supermarket where Luisa worked. Garzón parked far enough away to be able to watch the entrance without being obvious. We switched on the radio and fell into the age-old police habit of smoking while we waited. I dragged small stratified clouds out of my cigarette while my colleague surrounded himself in woolly cumuli. At five to eight, the last customers left the establishment and at eight they lowered the shutter. Half an hour later, the staff filed out through a secondary door. Luisa was alone, walking at the sluggish pace of someone who's not in a hurry to reach home.

"There she is," said Garzón.

We watched her move off, fleeting like a brushstroke.

"How could that girl have killed anybody?"

I nodded in silence, completely absorbed in Luisa's long, elastic strides. I carried on watching until her black overcoat disappeared from sight.

"Have you thought about that, Petra?"

"I have."

Everything was going smoothly. The manager was the last to leave and, as he was searching for his keys, Garzón and I got out of the car and marched over to him. We showed him our ID.

"Does Luisa López work with you?"

"She's just left."

"You see, she told us she had some evidence here, we'd arranged to meet but . . . we were running a bit late. Has she left anything for us?"

"No."

"Do you have any idea where she keeps her things?"

"Each employee has a clothes locker but if she's not here . . . "

I smiled:

"Don't make us go and get a search warrant, we'll only be a minute."

He stepped aside and let us in; he was serious and distrustful. He took us to the back of the building down a corridor jam-packed with boxes. At the end, it opened into a large, square room containing various metal lockers and cleaning materials.

"I think hers is number twelve."

"Do you have a copy of the key?"

He disappeared, increasingly irritated, and came back with a bunch of keys. He found one and gave it to me.

"Would you mind leaving us alone? We won't be long."

Suspicion hung about his head like an aura. He moved off reluctantly. I looked at Garzón:

"Shall we?"

His eyes were like those of a child at the end of a story. He nodded. As soon as I opened the door, a pungent smell of cheap perfume wafted towards us. Garzón was standing right behind me, looking over my shoulder, intoxicated. I could feel his heavy breathing like an ox's. A hanger supported Luisa's uniform, a blue jacket. On the floor were various cosmetics jars, a towel, a hair band and a pile of carefully folded newspapers.

"Have a look to see what's in those papers."

"Just a moment, Fermín."

But it was pointless asking for calm, Garzón's normally moderate rhythms were throbbing in anticipation. I understood that he felt like the handler of an excruciatingly slow puppet. I stepped back and invited him in:

"Why don't you carry on?"

He didn't think twice, he threw himself on the papers and started leafing through them. They contained information about the case, nothing logical that provided new evidence. Underneath, there was a little box, which he dived into. He produced two sweets in brightly colored wrappers, a mirror, a comb.

"There's nothing here."

He lifted the box out of the locker and stuck his hand inside. After feeling about, he produced a small bundle made with handkerchiefs. He placed it in front of me and slowly, taking care not to touch what was inside, he opened it. There it was, the blasted watch, the machine for marking flowers, the rapist's weapon.

"Here it is, Petra. Do you see it?" asked Garzón redundantly in a shaky voice.

A second face was clearly mounted on a ring of barbs, but it was best not to handle it till the experts had examined it. On coming into contact with that instrument, I felt pleasure and curiosity, followed by sheer horror. Something abstract had materialized, become actual fact. We'd been playing with the pieces of a gruesome puzzle, but now they were near. These barbs had pierced skin, made blood flow, been stuck in defenseless arms. Suddenly we heard a loud voice behind us:

"Don't move! What do you think you're doing?"

I turned around on the verge of hysteria. There were two national policemen.

"What the hell are you looking for?"

"It's all right, colleagues," said Garzón.

The manager had called the police. Completely normal, our behavior was so suspicious we left him with no alternative. We had to show our ID, give a superficial explanation. I was afraid the manager might have decided to alert Luisa as well. We asked the policemen to come with us to her house as reinforcements in order to effect the arrest. They got in their patrol car and followed us. As he drove, Garzón wondered out loud:

"My God! Obviously the girl's guilty but of what?"

"There's no way of knowing but everything seems to indicate she did away with Juan. No one else could have known where he was, removed his watch."

"And the subsequent rape?"

"You're going too fast, we'll have to arrest her and then question her."

In his noble elephant's noddle, he drove while bitterly deducing:

"Kill her own boyfriend, her brother, do you really think it's possible?"

"She's a tough cookie, remember what Ricardo Jardiel told us? She wasn't even willing to see and forgive her own mother."

He nodded, scandalized and philosophical in the face of evil:

"What complicated beings we are!"

We reached the Jardiels' apartment. Luisa hadn't escaped, she herself opened the door. Her expression showed nothing special, but a second later she saw the policemen behind us and her eyes narrowed.

"Luisa, you'll have to come with us to the station."

"What for?"

Garzón put his hand in his pocket, took out the small bundle of handkerchiefs and placed it in front of her.

"We found this in your locker at the supermarket."

She looked down and blushed.

"I'll just get my coat."

At that point, Mrs. Jardiel appeared. She gave us a surly look.

"What are you doing here?"

"Luisa will have to come with us to make a statement."

The girl passed next to her without a word.

"A statement at this hour? No way! We're about to have dinner. Haven't you interfered in our lives enough already?"

"I'm afraid it's serious, madam, she'll have to come."

Luisa returned, carrying her dark overcoat.

"Where do you think you're going?"

"With them, mother, I'll be right back."

"You will not!"

There was a momentary stalemate. The woman held her adoptive daughter by the arm, the daughter looked up and faced her.

"Don't, mother, I have to go," she said in a whisper.

Garzón gently nudged her out of the door. I took a step forward:

"We'll let you know from the station when you can come and see your daughter."

Her inflamed eyes bored into me:

"I spit on you," she said and landed a gob of saliva at my feet. I nodded bitterly, turned around and started to walk. The door slamming made the sad space of the landing echo. I descended the stairs in twos as if I were fleeing from the inferno. Accursed lineage, guilt that never sees the light of day. That woman, like a large tree, had cast a thick shadow around her, where everything was rotten and the sun never reached.

I had no choice but to inform García del Mazo that we had arrested the girl. He immediately called a meeting prior to the interview. Garzón was livid. The inspector lectured us on the advisability of giving the detainee a psychological test. The importance of this method resided not in the conclusions psychologists might reach concerning the features of her personality, but the time it took her to complete the test. It had apparently been proved that this was a crucial period to prevent any last-minute plans the accused might come up while it also gave the police the opportunity to get ready and handle proceedings without prejudices deriving from the euphoria of having made the arrest.

Luisa took two hours to answer such questions as *What would you do if you were shipwrecked?* The experts, meanwhile, studied the prints on the watch. It was understood that García del Mazo would attend the interview with us. When Sergeant Garzón found out, the color of his face became like a chameleon in a pool of blood.

"Outrageous! He's no right to interfere at this stage."

"Leave it, Fermín, the outcome isn't clear yet."

He gave me a sulfurous look, pitiful of my naivety.

As soon as I saw Luisa, it seemed to me she'd suddenly lost weight. Her sturdy body had shrunk and dark half-moons were drawn under her indifferent eyes. García del Mazo gestured significantly as if to say, *It's over, she won't put up much of a resistance.* He took the initiative.

"I don't have to tell you there's no point in your denying the evidence, so it's better if you tell us the truth, quickly and clearly. Cigarette?"

Luisa shook her head. Under her broken appearance, she appeared relaxed.

"The experts have confirmed that the watch found in your locker is the same one used to mark the rape victims. What was it doing in your possession?"

"Somebody gave it to me."

"Who?"

"The man who raped them."

"Do you know who that was?"

"Yes, the man who killed Juan."

"Tell us his name."

"I don't know it, some guy Juan knew."

"And he gave you the watch?"

"He sent it to me."

"What for?"

"I don't know."

"Who was this man?"

"I don't know."

"But you do know he was the real rapist and killed Juan."

"He phoned me up and told me."

"And you expect us to believe that?"

"It's true."

García del Mazo turned to us, gestured irritatingly. I went up to Luisa and asked her:

"Did you know Juan was in contact with his father, went to visit him and spent time in his pub?"

"No."

"Did you know . . . ?"

"I won't talk to you. You're to blame for everything, for the charges against him, for his death."

"Don't kid yourself, the only one to blame is the person who killed and raped, nobody else."

"I won't talk to you. If you're here, I won't say another word."

García del Mazo intervened:

"Inspector Delicado . . . "

I interrupted him:

"Don't worry. If I'm the problem, then I'll go."

Garzón made as if to follow me out, but the inspector stopped him:

"Stay here, Garzón, I might need you for something."

My colleague pulled a martyr's face and melancholically watched me leave.

I sat down in the corridor. Was Luisa covering up for someone? Dirty, obsessive, family ghosts, with their dead effigies feeding the hatred of a lifetime. A case for Freud. I approached the guard on duty.

"Has the detainee's mother come yet?"

"No, inspector."

"Has she called or asked about her?"

"I'll have a look but I don't think so."

He returned a moment later.

"No, she hasn't been in contact with the station."

"Fine. When the inspector and the sergeant come out of the interview, tell them I had some business to attend to."

He clicked his heels while I moved off, embarrassed at being the object of so much martiality.

Mrs. Jardiel wasn't pleased to see me. Nothing new there, but she at least let me in her home, invited me to take a seat in the lounge. Not a single question passed her lips.

"Your daughter will be charged with murder."

Not the slightest reaction.

"With the murder of Juan Jardiel."

"Has she confessed to it?"

"She will. We found the watch used by the rapist among her things. Juan was the rapist; she killed him in revenge."

"What about the subsequent rape and the other death?"

"They're under investigation. My colleagues are questioning her right now, I preferred to come here."

"Why?"

"Did you know Juan was in touch with your ex-husband?"

The impenetrable rock of her face cracked around the lips.

"Did you know he discovered where his father was, turned up in his pub, introduced himself? He went to see him often, they chatted, shared things in common. When we were search-ing for your son, it was your ex-husband who took him in."

"That's not true."

"It is true. Ricardo Jardiel's been arrested. I questioned him the day before yesterday, he told me all of this. Now he faces charges of obstructing the course of justice and aiding and abetting a fugitive."

She clenched her hands in her lap, then stood up and left the room. She returned after a while with a metal box. She sat down and opened the box, which was full of photographs. She passed them to me one by one. Photos of Luisa and Juan when they were small. Two tall, sad-looking children in oversized clothes and heavy shoes. Posing next to each other on a bal-cony. Juan on his own, upright and confused, slightly pathetic, gazing at a place somewhere between fear and a smile. The two of them together again in Catalunya Square, surrounded by pigeons pecking at their hands and head. Lifeless, docile figures allowing the camera to take photos, resigned and astonished, never caught unexpectedly in a joyful moment of play. I felt pity, poor them, poor all of us, over successive gen-erations inheriting hatred and sin, then passing them on with no more awareness than our own horror. She placed an enlargement in my face. Luisa dressed to the nines for her first communion.

"They never went without, never. I worked away, you understand, slogged my guts out for them, never asking for help or complaining to the neighbors lest anyone should feel sorry for us. My whole life was like this."

Her voice was dry and powerful, she didn't sob or hesitate.

"But in the end you can't change things. His father's a bas-tard, her mother's a whore, what can you expect? I always knew something similar would happen. Every day I'd wake up and wonder if it was the day they'd show their true colors. You say he's raped? I'm not surprised. She killed him? I imagine she's capable. I don't want to know, you understand, I did what I could, my conscience is clear. Now it's as if both of them have died."

"Come with me to the station, Mrs. Jardiel. You should talk to your daughter."

"I don't have a daughter."

"Will you not see her just this once?"

Her expression turned sour, she thought for a moment.

"Just this once. But don't ask me again."

That was the last thing she said. All the way to the station, she kept silence, huddled in her worn coat that smelled of dust. I asked the guard if my colleagues were still questioning the suspect.

"Inspector García del Mazo's come out. Sergeant Garzón's with the girl, I think she's signing today's statement."

I entered the room and took Garzón aside.

"Has she said anything new?"

"Not a word."

"Find García del Mazo straight away and come the two of you. I have the feeling something important's about to happen."

He made as if to leave.

"But sergeant . . . don't find him too quickly, you understand?"

He nodded and went out. Luisa was sitting on her chair, she didn't even look at us. I sent for her mother. As soon as Luisa set eyes on her, her features softened, but she didn't say anything. They squared up.

"Hello, mother, how are you?"

There was uncertainty in her voice, fear, a call for affection.

"You killed Juan, didn't you?"

Luisa's eyes opened wide in panic.

"No, don't believe what they told you, it wasn't me."

"You killed him because he was a pig, didn't you?"

"No!"

"You did the right thing. Now all that remains is for you to die as well. I've come to tell you not to call me, not to come back home, not to show your face there again. It's a shame I didn't give all the bread I fed you to the dogs. I've nothing more to say."

She looked at me:

"Can I go now?"

I nodded. My heart was thumping. I had to make an effort to stop my breathing from running out of control. She left, slamming the door. Luisa returned to her seat. I lit a cigarette, struggling to keep my hand steady. It was time to go on the offensive.

"You see how things stand, Luisa."

She slumped in her chair, gazed at the ground.

"You told her . . . "

"I didn't tell her anything but don't you realize? The judge will charge you with murder, he has more than enough evidence. Like Juan, you'll be charged with rape. Don't you think it'll all come out even if you don't speak?"

It seemed to me her eyes were full of tears.

"Your mother knows about the watch, don't you think we've enough evidence with the watch? Do you really expect us to believe the story about the unknown man? For God's sake, Luisa, come back to earth, the truth's out, can't you get that into your head? It's over!"

The tears started sliding down her face.

"Your mother knows, I know, we all know you killed Juan, the only thing left to know is if someone helped you and if that person raped and then murdered Salomé."

She covered her face with her hands. I missed Garzón.

"You love your mother a lot, don't you, Luisa?"

The first sob broke out.

"You love her and know how important reputation is to her, right? So when you found out Juan was a rapist on the run from the police, you were horrified. How could he have done such a thing? Then he called you from his hiding place and you decided to kill him. It was the only way to defend his honor and protect your mother from that nightmare. You arranged to meet. His pleas of innocence were pointless. You already suspected he was perverted, you'd seen pornography hidden away in his room, you knew he was a bit strange, repressed. It was easy to stab him, how could he have fallen so low? Then you removed the barbed watch and replaced it with one you'd just bought. First step to prove to the public he wasn't guilty. The second was to kill and rape Salomé, to clear Juan of any hint of suspicion. Who helped you, Luisa?"

She took her hands away and gave me a fright, her suppressed crying had made her features swell and redden.

"It was me on my own," she said.

The words came out of her mouth slowly and clearly.

"I had to kill her to stop her from talking."

"And did you rape her?"

"After I killed her, yes, with a large door handle I bought at an ironmonger's."

"But why that girl precisely, why not another chosen at random?"

She was distracted now, looking at the door. I repeated the question.

"It didn't matter to me who. I knew everything about that girl, on the telly they said what time she was raped, where she lived, what route she took every evening. Why look any further?"

Shocking, like everything that's simple and could so obviously have been avoided. We fell silent, the two of us staring at the same worn spot on the ground.

"You'll have to repeat your statement, Luisa, and answer all the judge's questions."

"Will I be sentenced to death?"

"We don't have the death penalty in this country."

"Good, then I'll go to prison."

"You'll be put on trial."

"I'll be O.K. in prison."

She didn't cry, wave her arms about, she stopped speaking, enveloped herself in an almost catatonic indifference. I got up and left. At that moment, García del Mazo and Garzón arrived.

"Where were you?"

Garzón gesticulated wildly.

"It was absurd really, half an hour playing hide-and-seek with the inspector. If I looked for him in the archives, he'd just left. He'd gone out for a coffee? I missed him. I thought we'd never meet up!"

García del Mazo wasn't listening.

"What happened?" he asked me.

"Luisa's just confessed."

"How did you manage it?"

"I got her mother to come, she was very hard on her, in the end she collapsed."

"Wonderful! Is she still there?"

"Why don't you take her written statement? I didn't go into details."

He rushed into the room. Garzón and I were left alone. I headed for a bench, slumped down.

"Are you not feeling well, Petra?"

"Give me a cigarette, mine are inside."

He anxiously searched for his pack and lit one for me.

"Perfect, Garzón, you were just long enough to make it look real."

"Oh, Petra, I knew that you'd . . . "

He interrupted his sentence, didn't see the need to go on and thank me for obstructing García del Mazo.

"So she confessed."

"Yes. She killed Juan Jardiel and Salomé."

"And the rape?"

"She raped her with a door handle."

"In revenge only?"

"And for the sake of honor."

"Whose honor?"

"Everyone's, Fermín, her mother's, Juan's, her own, honor is not an individual concept, it affects everybody, just like corruption."

He nodded, deep in thought. I rubbed my eyes, I felt sick, too much tobacco, too much coffee, too much fatigue.

"Is something wrong?"

"I don't know, life's so ugly . . . everything's so miserable . . . "

He put his bearlike paw on my back and patted me incongruously.

"The consolation, Petra," he said, "is that it's always been like that."

Some consolation. I dropped my head on his shoulder and, because he was wearing a jacket with thick shoulder-pads, I felt better.

14

There were all kinds of interviews, the most illuminating was the psychiatrist's. Luisa was declared responsible for her actions with no extenuating circumstances on the grounds of mental alienation, but her case was considered psychologically complex. A traumatic experience such as being abandoned by her parents in childhood would have been enough by itself to affect her deeply, but then came the worst. Her adoptive mother cleared the way for a personality that was almost pathological. The overriding dominance of a hard and bitter woman full of hate. The constant reminders that she'd been taken in as a result of sin, the daughter of a woman who was partly to blame for the family's misfortune. The strict upbringing based on fear and guilt. The sexual repression, the total lack of tenderness. And, alongside her, Juan. There arose between them a feeling of complicity, affection, and in both a deification of the mother figure, an acceptance of her principles as the only way out of the guilt they carried. Terrible contradictions of their true desires, their natural impulses. According to the psychiatrist, Jardiel had been led to rape the girls by the typical, unconfessed hatred of his mother, which spread to the rest of her sex. He marked them in an attempt to leave his impression, his influence on them, having not been allowed to exhibit a single photograph on the wall of his bedroom. In his case, a pathological state had developed more fully. He was, in fact, psychotic and would no doubt have been declared irresponsible for his actions by the judge.

The chief inspector congratulated us.

"Case closed!" he said, rubbing his hands. "And it wasn't at all easy, I can say. It's not every day you find a woman guilty of rape. The three of you made an excellent team."

"Thank you, sir . . . but I'd like to point out that the case was solved by Sergeant Garzón and myself on our own, without the need for outside help."

"I'm aware of that," he said solemnly.

García del Mazo came in and we all fell silent, he was bursting with happiness.

"Before going back to Girona, I'd like us to have dinner together. Because there's not a single loose end, now is there, colleagues?"

"It appears not. The judge has released all the suspects without charge."

"Then we can rightly feel satisfied. Case closed! And what are we going to do with the journalists? We'll have to call a press conference. Of course, after all the controversy this case has aroused, we can't just send a spokesperson, I think you should go, Petra."

"Me? No way! I've refused to collaborate all along on principle and now the case has been solved, I join the stars. No, I don't want anyone thinking I'm after the recognition."

"Well, then I'll have to do it. Does anyone mind?"

"Fine."

The chief inspector looked at me ironically. Of course it didn't even occur to García del Mazo to offer Garzón the chance to speak publicly. When was a sailor ever seen to give a press conference when the skipper was up to the job?

We spent the rest of the day taking it easy or at least that's what we should have been doing, but it was very difficult to find some peace with my colleague grumbling and cursing. García del Mazo taking the plaudits before the fourth estate was more than he could bear.

"I knew it, I knew this guy would end up grabbing other people's medals."

This business about the medals had turned into a real obsession. It was pointless my joking, questioning the validity of medals, drawing up humorous lists of them—medals worn by creaking heroes in parades thirty years later, Olympic medals, medals from dog shows—he didn't find it funny, he still thought I should have publicly restored my honor using the same means that took it. But all these reproaches were no more than a trickle of water compared with what came later. When García del Mazo gave the press conference, then came the waterfall, the torrent, the unstoppable flow, the tidal wave, the geyser, the flood.

The newspaper reporters were more or less unanimous in their conclusions. Some came straight out with it, others were more circuitous. The case had been solved after the arrival in the investigative team of an inspector from Girona, a man on the ball who used modern methods, a true professional. I'd be lying if I said García del Mazo encouraged them to think this, but it's also true he did nothing to prevent an outcome that suited him down to the ground. He became a celebrity overnight, gave interviews, posed for photographers, savored his moments of glory.

Ana Lozano pulled out all the stops on her program. With the help of actors, she put together a dramatized version of events I refused to watch. But Garzón told me nothing was missing, everything was realistic and well done, a work of art in the crime genre.

Finally, to protect the defendant's privacy, the judge imposed a ban on reporting the case. Everyone breathed a sigh of relief. Luisa began to receive psychiatric help in prison. She was quickly falling into depression. The doctor asked her adoptive mother to visit, but to no end. "I never will," answered a proud Mrs. Jardiel shut up at home, embittered—she had suddenly grown old. A sad, sordid, stagnant story, full of foul air and darkness.

García del Mazo returned to Girona. We never had that dinner of fraternity. I rejoined the Department of Documentation and, utterly at a loss, tried to remember how everything worked, it seemed so long ago, another world almost. However, the judge or Homicide would summon Garzón and me from time to time to provide further details, clarify points, work on the indictment.

Although all the fuss with the media had died down, my colleague was still annoyed and on the warpath; frankly he was unbearable. One day I ran out of patience.

"That's enough, Fermín! I've had it up to here with all this business. I don't care who's taken the credit. And I don't need my honor restored, you see what blasted honor can make people do. If you want to set the record straight, all you have to do is ignore the judge's ruling and give your own press conference. There you can have your say, but don't even mention me, understood?"

"Shame you now keep all your fury for me!"

He was seriously irate. He turned around and left without saying goodbye. The following day, he phoned me in the Department of Documentation:

"What are you doing after work, inspector?"

"What do you propose?"

"A quick beer in the Jarra de Oro."

"I'll be there."

He didn't refer to the excesses of our previous meeting, but nor was he entirely normal, his mood of protest had been replaced by a cynical, existentialist loss of spirits:

"There's no point," he said as soon as he'd pulled himself out of his beer.

"To what?"

"The police, duty, work, everything."

"Oh, come on, things will soon be back to normal."

"Petra."

"Yes?"

"I've something to tell you."

"Go ahead, I'm listening."

"Not here, at the bar. Over at that table."

I carried my mug of beer, wondering what fly could have bitten that great big steer. We sat down, he looked at me:

"It's about the smuggling."

I assumed a blank expression.

"The smuggling of tobacco, remember?"

I nodded.

"From one informer to the next, I've reached the heart of the operation. I know where the goods are, how they operate, who their contacts are."

"That's great! I expected no less of you."

"Here comes what I have to say. I'm being offered money to stay quiet and I don't know what to do."

I was amazed.

"A lot of money?"

"A hefty sum."

I took a sip, crossed my hands on the table.

"Take it, Garzón. As you said just now, all that duty's a waste of time."

"But there's no way I could stay quiet and remain in the police. The shame I'd feel if it was ever found out wouldn't let me live. The idea is to leave, take the money and cross the border, start again elsewhere, I think there's enough for that."

"Why not? Take the money. Go and join your son in the States."

"No! What would I do there? That is . . . that is unless you came with me, Petra."

Somebody banged a gong inside my head.

"Me?"

"You speak English and you like to change. We could set up a bar for Hispanics, like Pepe and Hamed's. I'm not making an amorous proposal, Petra, I wouldn't dare, we'd each live in our own apartment. But we're both solitary beings, we get on, we'd end up being grateful for the company."

I smiled, pulled my hair back, snorted.

"You've caught me by surprise, I don't know what to say! . . . It's complicated. You see, this damn case has brought me back to reality. Right now I just want an ordered life, to water the geraniums, to be alone. Small everyday details begin to strike me as a privilege. I think that for once I don't want to change the plans I've made, now more than ever they seem appropriate, I don't think I've made a mistake. No, as things stand, Fermín, I'll stay the way I am."

A long swig of beer tumbled down his throat.

"I understand."

"Will you do it?"

"I'll have to think carefully, I can't delay much longer."

We fell awkwardly silent.

"I really appreciate your suggestion."

He gestured self-deprecatingly.

"I'm serious. And I want you to know you're a great man, a wonderful colleague, a real sweetheart. But all I'd do is complicate your life."

"That's what I've been wanting all this time, a bit of complication!"

"Listen to me, go it alone, Fermín, I'm sure it'll work out."

He guffawed unexpectedly.

"Maybe I will, what the hell! I have to reach a decision by the end of the week. I could set up a paella stand under the Statue of Liberty!"

He wiped his thick lips, padded and homely like thick cushions.

That Saturday, Pepe and Hamed invited us to dinner in the Ephemerides and, when the flow of customers had dwindled, they joined us at our table for dessert and tea. They were very impressed by the outcome of the case. There were toasts, congratulations and comments. Hamed was afraid all women would feel driven by that story to defend their own and their husbands' honor. It could turn into a real disaster if it happened, because women are resolute in their decisions and never change their minds.

"So women aren't like flowers anymore?"

"For me they'll always be, so long as I have faith in love and tenderness."

"But the love here isn't at all clear," I observed. "It's sickly and ambiguous. The love between Luisa and Juan, what was it? Passionate, fraternal? The love between Juan and his mother, suppressed feelings of incest, love-hate? Luisa's gratitude towards her mother, doesn't killing her son suggest covert vengeance?"

"An unhappy affair."

"Unhealthy. Why else do you think the press was so interested?"

"That's too much!" Pepe retorted.

"By the way, how is your journalist friend?"

"Fine, thanks. I'm moving in with her next week."

"That's wonderful! For how long?"

"Indefinitely, perhaps forever."

"Well, my congratulations!"

He gave me a suspicious look. Garzón intervened:

"A toast!"

My onetime tender ex-husband was defiant. I smiled at him sympathetically, I'd reached the conclusion that making mistakes is about all a human being can do with his freedom. He was probably mistaken in thinking he'd be happy with that woman, as I'd be mistaken again, as Garzón would be mistaken, as

Hamed had been mistaken in thinking women were pure and ethereal.

"A toast to flowers!" I suggested. "Even those that have thorns," I added.

On the way out, Garzón was pensive. He accompanied me home and adopted a solemn air.

"Well, Petra, today's goodbye may be the last. This weekend I have to take my decision. If on Monday you go to the station and I'm not there . . . I want you to know it's been a pleasure working with you, I've learned lots about women and . . . in short, why go on? You know what I mean."

"Fermín, if this is goodbye, why don't you address me as *tu*?"

"No, I couldn't do that. So long as we're both cops, you're the inspector and I'm a sergeant."

"All right then. I wish you lots of luck and happiness. Write to me from time to time, tell me how you're getting on, send me a Christmas card at least."

"Don't worry, I will."

I kissed his fleshy cheek, which smelled of talc like a baby's bottom. I got out of the car and, without turning around, heard him drive off. Garzón was a good man, he had the kind heart of a sheepdog. I hoped, wherever he might be, he'd find a little peace to live in.

I spent the whole of Sunday doing the housework. My home was like a devastated region or a colonized, as yet uninhabited, territory. I polished the parquet, cleaned the windows, arranged my books (Pepe sure wasn't going to do it) and searched in the telephone directory for the number of a cleaning company that would come once a week to look after things. I organized myself as I should have done months earlier. But life is full of parentheses or rather the intervening period between a project and its completion can be lengthy.

I watered the garden. The geraniums were covered in

healthy buds which, come next spring, would explode in all their intensity. I collapsed on the sofa, I was tired, my mind erratic and lazy. Everyday delights, a bit of comforting sedentary life. I switched on the TV, a fashion show in Paris. Lanky girls like muskets elegantly striding down a red carpet. Shiny hair. I looked out of the window, felt well there. When night came, I'd make myself a cup of tea. From now on, I could be pleased that the harshness of the world wouldn't batter me every morning when I woke up. Reality consists of the many surfaces of a single prism, but there's no need to embrace them all at the same time. Better to think about crimes and rapes purely on a theoretical level and, above all, to forget about the hordes of young people washing hair, delivering packages or manufacturing screws in some dark corner of the city. A succession of placid, similar days, any change now would be for the worse. I decided that evil is just more matter formed from madness, a lack of culture, moral misery, accumulated pain, inherited poverty, harshness, inner orphancy. A model on the screen showed off an ornate dress inspired by the East. It was good, however unfair it might be, it was consoling that a woman could sometimes feel like an empress.

I slept deeply. The phone didn't disturb the early hours of the morning. I woke up to the sound of my alarm, had breakfast and went to work, what usually happens in an ordinary world. In the Department of Documentation, there were piles of paperwork. I realized I'd gotten out of the habit of applying a method, having spent so much time following the zigzag of events. I'd have to start again. I classified, organized, but at ten in the morning I could no longer suppress my curiosity: had Garzón left? I decided to take a break and have a coffee.

I went down the station's winding passages till I got to the Department of Homicide. I searched in the interview room, the boardroom, the chief inspector's waiting room. Suddenly I thought about the archives, opened the door . . . and there was Garzón, sitting at a desk surrounded by towering cabinets.

"Fermín! What the hell are you doing here?"

"I've been given a provisional office."

I looked him in the eye:

"Duty won the day?"

"Here you find me."

"That's good."

"I wouldn't be so sure, in a few months I might be feeling sorry."

"I wondered if you had time for a coffee."

"You bet!"

He got up in a flash, put on his oversized jacket and drew aside to let me pass.

We crossed the street to the Jarra de Oro, greeted by the guard at the entrance, who was used to seeing us together.

"We should go for coffee at ten every morning," said Garzón. "Breakfast in the boarding house is horrible, I'm always starving by now."

"What you have to do is find yourself an apartment, Fermín, I won't stop telling you. People don't stay at boarding houses anymore."

He burst out laughing.

"Now that is a good reason to leave! Yep, I'll have to start thinking about it seriously, it bothers me being old-fashioned. Do you want milk in your coffee?"

He thundered out the order. I looked at the striped suit he was wearing, his extended belly, and understood that, while we might never address each other as *tu*, we had laid the foundations of a long and beautiful friendship.

Barcelona, November 29, 1994